Samuel Bayard Dod

A Hillside Parish

Samuel Bayard Dod

A Hillside Parish

ISBN/EAN: 9783337327378

Printed in Europe, USA, Canada, Australia, Japan

Cover: Foto ©Andreas Hilbeck / pixelio.de

More available books at **www.hansebooks.com**

A HILLSIDE PARISH

BY

S. BAYARD DOD

AUTHOR OF "A HIGHLAND CHRONICLE," ETC., ETC.

———————

NEW YORK
DODD, MEAD & COMPANY
1893

A HILLSIDE PARISH.

CHAPTER I.

THERE was an unwonted stir in Clintonville, and its one long street was thronged with a muster the like of which had never been known in the history of this small, but reputable village.

All sorts and conditions of horses and wagons, loaded to their utmost capacity with men, women and children, came streaming in from the North, East and West "settlements," as the straggling farm-houses strung along the roads running through the valleys toward these quarters of the compass, were called; to the South lay "The Barrens."

It was the county town, and was perched upon one of the ridges that divide the head-waters of two rivers which meander among these highlands until they find their way to the sea, bearing on the bosom of their Spring freshets great rafts of lumber, or those unique structures called "Arks," laden with potatoes, pumpkins, cabbages, and all other kinds of country produce; which, but for the lack of an assortment of animals, are no mean effigy of their great prototype.

Nestled on a plateau of one of these hills, with

1

the higher spurs surrounding it, thirty miles off from the railroad, on the line of the old post-road from the Hudson to the great lakes, Clintonville was a place of great promise before those upsetting railroads left it far on one side, and raised some of its meaner rivals to an undeserved prominence.

It still retained a certain dignified superiority above these upstarts, in that it continued to be the county seat, and dreamed of a day when the railroad must come to it; just why, no one could say, except that the oldest and wisest men said, "it was bound to come."

In the mean time, and until the railroads saw it in the same light, the village was, perforce, content to sustain the dignity and prestige of the old Concord coach, with its six horses and genuine old-time driver, which plied regularly, once a day, to and from the railroad station, thirty miles away.

Across "The Barrens," down to the little village of Middleburgh, where a halt was made for dinner; then on, over the Shawnee mountain, a four-mile steady pull up-hill, then down to the railroad station at Weston; it was a good twelve hours' tour to go and come, with fresh relays of horses at either end of the route.

Clintonville was a straggling settlement, nearly two miles long, of white houses with bright green blinds, dotted along the main street (which was the old post-road).

Here and there a side street had sprouted from the main stem, as though to assert its growing power; but it never grew; it had all that it could do to live.

At the upper end was the judge's house, on an eminence, as befitted a judge. In the centre was the village green, sloping up from the street to quite a hill at the rear, and on this knoll was the court house, on one side, and the Presbyterian church on the other, furnishing the community with a perennial joke on the law and the gospel.

The band-stand, in the centre of the village green, was the scene of many a triumph by the village band, when the rustic swains sat beside their girls on the fence, and whittled or smoked while the band went through the programme which, during their season of hibernating, they had succeeded in mastering.

On the edge of the green was a famous well, and alongside the well was the village inn, with plenty of hitching room for the farmers' teams, where mine host, Sol Joyce, entertained man and beast with gossip and fodder, and kept even with the whole country on a horse trade, knuckling under to no one save his black-eyed, bustling wife, who was the only person who could thoroughly upset Sol.

It was around this village green that the excitement centred, and the horses were hitched, side by side, all down the border of the green and alongside the hotel, for it was a day to be remembered in the annals of this hillside parish.

For nearly fifty years, old Dominie Edwards had ministered to them, and it was scarce within the memory of the oldest inhabitant that they had been called to the serious business of choosing a minister, and they did not know how to go about it. This generation had grown up, with the good old man moving in and out, like a patriarch, among their families, and they had almost grown into the belief that ministers come among men as parents do, by a process of nature regarding which we have no selection; or that, like the prophets of old, they were sent of God.

But they were soon educated out of these old-fashioned notions into a fine critical judgment of the points of the various candidates, who came, as if the burial of the poor, old dominie had sprouted this crop of candidates, thick as the berries on the native black-cap bushes; and, after they had become connoisseurs of preaching and preachers, they were in that state of snarling uncertainty which would ensure the new minister, whoever he might be, a divided parish. Old quarrels had been revived, and personal differences and jealousies emphasized; and it was enough for some stout churchman, who had an old lawsuit pending against another member, to know that the " said defendant " was in favor of one candidate, to fix his choice promptly and finally upon another.

There had been put in nomination four candidates for this pulpit, where six hundred dollars a year, and a donation visit, was to remunerate the man whose sole thought and care was to be the burden of the spiritual welfare of this people; who, night and day, was to bear them on his heart; through summer's heat and winter's cold, was to trudge over those bleak hill-sides, unless, perhaps, he "got a lift," when his tired feet would carry him no farther.

Their intellectual life, too, was to be his care, for

there was no one else to organize and provide the means for a village library, lectures, readings, concerts, or whatever might tend to turn away their thoughts from beeves and wool, or cheese and butter.

The debate had run high, and each one had contributed his quota to the sum of perfections that would be required of the Apollos who was to have the privilege of leading this flock in pastures green.

Old Deacon Shrake, who kept the village store and had amassed a fortune, (estimated by his gifts at spending it, an ample fortune,) rose at this point to deprecate the turn that things were taking, for he saw that the tide was drifting toward no choice; and this had been the fatal conclusion of three previous attempts to choose a pastor.

"Brethren," he said, and every one turned to listen, for the Deacon's acquirements had won him a position of influence; albeit the farmers' hard-earned dollars had gone into his till—they respected the man that could coax their money from the stockings;—"Brethren, I think I can perceive whereunto these things leadeth;" the deacon dropped into what he regarded as scriptural phraseology, and with this for a text, proceeded. "We must jedge o' this matter in a plain, common sense way. To my thinkin' a minister is no more'n human, and bein' sech, he is to be treated in a humane manner; and hence the value of him is to be jedged on the same principles as you value any critter, or as I value the goods that I sell over the counter." Some thought this very dear.—"The price of the article has got to reggilate the quality of the article,—you can't buy more'n a yard o' silk for the same money that'll git a hull dress pattern o' calico. We want a six-hundred-dollar minister, and we hain't no right to expect a thousander for that price. Let us jest settle down to that, and, as the apostle says 'learn therewith to be content.'"

This at once turned the tide, and the senior deacon, Shelton, who knew the turn of the tide, like an old fisherman, took prompt advantage of it, and so won all the prestige of a personal victory.

Martin Luther Shelton had a confident way of stating his opinion, with a meaning smile, that seemed to pour derision on any one who dared to dissent. This confidence was begotten in him partly from the name he bore, which gave him a proscriptive right to lead on all matters theological, partly from the fact that he was the only son of the Rev. Amminadab Shelton. The old minister, known far and wide as Father Shelton, was paralyzed now, and so this namesake of the great reformer could state his father's opinion just as he liked to have it, without fear of contradiction,—and he embraced the opportunity.

He chewed tobacco, and spat with the same abandon with which he let fly his opinions, reckless whom they hit. He had a homely gift of telling a story, always fastening these stories on his father, with an unctuous tone that harmonized with his bland smile.

He lifted his tall form, in the midst of the discussion, and smiled on deacon Abijah Stretch, the signal that he would fall foul of him, and shot the following story at his brother deacon:

"About twenty-five years ago, my father, the Rev.

Amminadab Shelton, heard tell of a horse dealer, who was known through four counties as a square man on a horse trade." Deacon Stretch squirmed, and some unkind people smiled, for the deacon was never worsted in a horse trade. "Well," continued Deacon Shelton, having waited for this silent applause, as public orators do, "my father thought it was worth a fifty mile ride to see such a man, and much more to have a trade with him. And so he rode over to Delaware County and put up for the night, and next morning went out to see Sol Babington. 'I have heard tell of you, Mr. Babington, as an honest horse dealer, and have driven fifty miles to have a trade with you.' 'Very g-g-good, sir,' says Sol; for he stuttered like a bull-frog. 'I'll tell you,' says my father, 'what kind of a nag I want, and you can name the price; I leave that to you.' 'Very g-g-good, sir,' says Sol. 'He must be sound and kind.' 'Very g-g-good, sir.' 'And he must have a smart gait on the road, and be kind and gentle for a lady to drive.' 'Very g-g-g-good, sir.' 'And he must go easy under the saddle, fit for a lady to ride, and steady at the plough or haying, a good feeder and an easy keeper, spirited but kind.' 'Anything m-m-more?' says Sol. 'No,' says my father, 'that'll do.' 'Well, d-d-durn ye, there ain't no sech a horse,' says Sol. And, brethren, that's what I say about this minister you've been describing as the man to receive your votes for this pulpit, there ain't no sech a minister." ·

Deacon Stretch started as his brother deacon gave mouth to the "little sweer," but he did not rise to reply,—deacon Shelton had swept the field, and stood, a smiling victor, surveying his fallen foes; and, after a moment's vigorous chewing, he gave those foes a Laodicean rejection, and, with an insinuating tone, as though it were the height of folly to think of anything else, said, "I move we proceed to ballot for a pastor." "I second that motion," said deacon Shrake; and no one else gave a peep or mutter.

With many scattering votes, the main following was divided between two candidates, one a man whose hair was already sprinkled with gray, who was master of a style as florid as his face,—in his favor was urged his fluent, easy style of address and his experience as a pastor, culled from eight churches to which he had ministered; while his opponents urged that he was out of a charge, and that the very abundance of his previous ministrations was an item not in his favor; and, as a commentary on this constant flitting, they said his wife did not share his migrations.

The other prominent candidate was a young, unmarried minister, fresh from the theological seminary, and therefore with no experience, and hardly fitted to cope with the complex problems arising out of the divided condition of the congregation.

Perchance the older heads of the parish would have had their way, had not their candidate allowed his zeal to outrun his discretion, by sending to the senior deacon, along with his photograph, a letter in which he not only set forth his own claims, but enforced them with a solemn admonition, illustrated by example, setting forth the danger of those who might oppose him. The letter closed with the circumstantial recital of the speedy death of two men in other parishes who had been reckless enough to vote against him; closing with this prophetic warning,

"Touch not mine anointed and do my prophets no harm. Yours in the Lord,
ICHABOD CULLEN."

This did the business for Ichabod, and provoked so many to tempt Providence by voting against him, that young Henry Dinsmore was elected by a handsome majority.

CHAPTER II.

AND who was Henry Dinsmore? He was a young fellow of about twenty-seven summers, or winters, by whichever mode of reckoning you choose, who had gone through college without any great distinction or discredit to himself; though he came near making an early wreck of his richly freighted galleon by indulging his irresistible propensity to mischief, which garnished his college life with numberless incidents amusing to recount, but not so humorous to his preceptors in their execution.

From college he had gone to the study of the law, which offered him a fair field for the exercise of his talents and energies; but, when just entering on a career of great promise, he had thrown it aside for the study of the ministry.

His friends remonstrated earnestly, and especially was Judge Channing, in whose office he had entered, loath to part with the brilliant, energetic young fellow in whose career he saw great promise for his pupil, and no less comfort for himself.

"My dear boy," said the old Judge, "I am pained and surprised to hear of this notion of your giving up the law, in which you have a future of great promise, for the preacher's vocation. There will always be plenty of good preachers; but sound lawyers are rare. What in the name of common sense has put this notion in your head?"

"I feel that I am called of God to this work," answered the young man.

"Tush! nonsense, my dear fellow," said the judge, testily. "I am always afraid that a man is going to make a fool of himself when he talks in that way. The time for that sort of thing is gone by; there is as much need of good men in our profession as anywhere else in the world, and a sensible man judges of what he is called of God to do by what he can do best. You have a special gift at making your way with men in the world, and talents which will make you a successful and useful man in our noble profession; all these will be thrown away preaching cut-and-dried theology to a country parish, and catechising the children."

"I do not propose to preach cut-and-dried theology," answered Henry.

"Well, then, they will pitch you out of the pulpit," interrupted the Judge. "It is all of it cut-and-dried, some broad-cut, some fine-cut; but all of it is the same kind of stuff, when you get to the bottom of it."

"I am sure, Judge, that, feeling as I do about the work, it will interest me—I want to put all there is in me into my preaching. I shall be no good in any other profession; and I'm going to enter the seminary this Fall."

"At what seminary do you propose to enter on this modern crusade?" asked the Judge, sneeringly.

"At Princeton," answered Henry.

"Murder!" groaned the Judge, "they will dry the

very meat off your bones; and you can't call your soul your own when they're done with you." And the old lawyer felt both pity and vexation at this young fellow who was going to sacrifice a tangible future for some crazy whim-wham that had laid hold of him, as some diseases do, without premonition, and, apparently, with incurable virulence. But he had done his duty by the young man, and he must go his own gait now;—and so he did, and had spent his full three years at Princeton, and was now come forth a licentiate of the church, and a candidate for holy orders. Whatever the drying process had been, it had not quenched the ardor of that enthusiasm with which he had started on his career, nor weakened his conviction that his choice had been in obedience to a call of God, and he entered on his ministry with the buoyant faith of youth, strong to remove mountains.

He was a handsome fellow, tall and lithe, with a long, firm, springy step; his hair was dark and wavy; his eyes, deep-set and penetrating; there were firm lines about his mouth, indicative of power to make up his mind and hold it, with the full courage of his convictions, and a way of stating them, sometimes with solemn earnestness, sometimes in a quaint, whimsical way, but always so that none mistook his meaning.

His face was pale, not with the pallor of sickness, but with the scholarly reflection from books, away from the sunlight and far into the night, under the rays of the lamplight, which neither tans nor freckles.

This paleness of his skin was enhanced by his dark hair and the black mustache which graced his upper lip, rather to the dismay of some of the elders and elder spinsters, but to the delight of many a maiden; and some hearts throbbed to the eloquence distilled from under that "lovely mustache" which would have been callous to the persuasions of a bare upper lip.

The call had been placed in his hands, duly signed and attested by deacons, trustees and moderator; with the usual pertinent clause "and that you may be free from worldly cares and avocations, we promise and oblige ourselves to pay to you the sum of six hundred dollars, in equal semi-annual instalments, during the time of your being and continuing the regular pastor of this church;" no mention was made of the donation visit, but this was set forth in attractive colors in the letter accompanying the call.

Henry Dinsmore smiled as he read this. Did he remember the glowing picture which the old Judge drew of what "might have been" if he kept on with the law, and foretold just this kind of a rustic field as the reward of his ministerial aspirations? He smiled, but he did not voice his thoughts even to himself.

He wrote a letter of acceptance, and left the elders to select as early a day for his ordination and installation as they pleased, and acceded to their request to preach for them on the following Sabbath.

It was a beautiful June day as he drove up from the railway station, mounting higher every mile, until, from the top of Shawnee mountain, the eye took in at a glance the valley of the Muskingum lying far below, with the farms strung along the banks of the silver thread of a stream that meandered through the flat lands.

Old Tom Burton handled the ribbons, and chatted with the young parson, (who had the seat of honor beside the driver,) telling him the names of the farmers and scraps of the history of each family, as they drove along; but, first and last, recurring to his own experiences during the twenty-five years that he had driven on the road.   They had just passed the crest of the Shawnee mountain, where old rattle-snake Bill had his hut, near the ledges which were his stamping ground, where he hunted rattlers and tried out their grease, "which be a mighty savin' cure for rheumatiz'.   It ain't to be beat by no doctor's stuff, fur old Bill he says it's by the power o' this that the rattlers keep their jints movin', and it stands to reason if it kin keep sech a row o' jints as theirs a wrigglin', it must answer for the single jint of a man.   And, as Bill says, 'whoever heerd o' a rattler hevin' the rheumatiz'; and the Injuns used it to keep 'em supple."   Beguiling the way with such discourse, old Tom turned the crest of the mountain and started down the slope to the Muskingum valley, a four mile stretch, with a steep grade all the way; off started the horses, and, when Tom put his foot on the brake, it came forward easily, and then fell flopping against the side of the stage.   In a moment the sleepy, old driver gathered up his reins, and, with fire in his eyes, as he sat calm and erect on the box, seized the whip in his hand, and said quietly to the young minister, "Hold on tight, Dominie; and the Lord have mercy on our bones."

The long, steep grade was so straight that the eye could take it all in at a glance, until, far away, down at the bottom of the hill, where the road took a sharp turn at right angles, a "worm" fence seemed to stretch right across the way, with a broad, green meadow beyond. Along the side of the road ran a single guard-rail of saplings nailed on the top of posts, about three feet high. This served well enough to keep a man from driving over the steep embankment, of a dark night; but was no more than a bulrush against the momentum of the heavy coach.

Dinsmore kept his seat by clinging to the iron guard-rail of the seat as the stage lurched from side to side when they struck even a small stone. His face was very pale, and his breath came quick and hard.

Tom lashed his horses into a gallop. One of the wheelers made a false step. Dinsmore leaned forward, to see him fall; but Tom had him in hand and held him on his feet.

A chipmunk ran across the road. Again Dinsmore leaned forward intent upon seeing whether the agile, little fellow could escape two dozen trampling feet; and as they whirled past, turned to watch him scamper along the guard-rail as if to join in the wild race.

Then came one of those hummocks in the road, which the country girls call "Hug me tights," or "Thank you ma'ams," as their mood may be; it was no joke to face it now. Over it they went with a rebound that brought screams of terror and shouts of angry remonstrance from within the stage.

Not a word passed between the two men who sat, on top of the swaying, lurching old coach, face to face with sudden death.

The panting horses slackened their pace; the heavy coach crowded on the wheelers.

If one of them fell! Dinsmore drew a hard breath as the picture rose before him; but Tom plied the lash, now on the wheelers, now on the leaders.

They were nearing the foot of the hill. At that turn no skill of driver nor strength of horse could save them. At such a speed and with such a load the old coach could not be made to turn that corner; but it was a mercy that they were not to be slung over into the deep, rocky ravine.

Dinsmore turned and looked into Tom Burton's face, when they were within about fifteen feet of the turn. Tom was looking straight at the leaders; his lips were firmly set with a grim smile; his eye was bright; his hand was steady.

The leaders started to take the turn of the road. Tom was ready, and with rein and whip held them straight for the worm fence; for a moment they hesitated but Tom drove them, through the wreck of it, out into the soft, broad meadow beyond, with only a few scratches on his six horses, and a few bruises on his angry passengers. It was all over in less than ten minutes, that long, wild ride.

Tom said nothing in answer to the abuse which was heaped upon him; but quietly dismounting from his seat, after putting his whip in the socket and slowly wrapping the reins around it, examined his horses over with great care; and, when the passengers dismounted and gathered closer round him, to get the better crack at him, he drawled in reply, as though it were a collect from the liturgy,

"You can jest thank your stars that we had the Presbyterian Dominie aboard, and that he was just called to the church, or else your jaws would ha' been shet, world without end, amen."

Henry Dinsmore was a shade paler and very silent as they drove up, after dinner, over the barrens and down through the dark hemlock woods that lined the road, as it drooped through another valley, just before entering the village. The vision of sudden death suggested the thought that his life had been spared to let him enter on this field of labor; and now he felt not only that he was called of God, but that he had been saved by the hand of God. Was this for some great work? His ministry assumed a grandeur and solemnity, to his youthful imagination, akin to the work of the prophets of old; what wonder if this seemed to him the very refutation of the worldly wisdom and estimate which the Judge had put upon his life in a rustic parish, and his enthusiasm was kindled anew.

There rose within him high hopes and rare promises of what he might do among this people. The sordid side of what his compensation was to be, sank into nothingness before this aspect of his work and its rewards;—he would awaken these people, rouse their intellects, win their affections, engage them heart and soul with him. They should shake off the lethargy of their narrow life, and live a new life, in a larger sphere; touch the great living, thinking world

2

and be touched by it; feel the pulse of the great intellect of humanity, the *welt-geist;* and rise to touch eternal things, looking from the grandeur of the things seen and temporal to the glory of the things unseen and eternal.

He would rouse them to know the beautiful truths of science,—of art,—of literature and of religion; their feet should tread with him on the high places of earth, and look off to the battlements of the eternal city.

So he drove up over those wide barrens, through the dark, primeval forests, like a knight errant of the nineteenth century, to tread the enchanted ground where sordid and petty cares had thrown the spell of an enthralling sleep; he was bearing an Ithuriel's spear, at touch of which these sleepers should waken.

Who were these dwellers on this enchanted ground, and what sort of material do they offer for the realization of the hopes and aims of the ardent, young minister?

With the exception of the three or four storekeepers of the small, miscellaneous stores of the village, the Judge and two other lawyers, the doctor, two blacksmiths, a wheelwright, and that man of all trades, the village cabinet maker and undertaker, named Tim Mitchell,—all the rest were farmers, farmer's wives, sons, daughters and widows; and, as the rocky soil was not kindly to crops, and the late spring and early winter made but a short season, they were almost all dairy farmers.

Almost every house was furnished with a dairy

cellar, and the front yard was garnished with bright, tin pans, sunning themselves sweet.

The churns were often driven by water-power, and the water-wheels of those houses that were in a valley with a stream running through it, made them look like a succession of small grist mills. Where water-power was wanting, a stray bear was found following the uncongenial trade of making butter; or a great, fat sheep was on the treadmill (for mutton throve at this kind of work); or else a shaggy New-foundland dog was on duty,—when he could be found; for the trouble with these churners was that they were too keen of wit, and, keeping count of churning day, they were off to the woods, from dawn to dewy eve, so that churning day must be made a movable feast in order to secure these quick-witted servants, in whom conscience had but a rudimentary development.

The other main industry of this section was tanning, the evidences of which were the great piles of tan-bark which one saw stacked along the roadside, or met being hauled on sledges in the winter, and also the unpleasant load of fresh hides, which would frighten some horses into madness, and horrify the nostrils of the driver, for a mile or more. The tanneries made the streams run red, and drove the trout from the lower waters; but they brought business to the country stores, and gave the farmers steady winter occupation hauling the tan-bark.

Beside the maple sugar making, which was more a pastime for a winter's holiday, the only other industry was scoop-making. These scoop-makers were a tribe as distinct and apart from the rest of the community as though they were gypsies; they lived in a settlement four or five miles north-west of the town, near Pleasant Pond, a rude little hamlet of one-story shanties.   Their larders were replenished at the expense of a wide range of hen-roosts and sheep-pastures.   Here they fashioned, with rude tools, by hand, from the hard maple, those large wooden scoops with which sugar and grain are handled, and the wooden bowls in which the butter is worked.   They came to town with a great load of these scoops strung over their shoulders, or, haply, if they were well to do, hung panier-fashion on a donkey's back.   The stated barter of their wares was for opium, and all the country stores kept a tin case of the soft, dark, fascinating gum; for this dwarfed, stupid race were constant consumers of the drug, which they took in the simplest fashion, by rolling a small portion into a ball, about the size of a pea, and lodging it in a corner of the mouth.

CHAPTER III.

TO this community came the young minister, surcharged with his high purposes, to seek their realization. He found lodging at the village inn, and was given a warm welcome by the old Episcopal minister, the Rev. William Forrester, the length of whose ministry may be inferred from the fact that he always carried a faded green cotton umbrella of solid construction and broad dimensions, and told the young minister that he had acquired the habit because he owed his life to just such an umbrella. He had, in the early days of his ministry, paid a parochial visit to an outlying farm-house, and was returning home, when a pack of six wolves started in pursuit of him. He whipped up his horse, and had a fair show of distancing his pursuers, when, to his dismay, he came upon a tree fallen directly across the road. Out he jumped, to break down the branches and leap his horse over the trunk and drag over the sleigh; on came the wolves; in lieu of any other weapon, he picked up his umbrella and pointed it at the pack, with the effect of halting them, then, with a step forward and a great shout, he suddenly opened the umbrella, at which the pack turned tail and fled to a respectful distance; and, by repeating this at intervals, he made good his escape; therefore he always carried a green cotton umbrella.

Beside the old rector, there was young Fred Hutton, the dry-goods clerk, who went periodically to the city and came home with astonishing neck-ties, and the air of a man of the world, and a debonair style that was the admiration of the village belles and the envy and detestation of the rustic swains.

The two other boarders were Mrs. Hollis, the widow of a Presbyterian minister, and her daughter Amelia (Mealy Ann, the old lady called her), but she herself, having surreptitiously read several translations of some wicked French novels, always spelled her name Amèlie, with a tremendously acute accent on the penult, and with a breadth of pronunciation to the first letter that made it almost a groan.

She was fading into the forties, but was still young at heart, and capable of keeping Fred in practice; showing how entirely relative is our estimate of the flight of time.

Old Mrs. Hollis was sick with consumption, and was always nearing her end. She was able to endure all the pains of sickness better than exclusion from the news of what was doing in her little world, and thankful that her infirmities did not incline toward deafness. The watchers in the next room, on one of those nights when her dissolution had been announced, as they sat conversing in subdued accents, were startled, as by a voice from the tomb, when the old lady, in a ghastly but penetrating whisper, interrupted them, "Speak out loud, for mercy's sake. I could bear to hear it thunder better than to have you whisper." This meant much from her, for, of all things, she feared a thunder storm.

Her first greeting to Henry Dinsmore was, " I am very glad to see a minister safely settled over this church, and thank the Lord that you are not married, and have come to live in the hotel; for now I can have a good night's rest."

" Why so, Mrs. Hollis? " queried the young parson; at a loss to know why he should prove a narcotic to this old lady.

" Because I am terrible afraid of thunder," answered the old lady; " and I'm sure the Lord will not let the house be struck by lightning while a minister is in it."

" But you have Mr. Forrester here," he answered, smiling at the odd conceit that to his ordinary pastoral duties should be added this of serving as a non-conductor.

" Oh! yes," answered the old lady, with a grim smile, " but I never reckoned that the Episcopals was any protection against thunder and lightning."

And yet it seemed to Dinsmore that the old rector would be the more effective lightning-arrester, for he was a corpulent, slow-gaited, old gentleman, always with his green cotton umbrella tightly clasped under his arm, ready to stop anywhere and at any time to have a chat with anybody, and of an absorbent nature.

Forty years ago he had come here, to his first, and only, charge, and, six months later, he had brought his young wife, who stayed two weeks, and then suddenly left and never came back again; why, no one ever knew; she was living still, but never a letter had passed between them during these forty years;

this much the post-masters and mistresses covering that period could tell; more than this no one knew, save that her name never passed his lips.   Of course, there was a great stir at first, and a disposition to enquire who was in the wrong, but Mr. Forrester prudently baffled all such attempts, and quietly lived down the little flutter of scandal that followed her leaving, and that was the end of it.

Now he was old and failing, his speech was thick, his false teeth were all the while dropping down in the midst of a sentence and clipping it in an untimely fashion; but one soon became accustomed to this, so that it seemed only one of his personal peculiarities, and did not seriously mar his conversation.   He was genial and kindly to all, wise and politic in his relations to his neighbors of the other churches.

His weakness was strawberries, of which he always secured the first basket from the gardens of his parishioners, and bore them home in triumph, along with the dose which he had gotten at the apothecary's to overcome the painful fact that strawberries would not agree with him.

There were alternate services at the Episcopal and Presbyterian churches on Sunday evenings, as the village did not furnish a church-going element large enough to make two evening congregations; and the rector was diligent in his attendance at Dinsmore's evening service, where he sat in a rear seat and counted the attendance carefully, keeping tally as though it were a series of games, and reckoned with glee when the count was in his favor.

To him the young parson first unburdened his

heart regarding the mission with which he felt himself charged.

"I want to talk with you, Mr. Forrester, over the intellectual and spiritual needs of this community," said Henry one day, as the old rector and he were chatting, and the old man had been posting him about some of the family quarrels which offered dangerous pitfalls for the uninitiated.

"Yes, yes," said the old rector uneasily, "there are some of them who don't get to church more than once a year; but they would only make trouble if they did come, and it is just as well to leave them alone; but you must remember not to say anything about the widow Hollis when you visit Martin Shelton, for her husband and old Dominie Shelton had a great spat because Amelia Ann wouldn't take a shine to Martin. You'll have your hands full attending to those you have in your church, without bothering about outsiders; and do you go to Mother Livingston's to tea, and tell me what you think of her chicken-pie,—I haven't a member of my congregation that makes such chicken-pie as hers."

And so he rattled on, to the dismay of the ardent young enthusiast. He too seemed to have withered in this dry mountain air,—was there a fatality about the place, which blighted hope and enervated a man's vital force, and must he, in time, succumb to its influence? Now it was but another spur to his enthusiasm, this lethargy of all around him; another motive to his ambition; he would stir these dry bones and cause the Spirit of the Lord to breathe upon them, so that they should live.

There was another element of his parish, an out-lying band, which enlisted his keen interest. He came in contact with one of the scoop-makers, and this set him to inquiring into the history of this outcast tribe.

One cold November twilight he was walking briskly through the crisp air, on his way home from a turn at skating on Pleasant Pond; familiar objects were taking the outlandish shapes which they assume at this confusing hour, when he noticed by the roadside a strange looking object that refused to be classified.

The air was keen and raw, and he was in a hungry hurry to be home, but stopped to investigate.

It was a "Scooper," who, having taken a drop too much, had made a stone his pillow, and the bag in which he had carried the scoops his blanket, and the open sky his shelter.

Henry Dinsmore concluded that he was likely to see the end of his earthly career if he spent the night in such quarters, and therefore stayed the urgent appeals of hunger to set the "Scooper" on his feet again. This having been accomplished, in the face of his violent protest, and the scattered contents being restored to the sack, a loaf or two of bread, a piece of bacon, a few small packages of groceries, among which was the usual chunk of opium, then, with sack laid over his shoulder, the young pastor set the wanderer's face toward home.

"Who be ye, anyway, that are meddlin' in my affairs?" said the irate "Scooper."

"I am the new pastor of the Presbyterian church in Clintonville," answered Henry.

"It's a pity ye don't begin by mindin' your own

business. I know what ye think. Ye think I'm
drunk; I ain't too drunk to lick you; and I'll do it,
by Jove, the next time you lay your hands on me,
you good-for-nothing, beggarly, snivelling parson."

And off he went, muttering, over the hill; and a
grotesque silhouette he made against the faint, cold
light that lingered in the evening sky.

Here was another problem for his solution, to reach
this besotted band of outcasts who were far out of
hearing of the church bells, and beyond the pale of
any influence which the christian community, in which
they lived, could exert upon them. There were not
a few who, living in the far outskirts of the settlements, knew the minister only as he came among
them to marry them or bury their dead; but these
Ishmaelites were even farther outside the pale of
christian influence than this, they were married by
some uncouth ceremonial of their own, or by the
squire, and they buried their dead as they buried a
dog, without other ceremony than the funeral feast,
at which they drowned their sorrow in drink, or with
their favorite drug.

Clearly, there was but one way to reach these
outcasts, and that was to go in among them and
gain some personal hold upon them; and his first
essay in this direction had not been encouraging.

He was not daunted by this array of natural resistance in the material upon which he had to work,
but he was sorely perplexed. The general tone
around him was discouraging. It reflected the old
rector's policy of pursuing the beaten path, and
" minding his own business " as the " Scooper " put

it; that business being to preach in all weathers, no matter how stormy, attend every funeral and wedding at which he was called to officiate, to baptize the babies, and eat the chicken pies and all the rest of the hospitable offerings under which the tables groaned when the minister was asked to dinner,—this, with the accurate memory of the children's names and birthdays, was enough to keep a man busy.

And these sentiments of the kindly, old rector, who was universally popular, were re-echoed by the elders of his own church session, who thought the flock of God was the true field of labor for the Shepherd, and it was enough to fill his heart and mind to prepare suitable, spiritual food for them; and they were wary of committing themselves to the endorsement of any other plans or schemes than this strictly ministerial work.

So that, before long, he began to think that he was "the voice of one crying in the wilderness;" but this only made him feel more strongly the prophetic impulse rise within him,—resistance called forth his energies to overcome it.

The Sunday after his installation, on which Henry Dinsmore was to preach his first sermon as pastor of the church, was a fair June day. The window of his room opened on the balcony that overlooked the village green.

The merry robins and the noisy blackbirds that were nesting in the trees on the green, had stirred his restless sleep with their matins, and the vagrant wind sent whiffs of the honeysuckle in at the open window.

It was useless to try to sleep again, so he walked up and down the balcony until breakfast time.

From the corner of the village green nearest to the Inn a straight path led to the steps of the gray stone court-house, with the grated windows of its cells looking out toward the church. From the other corner, as straight a path led to the porch of the white church with its green blinds. They crossed in the centre, forming a great X in the green sward.

After breakfast he came up again and paced the balcony, reviewing the past and forecasting the future. What a glorious day it was; how full of bounding life his pulses beat.

An hour before church time the wagons from the country began to come in; there would be a great congregation to-day.

He watched the people gather in groups in the church porch and on the grass in front.

Half an hour before the time of service, the bell rang out. It startled him, for he had forgotten the country custom. Then, as he stood there listening to it, he felt a thrill of excitement, as the air throbbed with the sweet tones, and the listless wind carried them out over the hills and down the roads where the wagons were bringing his people to church.

The tender glory of the summer day, the gathering of the people, the sacred mission with which he felt himself charged, the far floating angelus from the belfry, stirred him, excited him, elated him.

As he passed out from the Inn, if he had followed his impulse, instead of walking up the two sides of the triangle which the path traversed, he would have vaulted the fence and made across the sward on a run.

But his feet were shackled by the decorum due to the many eyes that were fixed on him from the moment he left the porch of the Inn.

He could see a movement among the people as soon as he came in sight, a sort of huddling together.

The two sides of that triangle seemed half a mile long, as he measured each step that he took and wondered whether he was walking with becoming gravity.

As he neared the church, the groups of people fell back and those in the porch retreated into the church and took their seats. Only here and there one who had met him ventured to bow. Two of the elders came forward and shook hands with him; and those who were near enough craned their necks to catch even a word of what the young pastor said, and repeated it, with pride, to those who were not so venturesome.

Dinsmore tried to look pleasantly on them all and give an inclusive bow to the various groups, as he passed them; but any notice from him served only to embarrass them.

As he sat in the pulpit watching them assemble in church, and pew after pew was filled, until the church was crowded, and the assembly sat still and expectant every eye fastened on him, there coursed through his brain again and again like vivid flashes, the hopes and ambitions that had led him to this position.

He was at the threshold of his ministry. What lay behind the veil?

Under the impulse of such thoughts as these, he stood up before them without notes save a small bit of paper which he twisted nervously in his hands until anything written on it was soon past reading, and looking the congregation over, with a flash in his eye, and a twitching in the corners of his mouth, he began in a low, conversational tone to talk to them.

"This is a very sacred moment to me when I begin my ministry among you. I have come to you not only in response to your call, but in obedience to a summons from the head of the Church. On my way hither I have been saved from sudden death, and such a scene stirs the depths of the spirit. For what purpose am I here? and is my mission to be one of good or ill? My effort shall be to make my coming here a blessing, and the words of the great apostle to the Romans, Chapter 13, 11, embody my first conception of my work. 'Knowing the time, that now it is high time to awake out of sleep; for now is our salvation nearer than when we believed.'

"To know the time, the period in which we live, the great trend of our age, this the apostle assumes as the basis of the christian's duty. Ours is a time when all questions are being mooted, when foundation truths are rising to the surface, as in the great, formative, geologic periods when the granite was upheaved to the mountain tops, and the physical features of the earth were established.

"Men are questioning nature to make her unlock her treasury and yield her resources for our use, and tell us the secrets of her laboratory, and 'we must not be afraid to open our eyes before the face of nature.'

"Men are questioning the old forms of belief, and are formulating new ones. Some are asking, what shall we believe? Others ask, shall we believe anything at all? Has not the era of faith passed by? Is not this the era of experiment, observation and test, out of which is to come the science and religion of the future, both resting on the same substantial foundation of deduction framed by a rational process, and therefore within the grasp of every intelligent mind, a tangible, reasonable, human religion, capable of demonstration? In the midst of this molten mass of thought and feeling, the Christian Church of to-day is bound to rouse herself. She has passed through the era of persecution, sealing her testimony with her blood; she was awake then, she must not be found asleep now.

"The time when these words were spoken was not unlike our own times. There was a decay of fixed belief, a revolt against traditional religion, a contempt for its priests and oracles. The problems which are agitating us now, were then under discussion; some of them had been settled, others were being debated with a freedom and acuteness, with a force and elegance, which throw into the shade our modern philosophers. There were pessimists and optimists, stoics and epicureans, rationalists and agnostics, in those days, as there are now. The present phases of thought are but a recurrence, within a vast cycle, of the intellectual comets of that day; the repetition, in nineteenth century phrase, of the old Greek forms of thought.

"But it all had the effect of rousing the cultured

apostle, who was a classical scholar as well as thoroughly taught in the school of Gamaliel. When he stood on Mars Hill, and saw Athens full of idols, his heart was stirred within him; when he looked at the current thought of his time, he makes this stirring appeal, 'It is high time to awake out of sleep.'

"This summons is enforced by the fact that the world around us is awake. Go to a public library and search its alcoves of Science, History, or Fiction, and you will find the volumes full of these stirring questions.

"Scientists are telling us that a man cannot be an honest and effective searcher after nature's truths unless he first repudiate religion. Philosophers are telling us that but one conclusion can be reached by the untrammelled thinker, viz: Agnosticism.

"Novelists are presenting us heroes and heroines whose sole interest lies in the fact that they have discarded the restraints of moral law, or who enter into a battle with unbelief only to succumb with easy grace.

"Yes, you will find preachers filling the pulpits of Christian churches, owing their position in the community, their influence, yes, their daily bread, to those churches, and, all the while, using their ministerial position to undermine the creed of the church which they have sworn to uphold in their ordination vows. All these are awake, noisy, active, bustling, loudmouthed; therefore it is high time for us to awake out of sleep.

"I shall in the future have something to say as to the attitude that it becomes us to take toward these

3

forms of belief or unbelief; now I will confine myself to the single thought of the text.

"There are three spiritual narcotics against which I
would warn you; Selfishness, Worldliness, and Orthodoxy. When we have centred our thought upon
ourselves, and our own interests, and the petty concerns which involve us alone have become the chief
object of our thoughts, then we are lulled into a pro-
found sleep toward everything else, our ears are deaf,
our eyes are closed, our hearts are hardened, to the
trials, sorrows or struggles of those who are nearest
to us; and as for the great outside world, it is as
though it were not. For such there is no claim that
can assert itself for a moment beside the unremitting
demands which self makes upon our whole time and
thought. But the spirit of this age rebukes this selfishness at every turn, and re-echoes the divine word,
'No man liveth unto himself,' 'All men are of one
blood;' and the age summons these sleepers to
awaken, with the emphatic reiteration which it makes
of the universal brotherhood of man.

"But where selfishness has not hardened the heart,
worldliness often makes it foul. There is a sordid
canker about a man's heart when he has come to regard the gain of riches, the increase of flocks or
herds, of land or money, as an end in life. Then
all the evils which attend upon the degradation of a
higher nature to base and ignoble ends, flock into
the man's heart, and make it their home,—avarice,
.ust, envy, malice, covetousness, uncharitableness,
like ill-omened birds, find places to hatch their brood.
His fellow men become the objects of his prey, and

he is little better than the ravening wolf that lives
only to devour the weak or defenceless. How such
an one gloats over the conquest, by cunning or even
by deception, of the innocent and honest victim of
one of his shrewd bargains; and soon cunning ripens
into treachery and fraud, and the man's whole moral
nature succumbs to his greed of gain. Conscience is
stilled, honor is hushed to sleep, pity and compassion
are slain, in the heart where this greed of gain has
gotten the mastery. My friends, this is no time in
which to let the world see such a vice creeping in
among those who call themselves Christians. It is
an age of charity, of freedom for the oppressed, of
equal rights, of the organization of labor against op-
pression; and whatever body of men would lead the
thought of to-day, must be on the right side of this
question. It is high time to awake from the sleep
of worldliness, and let the world see that we are alive
to the wants and sufferings of our fellow men, and
feel for them, and have a remedy for them; or to let
some one who has such a remedy take our place.

"But there is a deadlier drug than either of these;
for it is a self-evident truth that the man, or body
of men, who are infused with selfishness or worldliness have no mission in our time but to hide themselves out of sight; the man that acknowledges either
of these as the prime motive power of his life, stands
self-convicted.

"But there is a spiritual narcotic that is well-nigh
irresistible in its hardening influence. A cold, comfortable, self-assured, Pharisaic orthodoxy, resting
securely in the form of godliness without the power

thereof, intrenched in the security of its pure, un-
adulterated theology, the assurance that it alone possesses the 'faith once delivered to the saints.' For
the outside world it has the cold comfort crystalized
in the term 'uncovenanted mercies.' It can whine
hymns, recite scripture phrases without limit, can
even pump up a few tears for seasons of special religious fervor, and in general can go through all the
formulas of a wordy religion, but, at bottom, the heart
is hard as the nether millstone. Its repose is complete, its lullaby is in the correct form, and you can
teach it nothing, for it has all the stock phrases and
arguments at its finger ends.

" But how fatally it has made torpid all those attributes of heart and mind which religion is supposed
to awaken and stir, you will see when you bring it
into contact with any of those forms in which the
life of our time manifests itself.

"Send the heart burdened with real trial and sorrow to such an one, and its stock phrases are like the
stab of cold steel. Send the doubting and perplexed
to such an one with the stirring questions of the time,
asking bread, and he is given a stone, or the self-
righteous theological wrath of this strait-laced for-
malist is roused because the enquirer drops his 'h '
in Shibboleth. Such religion will not pass for christianity in our time, and we may as well awaken to
the fact. It is high time for us to wake up to it, and
cast off the grave-clothes of a dead orthodoxy, and
show the world a living faith, working by love
and purifying the heart, and making us love our
neighbor as ourselves.

"And the reason given by the apostle should give another impetus to our awaking, 'Now is our salvation nearer than when we believed.' Yes, every such stirring of the dry bones, every such shaking of the nations, brings the salvation of the world so much the nearer. Every time that the tree is shaken the dead twigs and leaves, the sickly and worm-eaten fruit falls, and the ripe fruit has the larger flow of sap put into it. Every crisis which the church passes through, every assault which she undergoes, brings out the truth, sets it in clearer lights, casts off narrowing forms and modes of belief, broadens her sympathies, strengthens her influence.

"Viewed from any possible standpoint, the result must be to bring our salvation nearer, to emancipate us from vulgar errors, to put us on the true path to the final and ultimate form of religion. If Christianity is all wrong, her foundations uncertain and vague, her teaching misleading, her morality insufficient, her revelation unsatisfactory, we are about to learn that, if the combined assault of men and women can show it; and our salvation is nearer than when we believed, for now will the philosophers tell us wherein our salvation lies. But if, on the other hand, Christianity is right, then will she surely be able to vindicate herself now as she has done in the past, and as every possible assault is being made, we may anticipate that her endurance of this crucial test must stop the mouths of her enemies, or, at least, leave her friends firmly established in the faith; and therefore our salvation is nearer than when we believed. For my part I am ready for the issue, but let us meet it awake; wherever the truth may lead us, wherever an honest, open-eyed, candid, consideration of the arguments on both sides of this grave question lands us, there let us stand firm and un-wavering, and say as Philip said, 'now we have seen with our own eyes, and know ;' but do not let the issue find us asleep.

" This then, is my conception of my mission among you, to stand side by side with you, with eager and searching heart, gazing open-eyed at these great questions, asking only to be led into the knowledge of the truth.

" But let us understand distinctly, that Christianity is not on trial any more than infidelity, that there is no presumption against her truths, that we are not entering into a warfare, but are honest searchers after truth; if infidelity, so-called, can show us a deeper religious philosophy, a higher view of the nature and destiny of man, a better morality, more inspiring motives, holier lives, purer and sweeter con-solation in sorrow, and character moulded on higher principles, and all this on the basis of a clearer and more substantial revelation than the teaching of Christ, then, in the name of truth and purity and goodness, let us turn to infidelity.   But everywhere where our eyes behold the light which is purest, sweetest, strongest, most invigorating, thither let us turn, and walk in the light."

There were various comments on the young domi-nie's stirring sermon; the young people were charmed with it, his voice was so lovely, he was so handsome and so much in earnest.

Deacon Shelton said, "He means well, and is not too old to learn; there is power in the young man." This the deacon was fain to acknowledge, for the sermon had kept him awake, while in the old dominie's time, being full of unshaken confidence, he could always take a comfortable doze after sixthly, and feel sure of the result; but under this young man he was restless; so was Deacon Shrake, especially when the fruits of covetousness were being delineated.

CHAPTER IV.

A T the Fall meeting of Presbytery, Henry Dinsmore had an opportunity of seeing something
of the social life, as well as the ecclesiastical work
of his fellow presbyters. He had never been thrown
into any intimate association with ministers, and had
gotten the notion that a solemnity, amounting almost
to austerity, marked their social intercourse; that the
grave and earnest debates, rising sometimes to a degree that might be called heated, which characterized
their discussions in the meetings of the Presbytery,
were transferred to the recess between the meetings,
and were carried on over the dinner table.

Especially did he hold in awe a certain Dr. Henry
L. Bainbridge, who was one of the war-horses of the
Assembly, who stood for all that he regarded as the
essentially old and orthodox views in theology, with
a vehemence of thought and utterance, with a fire of
eye and thunder of voice, and strong speech, rising
often to eloquence, that made him an antagonist to
be dreaded.

In this region the meetings of Presbytery were
largely social, as well as religious, gatherings. Most
of the ministers, with their elders, drove to the place
of meeting, over the hills and through the valleys;
and, as one drew nearer to the village where the

meeting was to be, from converging roads, there would gather a number of these carriages, and the long string of vehicles would jog merrily along with salutations shouted or waved from one to another. At some comfortable farm-house by the way, well known for the hospitality of its good man and the chicken-pie of the good wife, the caravan would halt for lunch, and take up their way, mightily refreshed in mind and body. The meetings always lasted three, and often four, days, and gave the pastors time to talk over with each other the trials and the prospects of their work, and discuss all sorts of topics that could not come before the Presbytery as a body. Those who lived in the larger towns could generally command the services of one of the regular stage lines; and these were full to overflowing.

On one of these stage-rides Henry saw something of the humorous side of the great Boanerges, whose name was such a terror to the younger ministers, and it dispelled his fears, once for all.

They had halted for dinner at the half-way house, and as the ministers and elders gathered around the stage door to resume their places for the afternoon journey, there came, elbowing through the crowd, a poorly dressed man, far gone in his cups. Dr. Bainbridge had taken his place on the rear seat, with a brother minister beside him; the driver shoved the drunken man aside, and told him roughly that he was not fit to ride on the inside with gentlemen, nor on the outside, for fear he would break his neck. The poor fellow stood, in maudlin hopelessness, staring into the stage.

"How, the dickens, will Nance and the kid git along without me to-night?" he said, almost in tears.

"They'll do a blamed sight better without you than with you," retorted Tom Burton roughly. "Git! I tell you, for you're not goin' to ride inside with these gentlemen."

"It's hard on Nance," said the poor drunkard ruefully. "I'll have to stay here all night, and if I do I'll git drunk as a beast before night. Yes, I will; I know I will."

Then Dr. Bainbridge leaned out of the stage, and told Tom to let him come in, and they would look after him. Up mounted the poor fellow, and sat himself down on the middle seat, with his back to Dr. Bainbridge, and, facing him, on the front seat, was the Doctor's elder. The tipsy fellow leered triumphantly at Tom as he shut the door and put up the steps. Tom muttered, "They'll have their full o' ye before they've gone far;" and mounted to his seat.

Everything went smoothly enough with this uncouth guest of the parsons, until, after a half hour's blinking with owlish and studied gravity of demeanor, he addressed the Doctor's elder.

"Who be ye fellows anyway? Hang me! ef I can make ye out. You're a'most the queerest lot I ever struck."

"We are Presbyterian ministers and elders, on our way to the meeting of Presbytery," said the Doctor's elder.

"Give us your flipper, old chap," said the tipsy man. "My name's Bill Nash, and I'm a Presbyterian and an Old-school Presbyterian," and he smiled a genial welcome on them all as he shook hands with Elder McBride. Then drawing himself up haughtily, he said, "I hope you ain't New-school men."

"Oh! No," answered Mr. McBride, "we are all Old-school men, dyed in the grain."

"That's right," said Bill, heartily, "now I feel to home. Why, I've been an Old-school man a great many years; I'm one of Dr. Bainbridge's men; he converted me."

There was a roar of laughter from the whole stage, and Henry Dinsmore looked quickly at the Doctor to see how he would take the laugh; his mouth was twitching, and his eye twinkling. The mischievous elder kept stirring Bill on to talk, which was not hard to do, as he had the proud consciousness that, somehow, he had made a hit.

"Do you know the Doctor?" said Bill to the elder. "He's a great man on theology, and has convertin' power not to be beat by any man I ever see."

"Yes," said the elder, "I know him."

"Did he convert you?" said Bill, leering at him, "you look like one of his boys; I allus think I can tell 'em at sight."

This time the laugh fell on McBride, in which the Doctor joined, so heartily as to draw Bill's attention on him, and facing round, with some difficulty, he bore down on the Doctor with

"What's the matter with you, old crony? Do you know Doctor Bainbridge too?"

"Yes," said the Doctor, "I think I do."

"Well, you needn't answer that way," said Bill, with a touch of contempt in his tone. "Either you do know him or you don't. There ain't any mistakin' him. Does he know you?"

"Well, yes," said the Doctor, "I guess he does."

"There you are 'guessin'' again," said Bill angrily. "Can't ye give a straight out, honest answer to a fellow? Do you know Dr. Bainbridge?"

"Yes," answered the Doctor, soberly, amid the smothered laughter of the rest. "Yes, I know him to my cost. He has given me more trouble than any living man."

"Well why don't you shake him off, and be done with him, as I have," said Bill, sympathetically.

"I can't," said the Doctor. "I can't get rid of him."

"Well what's the matter twixt you and him?" said Bill; then, with a knowing wink, "I know what's the matter. You've been tradin' hosses with the Doctor."

A tremendous roar greeted this solution of the trouble which Bill had given with a tender sympathy and a wise shake of the head, that added an irresistibly comic flavor to his words. Encouraged by such applause, he plunged on, "You mustn't do that, you know, for the Doctor's a keener on a horse. He was bred in the blue-grass region; and there ain't divinity enough on earth to knock hoss out of a man if it gits into him early. There ain't a man in this State drives a finer span, or knows how to handle the ribbons better than the Doctor. It'll do to go and hear him preach, as much as you like; that won't hurt you a bit, and it may do you good; it did me heaps o' good; but don't you never be fool enough to swap hosses with him again."

Peals of laughter encouraged Bill as he cornered the Doctor and delivered him this homily on horse-trading.

When they reached their destination, Bill fired a parting shot of admonition at the Doctor to keep clear of horse-trading with Doctor Bainbridge.

As they got out of the stage, Bill stood a little to one side, while a crowd gathered round to welcome the party on their arrival; and the famous Doctor was the recipient of special attentions.

Bill stepped up to his friend the elder, and asked him "Who is that old feller that got done in a trade, him with that old soft felt hat and big necktie?"

"Why, that's Dr. Bainbridge," said the elder.

Off lurched Bill, with eager but unsteady gait, and, pushing his way into the crowd, almost threw himself on the Doctor's neck, as he astonished the Doctor's circle of friends with his maudlin greeting—

"Why, Doctor, don't you know me? I'm Bill Nash, an Old-school Presbyterian; you converted me."

Those who had winced under the Doctor's invective certainly had the opportunity, for once in their lives, of seeing him quail and leave the field to his adversary, without even trying to make a stand.

But, for one at least, it opened a new side to the great theologian's character, and made Henry Dinsmore feel that he was not unassailable, and therefore, he felt, not unapproachable.

There was great magnetism about the man, a sense of breadth and fulness to his nature, a large-hearted generosity, which made one feel that there was room for you in his great heart, if you could find your corner. He was a born leader of men, and would have been distinguished in the state or in the army, if that had been his chosen path.

To him therefore, in the intervals of the meetings of Presbytery, Henry Dinsmore unburdened his heart regarding his purposes and their realization.

"Well, my dear young brother, the first thing for you to learn is that the Lord makes men; they are not the creatures of circumstance. The second thing to learn is that He has made all sorts and conditions of men, in order to compose the great unit which we call humanity; thirdly, that each one of these units has its place and value in the mass, even the ciphers; and you have got to respect each one for what he is worth; then study what he is, then try to develop him into his best. You can't create him over, and you would make an awful mess of it if you could; you can develop him, with God's help; and that is your mission in life.

"There are some people, who know nothing about us ministers, who think that because we have settled convictions, have thought out and set in order our views on religious truth, that, therefore, we think all men who are religious must think just alike, must feel just alike, and act just alike. Well, they are welcome to their opinion, if it amuses them; but there is not one grain of truth at the bottom of it."

"But, Doctor Bainbridge," interjected Henry, who

was startled by this train of thought, "we are certainly bound to teach the standards of our church, and the theology that has been her glory and has made her the defender of the faith."

"Of course you are bound so to teach, if you are a Presbyterian minister, for that is what you have pledged yourself to do, because you declare it to be your own free, honest conviction. But there is no compulsion about it. You come forward and say you heartily believe a certain system of doctrine and want to preach it, and we tell you to study it carefully and understand fully and precisely what it is, and at the end of that course of study, we examine you thoroughly, and ask you to state whether you adhere to those views with which you entered upon your course of study, and leave you to say yes, or no. If you declare your belief in them, and you desire to preach and teach them, we give you our license and authority, which commends you to all our churches, as a man fitted, in our judgment, to teach and preach. We do not ask nor expect that the Methodist ministry or the Episcopal ministry shall teach this theology, and, even in our own church, we recognize a very broad margin of individual opinion as allowable."

"We certainly are reputed to be rigid in our doctrines and in our enforcement of orthodox views," said Henry.

"We are reputed to be a great many things that we are not, sour-visaged and grim in conduct and belief; and you have found how far away our merry gatherings are from any such reality as that; so that

the fun and good stories of our ministry are a proverb among our people.   I abominate that word rigid,
nor have I ever in my ministry seen any attempt at
a rigid enforcement of our doctrine or mode of worship.   We have the ecclesiastical care and charge of
a certain set of congregations, who accept a certain
interpretation of scripture, and have formulated that
belief just as clearly, precisely and definitely as we
know how, and yet without malice or bitterness
toward any who believe differently from ourselves.
A man comes to us, neither driven nor coaxed thereto,
and says, I believe as you do, will you authorize me
to preach among your people? We examine him
carefully to see that he does understand distinctly
what he believes, and license him to preach. This is
the only course consistent with good faith to all
parties, and implies neither rigidity nor force on our
part.   I am sick of this balderdash.   A man is free
when he comes to us, and he is free to go just when
he pleases; he is not, of course, free to stay and
profess to believe one thing and teach another; that
is dishonest to himself and to the people of our parishes.   But I say always and ever, let a man preach
what he believes; no other preaching is worth a
rush.   If he believes our standards, let him preach
them, heart and soul, and stand up to his belief; if
he does not, let him go to the church whose standards he can accept and preach to them; but if he believes nothing, then, in God's name, let him stop
preaching, and go to some honest trade, into which
he can put his whole heart and strength."   The old
Doctor grew earnest, and thundered forth these sen-

tences on the young man as if he were the imperson-
ation of a great assembly.

"I am not one whit at a loss as to my own belief,
Doctor," said Henry, amused at the way in which
this speech had been hurtled at him. "I am very
certain and hearty in my acceptance of our standards, strictly interpreted; but I am very uncertain of
my power to cope with the difficulties of my work.
Those mountain farmers seem to have fallen asleep
on their hill-tops; and I do not know how to wake
them."

"My young brother, let me counsel you a bit; first
of all be sure of your facts. You know that the
signs of life are not always the same. There is a
quiet, reserved manner, often seen in people who
have lived apart from their fellow men, which is the
result of shyness and diffidence that is timid in giving
expression to feeling, but which only exemplifies the
proverb 'that still waters run deep.' Underneath
that silent, shy reserve, lie the thoughts and passions
that find utterance in those who have the power of
utterance. So, before you begin to wake these
people, just study them a bit, and see which are
awake; for if you do not, some of them will give you
a start. Then remember that every human soul is
an individual flower, fashioned by the hand of God,
and developed by experiences peculiar, in some respects, to itself, and different from any other. That
product is not to be roughly laid hold of by you, to
shape according to your will and change to suit your
own notions. Reverence the human souls with which
you have to deal; the meanest of them can teach

4

you something; study and ponder well the experiences through which One wiser than you has led and formed them, and, out of this study, learn how you may lead them onward and upward. Be content if you see that they are growing and developing naturally and sweetly under God's gracious influence, as flowers grow, slowly, under his sunshine and dew; and study them, so as not to make the mistake of trying to shape them all after one set pattern.

"Above all, teach them, by precept and example, that religion is not a matter of creed or forms of belief in words or worship, but that it is God's truth transforming life and heart, belief converted into action. How often have I seen men steal the livery of heaven to robe the devil of their pride and indolence, when they declared their trust in God's grace and in His transforming power, etc., etc. *ad nauseam;* by all of which they meant only to shelter their own lazy indifference to exertion. God's grace is the man nerving himself to do what is right, and to shun what is evil; and the man who prates of trust in God, and goes on doing his own way, is one of the saddest instances of the perversion of truth into a blinding error. We must be earnest, and we must be honest about this matter of religion; or else there is no use of bothering ourselves about it at all."

Such a talk as this with such a man was an era in the young minister's life and as he told of his own plans and hopes the Doctor listened with interest, with here and there a pungent, and often witty, parenthesis thrown in.

This conference made these two men warm friends, and brought them into correspondence; and many a visit, helpful and suggestive to the younger man, in after years, was the outcome of this first meeting; for it was the Doctor's aim not to quench, but only to temper the ardor of youth.

CHAPTER V.

IT was hard for the restless, earnest spirit of Dinsmore to find a field for its exercise, in the still life of this out-of-the-way community. There were no mills, with their scant-paid and overworked operatives, in whose behalf he could exert himself by remonstrance with their employers. Among these well-to-do farmers there was, here and there, one who, through shiftlessness or misfortune, needed help; but the help was forthcoming from some kind-hearted neighbors, before Dinsmore could find a chance to let any one know of it; and he himself often knew of the distress only by hearing of its relief. It was of no use to organize a charitable society where want was sure to call in some kind neighbor before it was apparent to any outsider.

In the village there was an organized aid society of the most efficient kind that he had ever seen or read of; it was in session every day, and its president, secretary and visiting committee acted in perfect harmony, for they were united in the person of the widow Livingston, who was, in the literal sense of the words, a "mother in Israel." She was one of those in whom charity had wrought her perfect work, and, instead of exhausting itself in soft emotions or gentle words of pity, wrought itself out in deeds of kindness.

She had been for a long while, a widow; her only daughter had died some twelve years before, at the age of twenty-one, and her son, who was now about thirty, had never married. She had nothing at home, on which to expend the wealth of her motherly feelings, and therefore her heart was full of sympathy for all who were in need. Her very aspect was typical of her character. She was short and fat, with broad shoulders, and no neck at all, her head being set down on her shoulders, as a hen withdraws her head into her feathers when she nestles with her brood under her wings. A broad, white kerchief round her neck, always spotless and unruffled, was a sort of pillow for her chin. She had small, cosey eyes, which had never been large or restless. The forefinger of her right hand was crooked at the first joint, and she had an odd fashion of passing it over her lips as she talked with you, in a way that suggested that she was not telling you all that she knew.

Her knowledge on the subject of the good things that go toward making one of the chief of our creature comforts, was amazing; and in particular, her knowledge regarding the art of cookery for the sick, the jellies and broths that would tempt the nerveless palate of the invalid, and the toothsome cookies and ginger-snaps that would make the children's eyes glisten and their mouths water, all this witnessed not only to her culinary attainments, but also to her broad humanity; for never having known a day's sickness herself, being blessed with a solid and hearty appetite, she had gained her knowledge, not from her own experience, but from her sympathy with others.

Her art in dishing up and arranging these dainties .
was, in itself, a triumph of Christian charity.

She knew how the delicate sensibilities of an invalid were won by a neatly arranged menu.   In her
pantry there were baskets of various sizes and shapes,
but each vieing with the other to look neat and tidy.
" They keep themselves clean," she said.   On the
shelf above these, was an array of pet little dishes,
which she had picked up from time to time, with the
discriminating taste and pleasure which the connois-
seur in china feels when he has secured some gem
for his collection.   There were little pipkins, and
tea-pots, and broth bowls, and jelly glasses.

Underneath the shelves, was a drawer filled with
the whitest of linen, and with red and yellow doilies.

In the locked closet, next to the china shelves,
what was there not ?   A child whose eyes had once
rested on those hallowed depths, whose nostrils had
been saluted with the ineffable odor wafted from it,
never forgot it ; nor could later gastronomic enjoyments at all equal or efface the memory of that whiff.
There are grown men and women to-day, who have
eaten pâté de foie gras and truffles and all that the
cafés of Paris can offer, who, through it all, retain
a distinct recollection of the odor from Mother Livingston's charity cupboard.

It was of her chicken pie that the old rector had
spoken so affectionately, and you may be sure that,
for her own pastor, the old lady killed the fattest
hen that she could find, and made the puffiest paste
that she could roll, and was really fidgety as to how
the oven was going to bake that afternoon, and

came near spoiling the fire by peeping into the oven so often. She knew that she had a reputation for her butter and her chicken pie, and she was very proud of that fame; she did not know that any one ever thought or said anything about her charity cupboard, and she was not a bit proud of that, for any one could make jelly and broth, and do that plain kind of cooking, for sick folks; but pie-crust was another thing, altogether.

It was only by accident that Dinsmore discovered the charity cupboard; and, when he saw it, he was somewhat disconcerted. This was one of those dull natures which it was his mission to arouse to a wider view of life and its opportunities, and he felt how wisely Dr. Bainbridge had counselled him, to be sure of his person before he tried the process of arousing. He pictured to himself the scene of his coming to the widow Livingston and suggesting that she was leading a purposeless life, and, having no family duties to occupy her, that she might find employment in ministering to the wants of others; and, after he had freed his mind of such pastoral counsels, she would have led him back to her pantry, and showed him the charity cupboard. The very thought of it made him feel hot all over;—but, mercifully, he had escaped this, by heeding the good Doctor's counsel, first to learn what was in a man before you tried to lead him out.

"Well, how d'ye like our folks, Mr. Dinsmore?" said Mrs. Livingston, after the chicken pie, which had fulfilled all her best anticipations, had been despatched, along with the rest of those numberless dishes which go to make up the supper at which the country pastor is the guest.

Henry wished that the question could have turned upon the country, rather than the people; on the former he could have been enthusiastic, on the latter he could not.

"I can hardly answer your question, Mrs. Livingston," he said. "There are some very good people here, to whom I am already in debt for kindness shown me; and I am sure that I shall come to love my people as I hope that they will come to love me." He was embarrassed by the shrewd little eyes blinking at him, and the crooked forefinger passing over the mouth, so that he could not tell whether the old lady were smiling or not. It was very perplexing, and he was more at a disadvantage with this plain old country woman, than he had felt in the presence of women of the world, in society; but he was immensely relieved by the reflection that he had not read her a lecture on practical charity.

She questioned of one and another; whether he had called on them, and found them at home, and talked with them; and what he made out of the widow Cranston's state of mind; and whether he thought Amanda Williams, the lame girl, would ever be well again; and so on from one thing to another she gossiped along, in her gentle way; telling him, in her homely fashion, heart histories, sad and deep experiences of life, its sins and its sorrows, which he had not at all discovered in his intercourse with these people, who seemed all cast in much the same mould, as far as he could see, and who spoke in the same

restrained, commonplace way. It was a great lesson
to the ardent, young minister, with his grand plans
and schemes, and he was not above laying it to heart.
When she had gone the round of her humble friends,
she had nothing to say about her well-to-do neighbors, for she and they had only touched hands or
exchanged courtesies; but with these others she had
touched hearts and exchanged experiences.

And then, to Dinsmore's further discomfiture, she
turned upon him. "I did want you to come and live
with me, seein' as your mother wan't comin' to look
after you," she said heartily; "but, you know, it
don't always do for the minister to live with one of
his people; but he ought to hev a home of his own,
—some of our folks don't feel as if a minister was
real settled like among us when he's jest stoppin' at
the hotel, like a summer boarder." Then she passed
her forefinger over her lips, and Dinsmore thought it
hid a smile.

"Well, my mother can't come to live with me, Mrs.
Livingston; and I don't see just how I can have a
home any other way," he answered.

"Others has done it," she said; and then Dinsmore was sure the forefinger hid a smile.

"Oh! yes, I know there have been hermits; but
the day for them is past," he said, rather put to it.

"Yes, I never had nothin' to do with any hermits,
but I gather, from what I've heard o' them, that
they hed such dirty and disagreeable ways that it
was a mercy they lived alone. But my opinion is
that a young minister is not up to the full of his usefulness until he's married." She had done beating

about the bush. "There are 'various hindrances he meets,' as the hymn says, when he's unmarried. The young girls are thinkin' about it, and the older ones talkin' about it; and it does 'em no good. I hope you're thinkin' about this, Mr. Dinsmore; for I'm makin' it a subject of prayer."

The young minister smiled; it struck him oddly, this motherly old woman with this devout interest in his matrimonial affairs.

"It might be more to the purpose, Mrs. Livingston," he said, "if you would advise me what sort of a wife to get; or, better still, tell me where she is to be found."

It was far too serious a matter with the old lady for her to appreciate the whimsical side of the matter, which the young pastor could not help seeing.

"A good wife is from the Lord," she said, reverently, "and a minister of the Gospel must trust to the Lord for this, as for all things."

Dinsmore knew of no dispensation of Providence that touched this question; but he did not venture to raise any such doubt in the old lady's mind.

"And yet, Mrs. Livingston," he answered, "Providence requires us to do our share, in all concerns of this life, at least; and I need some one to tell me which way the path of duty lies, in this matter."

"I have seen a deal of marryin' in my time," said the old lady, in a dry tone; "but never saw the need o' any outside help when two young folks was enquirin' how they'd suit each other. They generally find it out, one way or another."

"But, in this case," said Dinsmore, "there is, un-

fortunately, but one person, and he needs some one
to help him find the other."

"There are considerable many to give him a lift in
that direction, without his askin'. Mebbe if you
was to give it out among the pulpit notices, you
might get all the help you wanted, and more too,"
said the old lady, with twinkling eyes. "I hev
myself heerd more than one who felt awful sorry for
you, livin' alone at the hotel; and I hev seen more
worsted-work slippers in the past month than was in
this parish for forty year back; and the prayer-
meetin' is fuller of the young girls than ever it was
in the old Dominie's time. Mebbe it don't signify
anythin' special; but I don't know as there's any
more religious interest among the young girls than
there was; mebbe there is, though. Now I don't
want to say anythin' upsettin' to your pastoral work,
Mr. Dinsmore; for they'd ha' done the same by any
young minister that come here. I only want you to
see that it wouldn't do no harm for you, as minister
o' this church, to be settin' your mind on this question. It does seem awful lonesome like for ye, too;
I don't wonder the girls feel it. You can't allus be
studyin' and writin', nor gaddin' around every evenin'. And there is some things it would do you a sight
o' good to talk out; and you dursn't talk 'em to any
one in town. And there is some things a woman
can see and tell her husband, even if he is a preacher,
and there ain't no one but his wife as can tell him.
There is some ways o' workin', too, that a minister's
wife can go into, that he can't do himself, let alone
that he hasn't the time to tend to them. There is

ever so much small work to be done in the world,
that don't signify, except where you count it all up,
and then it amounts to suthin'. And our folks has
a great interest in a minister's wife, and thinks a
powerful sight of her; and she seems to fetch her
husband closer to us, and make him more interestin',
except it be to the young girls, and they git older,
right along."

Here was home-spun truth for the young parson,
who smiled at the quaint touches in the homily; but,
none the less, saw that it was, at bottom, good, sound
sense, well harrowed in and planted deep.

"I'll think of it, Mrs. Livingston," he said, "and
I am sure it is ever so kind of you to take so warm
an interest in me."

"Well, if you fall to thinkin' on it, that is all I
ask; for a good man, if he once puts his mind to it
seriously, can come to only one conclusion, that the
Lord meant all men to be married, especially ministers." Then she added, with a tremor in her voice,
"I've had experience of both ways, Mr. Dinsmore,
a happy married life, and after that a life all alone;
and I know how the happiness of life is more than
doubled, if you have some one to share it, and trouble
isn't half as heavy if there is two backs to bear it."

Dinsmore was touched by the pathos of this little
outburst of sentiment, and rose to go, with a sincere
respect and regard for the stout little old dame, who,
under such a commonplace exterior, had a heart so
full of human tendernesses.

"Whenever you feel kind o' lonely, and as if you
would like to see your mother," she said, in parting,

"why don't you come down here to tea and let me give you a good supper, sech as the hotel can't get up; for there is nothin' like tasteless and onwholesome vittals to give a man homesickness, especially if he was used to good meals at home. And jest fetch along your slippers, and, after supper, you and my son William can sit and talk over your trout fishin', or play a game of chess; and we'll have some nuts and apples and cider, and you and William can smoke a segar and make yourself to home."

"Thank you, heartily, Mrs. Livingston; and I will surely fight off the next attack of blues I have, in just that way," said Dinsmore feeling his heart warm toward the motherly old dame.

"Do, do," she answered; and he left for home.

But he began to ponder along the way. It was not home, but only the veriest counterfeit of it, that bare little room in the country inn, with its bright red, three-ply carpet, its window without curtain or shade, its stained bedstead with a lumpy husk mattrass, underneath which the scant straw mattrass rustled as he got in bed, and, through them both, he could count the slats of the bedstead. The washstand and bureau were washed with the same stain, which was supposed to give them the outward seeming of mahogany, but came nearer to the color of raw veal.

Over the bureau hung a looking glass, on a nail driven into the wall, and this was the sole piece of furniture that rose above the commonplace. Some twist or fold in the glass caused it to reflect one side of the face about a quarter of an inch lower than the other; and Dinsmore found it the most entertaining object in his room.

For the rest, there were two rush bottomed chairs, and his own study table and easy chair from home, looking sadly out of place and lonely among their incongruous companions. His book-shelves had been made by Tim Mitchell, the undertaker and cabinet maker; and, thereby, he found that Tim had come to regard him as, in some sort, a partner in business, and bound to give Tim the *entrée* to the houses of his parishioners when there arose the sad occasion for their joint services in the house of mourning. For there was a rival undertaker in town, who was a wheelwright by trade, and Tim regarded him as an interloper and entitled to no consideration; and offered Dinsmore the courtesy of a seat beside himself on the hearse, either going to or coming from funerals in which they might be jointly interested.

But, to-night, Dinsmore was not thinking of the little undertaker who dropped his "h"s, in true cockney style, and wore his long crape weepers with such pride; for his mind was full of the home question. He came to his room; it was dark and cold. He lit his student-lamp, and the fire; but they did not, at once, dispel the chill. No, it was not a home; it was not cheerful, encouraging, helpful, inspiriting, it was the reverse of all this; and, as the room began to warm up, and it grew a trifle less gloomy in its aspect, what wonder if the "young man's fancies turned to thoughts" of some one to love?

He sat by the fire and drew pictures, castles in the

air, with cosey home surroundings, and comfort in every nook and cranny; but with whom? Ah! there was the rub. And yet there was a face and form that dwelt in that home. Therefore we may conclude that Dame Livingston's seed had not fallen on the wayside, beaten hard by the tread of many feet, nor yet on the stony ground where there was no deepness of earth.

CHAPTER VI.

DURING the following winter Dinsmore determined to realize some of his purposes regarding the people at large; and with this in view, organized a reading class among the young ladies of the village, which met at the Judge's house in the afternoon; and a debating society for the young men, that met over young Livingston's store, in the evening. In the latter effort he did not meet with a very gratifying success. It was his plan to enlist their interest in living questions, and not to cultivate the art of uttering with facility dreary platitudes on well-worn themes. This he endeavored to impress upon them in a preliminary talk with a few of them, who were invited to dine with him and discuss the matter.

With this end in view, and also in order to break the ice, which he was aware formed quickly on all these gatherings which were not in the nature of a frolic, he proposed that, at the first session of their society, which they decided to call the Clintonville Literary Circle, he should give them a talk on some theme which they themselves should select.

Fred Hutton was foremost in the scheme, lively, self-confident, and not averse to assuming the responsibility of leader. Fred was not stupid, but he was venturesome to a degree that often landed him in a position where he appeared stupid enough to all eyes save his own. He affected literature. It was only the Sunday previous that Dinsmore, as he passed through the sitting-room of the Hotel, had noticed Fred close and cover quickly with his hand, a book which he presumed the young parson would not have commended for Sunday reading. The yellow cover protruded in tell-tale fashion from under his hands, and to Dinsmore's query as to what he was reading, Fred's apt response was, "The life of a minister." It was the first volume of "Les Miserables."

Fred was made chairman of the committee to select a theme for this opening talk.

What was Dinsmore's horror, when, three days later, he received, in Fred's clerkly hand, the following as the result of their incubation.

"Dear Sir:

We have selected as a subject which will be both attractive and useful to us all, for your inaugural address at the opening of the Clintonville Literary Circle,

'The causes of corrupted morals and the impediments to social fruitions or enjoyments.'

Yours respectfully,

F. Hutton, Chairman

of special com. Clintonville Lit. Circle."

Dinsmore groaned inly and made a wry face over the marvellous conglomeration of words, and wondered by what process of invention a parcel of young men lighted on such a theme, and determined that, for the future, the selection of subjects for discussion had better remain in his own hands. He made up his mind to talk to them on the subject of mental culture as a means of pleasure and profit, and to take as his theme Leighton's pregnant caption quoted in the Aids to Reflection; "Your blessedness is not,— no, believe it, it is not where most of you seek it, in things below you. How can that be? It must be a higher good to make you happy." With Coleridge's comment, "All lower natures find their highest good in semblances and seekings of that which is higher and better. All things strive to ascend, and ascend in their striving."

It was a plea for thoughtful reading as a means of culture, for the attitude of mind that dwells with truth; and the text of his discourse was "Attention fixes the mind upon truth. Reflection fixes truth in the mind."

He mingled plenty of illustration and some anecdote with his talk, but while they looked on him with their eyes and heard him with their ears, he had not any strong hope that even the ghost of his meaning penetrated past the gate of the senses. Fred was, perhaps, the best read young man there, the most wide-awake, with the largest horizon of life; and as a result of the young pastor's talk, suggested that the subject of their first debate should be, "Is reflection an aid to thinking, or thinking an aid to reflection?"; without declaring any preference as to the side that he would take in the debate.

Dinsmore was too much dismayed to do more than negative this, and promise that he would read them some selections from various authors at their next meeting, and then announce a subject of debate for the ensuing week.

He was thoroughly disheartened, however, and felt that he had before him a task requiring the same sort of faith that would move mountains; for not one of the hearty, healthy young fellows about him had done more than sit in open-eyed wonder, save only the frisky young clerk.

With his young ladies class in literature on the following afternoon, his success was more encouraging. Miss Amelia Ann was there, vivacious and full of suggestion. She had a host of favorite authors, and was ready in quotation of her pet passages in prose and poetry. The meeting was held in the parlor of the Judge's house, and Mary Lowther, the Judge's daughter, was a very well read and highly cultivated girl. She had been to a New England school, and had spent her school days in thorough, hard study. She was no book-worm, but a genuine, sincere, and very intelligent girl, full of life and spirits. She was rather under than above the medium height, brown as a gypsy, with ruddy cheeks, dark hair, and with eyebrows, not delicately pencilled, but bushy and black. Her teeth, which were white and regular, seemed whiter by contrast with her dark coloring, and she showed them freely when she laughed, which she did very often, with a ring in her voice, made more contagious by her sparkling eyes. At first Dinsmore did not think her pretty at all; then, after talking with her, he thought her very pretty; and, as he came to know her better, he never thought of her looks at all.

But he recognized in her, very soon, one who would be an effective helper in all his plans to bring into the circle of the village girls something of the higher life that is gained by the knowledge and love of good books. Her taste was refined, cultivated and genuine. She formed her own opinions, and was enthusiastic in her love of both good literature and good music.

They were partners from the very first meeting. It was at her suggestion that the young ladies class in literature was formed without any name at all. That it should not become a mere desultory reading, at the mercy of this or that one's whim, she suggested that Dinsmore should read to them passages of his own selection, prose or poetry, while the ladies brought their work, and, after the reading, he should comment on the passages read, telling them something of the authors, and they should ask him questions or make their comments. This plan worked admirably to relieve these meetings of the stiffness and terror attendant on the sessions of a society. The burden lay on the young pastor to supply the entertainment and direct the train of study; but in all this Mary Lowther was an effective aid.

Miss Amèlie Ann Hollis was the only one of the circle who did not heartily approve of this plan. She had some essays and poems, a few of the latter having occupied a corner in the county paper. These fugitive verses she had purposed to read; but alas!

Coleridge and Keats and Wordsworth had supplanted her.

Once she made an ineffectual effort to stem the tide. The afternoon's reading had been devoted to "Dreams." Dinsmore had read Leigh Hunt's essay on Dreams, and then some examples of the dreams of the poets and prose writers.

After the reading, when various questions had been mooted, Miss Amèlie observed

"My father always forbid us children telling our dreams; he said it was both tiresome and foolish."

"I've no doubt he was right," said Sally Hill, the village belle, who was pretty and pert, with her pink cheeks and saucy lips, and as full of life as a kitten; and to whom the "Ancient pride of the village," as she called Miss Amèlie, was as the ball of yarn to the kitten, something to be tangled.

"I was not seeking your opinion, Sally," said Miss Amèlie, with some asperity. "We do not have to ask for that. It comes unasked, and, like all unsought blessings, perhaps is not appreciated as highly as it deserves."

"It is like the rain that comes on the just and the unjust alike; Eh, Mealy?" said Sally, with a wink at her neighbor.

Miss Amèlie turned, with dignity, from this fruitless controversy.

"I meant to ask you, Mr. Dinsmore, whether you thought it was as profitable to read the dreams of men, as their more earnest thoughts; and whether reading will cultivate one as much as to write ourselves?"

Sally Hill giggled aloud. "I have torn up all my compositions, but I suppose I could write them over again," she whispered, loud enough for Amèlie to hear. "My verses are still unwritten."

Mary Lowther interposed with the suggestion,

"For this season it might be better for us to read, and after we are more used to discussion of literary matters, we might, next winter, try our hand at some simple essay or impression of what we felt and thought about the pieces we had read."

She said it brightly and pleasantly, as though entering into Amèlie's plan, and postponing it only so as to ensure its success. But there was a finality in her tone that displeased Amèlie, who had so little distrust of her own powers, that she had already a half written essay on the "Genius of Keats."

Dinsmore began to feel the torments of arousing an inertia of motion leading he knew not whither, and thanked Mary Lowther, with all his heart, for extricating him so deftly, and conveyed his thanks by a look of relief so genuine that it made her eyes twinkle though she had to smother the laughter that it was a pain to suppress.

"Don't you think we can give a better opinion after we have heard all parties, Mr. Dinsmore?" she said, so as to draw his answer out to her, and save him a direct reply to Amèlie.

"I do indeed," he said. "I think it no easy task to see the beauties of an author, and a still harder one, so to point them out that another shall see as you see," he answered, with a sigh of relief. "I think, too, that, if we freely talk out our impressions

here, and compare views, we shall learn both to form
and express our opinions. Which of the poems that
I read this afternoon appeals to you most strongly,
Miss Amèlie?" he said deferentially.

"I think Byron's Dream is divine," she answered,
half closing her eyes, with her lips slightly drawn,
and a pinched expression about her nostrils.

"Did you feel any interest in Kubla Khan?" he
said, perplexed.

"I felt that it was ragged," she answered; "it
lacked finish and fulness."

Dinsmore felt that so far as literature was concerned, here was mission ground, and whether the
inertia of rest evinced by his class of young men, or
the inertia of motion as illustrated by Fred and Miss
Amèlie were the more unpromising field, he was at a
loss to say. Just now, he felt the latter to be the
more trying.

But this was, after all, the lighter side of his pastoral duty, however he might fail or succeed in
arousing their love of literature, his true work
touched deeper problems than this. At the lower
end of the village, near the Judge's house, lived
Bill Bennett, the black-smith, and, on his way home
from the Judge's that afternoon, Dinsmore encoun-
tered the sturdy smith, under rather exciting circumstances. He had, more than once, stopped to
have a talk with Bill, at his forge, and had stood in
admiration of the stalwart, swarthy fellow, as he
watched him swing the heavy sledge and let it fall
with a resounding blow that made the anvil ring and
the sparks fly, or bring it down so gently that you

hardly heard it fall. His admiration was heightened by an attempt which he himself had made to wield the heavy sledge; the sturdy smith standing by the meanwhile, with a lurking smile on his lips, and the brief comment, "You may be death on theology, parson, but you ain't worth your salt at the anvil."

Bennett was not in his shop, but as Henry passed the house he heard the piercing scream of a woman's voice and was horror-stricken to see the smith, with his black eyes, gleaming, like his forge fire, mad with drink, literally dragging his wife, by her hair around the corner of the house; she screaming "Murder!" It made him sick to see it and, as he hurried to her assistance, Bennett let go his hold of her, and stalked into the house.

Dinsmore hastened to the terror-stricken woman and, at her entreaty, helped her to her sister's house, over the way.

"What does this mean, Mrs. Bennett?" he asked, when she was somewhat recovered from her hysterical fright. "Its all for nothin' at all but the liquor that's in him" she sobbed.

"Does he often treat you so?" he asked.

"Well no, not very often; but he's ornery to-day," she sobbed.

"Have you done anything to provoke him especially," he asked; feeling that some unusual provocation must have called forth such brutal conduct.

"Well no! I can't say as there was. You might ask him," she answered.

After much persuasion, she and her sister agreed to go back to the house under Dinsmore's protection and send for Bennett, telling him that the pastor had called to see him.

After all, this quiet parish had its quota of tragedies, as well as the great world outside.

Over the way marched the small procession, the two frightened women and the young pastor, whose pulse beat several degrees higher than the normal rate.

Without venturing beyond the foot of the stairs, Mrs. Bennett called to her husband " The Dominie's here Bill, and wants to see you."

" Tell him I'll be down, when I've brushed up a bit," he answered, fiercely enough to show that his anger still burned hot. It was with many an uncomfortable qualm that Dinsmore awaited his coming.

Presently he came down the stairs, with a firm step, for he was one of those drunkards who did not reel, but grew mad with drink. He had dressed himself with scrupulous care, his shirt which was without starched bosom, was clean and white, unbuttoned and rolled back at the neck, showing the strong muscles of his chest; the sleeves were rolled up to the elbow and the brown, brawny arms showed sinews like steel and muscles hard as iron. His eye gleamed fiercely as he entered the room with a swift, stern stride, and walking straight up to Dinsmore, held his clenched fist close under his nose, and said " Parson, do you know that one tap o' that would send you to heaven; short cut." It was a somewhat thrilling experience.

" If it is a question of fighting, Mr. Bennett,

please let me have a chance to run; for you can knock me senseless, before I could think" said Dinsmore. "I came here to talk to you; I can't fight you. Won't you sit down and let us talk this matter over," and he moved to make room for Bennett, on the sofa.

Bennett glared at him a moment and then, bringing a chair, seated himself, directly in front of Dinsmore, with their knees almost touching, set his arm on his knee, his chin in one hand, and glared at the young minister, at short range.

"Now blaze away, Dominie," he said, "What hev ye got to say to me; this business is of your own seekin."

"Yes. I have this to say Mr. Bennett," said Dinsmore, looking him full in the eye, "that it is a shameful, brutal, cowardly thing for a strong man to treat a weak woman, as I saw you treat your wife; and I would not have believed it of you, if I had not seen it with my own eyes."

"Them is rather stout words, parson," answered Bennett "and I wonder whether you are altogether prepared to stand to 'em; Eh?" and he glared on Dinsmore.

'I am prepared to stand to them," answered Dinsmore; "and further to say that there is no excuse for such unmanly conduct."

"You may be wadin' in deeper than you know of, parson," retorted Bennett, with a grim smile. "Suppose we discuss the question a bit, parson."

"I am not ready to discuss such a question. The man is a coward and brute who treats his wife so shamefully, the girl he courted and married and promised to love and care for," answered Dinsmore, hotly.

"Well, leavin' aside this pint on which your mind seems to be so well sot, parson; hev ye any objection to discuss the question as to what led to the unfortunate circumstances that seem to rile ye so," answered Bennett. "Would you be willing to answer me a question or two."

"Yes," answered Dinsmore "I am ready to hear what you have to say."

Bennett paused, and the two sat looking one another full in the eye. There was a triumphant gleam in Bennett's eye and a self-confident smile on his lips, as he lifted his chin from his hand, leaned back in his chair, and said

"What is the fifth Commandment?"

Henry was so astonished at such a question, that for a moment he could not summon the familiar words. Bennett smiled, as though this was a point scored in his favor, and, before the young minister had a chance to collect his scattered wits, recited "Honor thy father and thy mother that thy days may be long in the land that the Lord thy God giveth thee" then winked triumphantly at Dinsmore and said, "That's the tune, parson, isn't it?"

"Yes" gasped Dinsmore "that's right."

"I thought there couldn't be no dispute between us on that pint" retorted Bennett; while the two women sat aghast to see the parson thus beaten, on his own ground, by Bill.

"But what has that to do with this miserable business, Mr. Bennett" said Dinsmore, essaying to assert himself, after this downfall.

"It has got a blamed sight more;—if you'll excuse the word parson, I'll stick to it—its got a blamed sight more, I say, to do with this business than you know for; and I'll just let you into that, if you'll give me the chance to be heard."

"Now he's goin' to tell a pack of lies on me," whined Mrs. Bennett, from the other side of the room.

"Shut up," roared Bennett; "the parson and me ain't goin' to stand no woman's clack in this here business; and if you don't hold yer jaw, I'll hold it for you; do you mind?"

"Mrs. Bennett I think you had better let Mr. Bennett and me talk this matter over alone" said Dinsmore, firmly.

"Right you are parson, women don't understand these pints o' theology. Now I'll drive ahead. Bein' agreed on the fifth commandment, we're not a goin' to quarrel on small pints. I hev' a boy named Bill, and when he come o' eighteen years he was hankering for a silver watch that I had allus carried. I told him, when he was twenty-one, it was to be his; in the meantime I would lend it to him.

"Well I lent it to him, about two weeks ago, and, about three days after he had it, I found he warn't carryin' it, and asked him what was gone with it; and he told me he had lent it to one o' his chums, and later on said he'd spouted it for two dollars; and, every time I asked him about it, he had a new story to tell; and, when I found out that he was givin' me a pack o' lies, I told him he could leave the house, and not come back until he brought me that watch. Well, after I had chased him out and told that woman," with a scornful emphasis on the word, and a contemptuous jerk of his thumb over the shoulder toward his wife, "that miserable woman, that had promised to love, honor and obey me, jest the whys and wherefores o' the hull business: what does she do but feed the cub, three meals a day regular, when I was down to the shop to work; and give him the money for his night's lodging into the bargain, jest to encourage him in stealin', lyin' and disobedience; and, when I told her to take herself off along with her cub, she up and told me that I could clear out myself. Now what I want to put to you parson is; hadn't I the right to demand that watch back?"

"Most certainly you had, Mr. Bennett" answered Dinsmore.

"Right you are parson. Secondly hadn't I the right to say to that boy, you shan't come to this house unless you bring me that watch?"

"If you chose to take such harsh measures, you doubtless had the right to do so;" answered Dinsmore, with some hesitation.

"Well, I did choose to; and so that pint is settled" answered Bennett. "Then thirdly, had my wife any right to uphold that boy in his disobedience?" and his eye gleamed with satisfaction.

"No, she had not" said Dinsmore firmly.

"Well, that settles the case" said Bennett grimly, as he rose to his feet "and I congratulate you, parson, on the level head you keep on your shoulders."

"No; I don't think that it does settle the case. I have two or three questions to ask you Mr. Bennett, if you will sit down for a few minutes."

"Certainly, parson; with the greatest of pleasure" answered the blacksmith, and, with an elaborate bow, he took his seat. "It is a real pleasure to talk with a gentleman who has sech a clear head to see a pint, when shown him and an honest tongue to own when he's beaten."

Dinsmore looked him quietly in the eye, for a moment.

"I feel as if I had come to know you better this evening, than in all the months I have been here, Mr. Bennett; and there is the making of a man in you," said Dinsmore, cordially; for his heart yearned toward this poor mortal in the toils of the demon's net.

It was Bennett's turn to be startled now. He had braced himself for an assault; but not on this side.

The women too were aghast at the turn things were taking, and felt that their champion was betraying their cause. After a minute's silence, which seemed ten, when it had become almost painful, Dinsmore continued "I want you to come to church, Mr. Bennett."

"By G——" began the smith.

"Hush" said Dinsmore raising his hand.

"Well, parson, I must put sommat to it. Be hanged if I don't. I will, so help me God, I will be there next Sunday," and his voice began to quiver, with maudlin sentiment. "I want to hear you preach, parson. I love you, I do. I'd like to be converted by you, parson."

"There! that will do" said Dinsmore. "I must go home to supper. Your wife will not fear to stay with you to-night. You will for my sake promise to treat her kindly. I will see your son to-morrow, and will talk over this with you, when you are feeling all right. You will promise me to do nothing more about it; until you and I have talked it over" and Dinsmore held out his hand, with a genial smile, to the poor fellow. After a moment's hesitation Bennett took it and gripped it until the blood flew into Dinsmore's face and said, almost sobbing

"I will, so help me God. You've downed me parson, you have; and jest when I was sure I had the better o' ye. I don't see how you got the under holt; but I'm downed. I am" and he dropped into the chair and bowed his head on his hands and sobbed.

How it touched Dinsmore. The tears came to his eyes.

"We are friends, Mr. Bennett," he said "firm friends, from this day forth, and, so help me God, I mean that you shall be such a man as nobody can down." Turning to Mrs. Bennett, he said "I think it would be better for you to say nothing more of this, Mrs. Bennett, until your husband and I have had a chance to talk it over."

And so he left them. That night he was wakened by the sound of a man's voice under his window which fronted on the village green. There on the fence sat Bennett, muttering curses at "the snivelling, little parson that stuck his nose in other people's affairs. And he thought he downed me, he did; when I could ha' knocked him to kingdom come, if I'd a mind to. I'll do it, next time; and he won't go off crowin' over Bill Bennett;" and he wound up with a curse full-mouthed and deep.

The next day, Henry met him on the street, and, as the young minister came near, Bennett drew back off the narrow side-walk and stood with his back close against the high-board fence, with his hand to his hat in military salute and his eyes on the ground, every feature rigid. Henry lifted his hat, gravely, and passed on.

On the following day, as he passed the shop the furnace was in full blast, and the anvil rang to the swift swinging blows, which the young minister was glad to hear. As he was making up his mind whether or no the iron was hot for him to strike, Bennett came to the door, and, with an evident effort, said

"Parson I have a word for you."

"All right, Mr. Bennett" said Dinsmore, cheerily, "there's not a man in the village I want to hear from as much as you."

"Parson," said the smith solemnly, "I want to explain to you, that I am obliged, sometimes, for a weakness of my innards to take a little quinine and, to make the quinine go to the spot, I am obliged to use a little whiskey. Well, between 'em, they have a curious effect on me, and they set me to thinkin', and sometimes to sayin', exactly the contrary o' what I really think and feel; and, most times, this comes on me late at night. That's all parson."

Henry put out his hand to him and, while he held the great brawny fist in his, said

"That's all right, Mr. Bennett. I think we understand one another, perfectly; and we are going to be firm friends after this, and I am going to see you at church every Sunday."

"Right you are parson, so help me God" said the smith, returning the firm clasp of his hand; "and bygones is bygones."

"Not only between us; but between you and the whiskey bottle too, Mr. Bennett" said Dinsmore, pressing his advantage.

"Do you want me to sign a pledge parson?" said Bennett, doubtfully.

"No, I do not, Mr. Bennett," answered Dinsmore. "I want you to be man enough to see the evil of the thing, and to feel how it debases you, and make up your mind that, by God's grace helping you, it shall not pass your lips. This is a better way than signing a pledge. Weaker men may need the force of a pledge; but you have brains and conscience enough not to need such help. God and your own brave spirit will pull you through."

"Parson it does hearten me to hear you talk like that. Do you think I can," he said humbly.

"I know you can, and will do it" said Dinsmore, brightly.

"Hanged if I don't come and hear you preach, if you can talk like this" answered the smith.

And, sure enough, from this time forth Bill Bennett was at the head of his pew, and every day the ring of his anvil, as Henry went by, was like music

6

in the young pastor's ears; and, when other plans and projects came to grief, it made his heart glad to go into the smithy and have a chat with Bill.

He made it his business to seek out the wayward boy, release the silver watch from pawn, and secure its restoration to the father, and, on the evening of that day, went to supper at the Bennett's.

"It's not for the like o' us to have the minister to supper" said Bill, when Henry proposed to take a meal with them.

"If I'm good enough to preach to you, I should think you might let me eat at your table," said Dinsmore, with a smile.

"Oh Lord! parson that's not the way I meant it" said Bennett, in dismay.

"Yes" answered Dinsmore "but that's the way I shall take it, unless you ask me to supper."

"Well then, for gracious sake, come to supper tomorrow night" said Bennett.

"It was the proudest day of my life" said Bill to his customers of the next and many ensuing days, "when I hed the parson to supper. My! didn't he eat, and said the things was good; and didn't he make himself to home and talk right in with us."

From that day customers were regaled with bits of Dinsmore's table-talk or scraps from his sermons, so that he got the nick-name of the "parson's Billy," and the scoffers called his shop "The Bethel Blacksmith's shop." It was well that their jokes were turned on him and not on the minister; for Bill would have sealed his testimony to the parson with the blood of those who spoke lightly of him.

CHAPTER VII.

OUTSIDE of the range of the ordinary life of Clintonville, isolated from all influences that could lift them from their degradation were the Scoopers, in their hamlet in a swampy hollow, northwest from the village. Dinsmore had, once or twice, walked nearer to it, on his way to or from some visit in that neighborhood, but his approach had been a signal for the inhabitants to retire to their huts and for the snarling half fed curs, with a starved and wolfish aspect, to come out from their lairs. These outcasts seemed altogether unapproachable. Nor did enquiry from the farmers round about elicit much information. They regarded them and their dogs, which harassed the sheep, as much on a par, and their attitude toward them was exclusively defensive. The only person in the tribe who excited the least interest among outsiders was the "witch-woman," as they called her, old Barbara Fisher. Of her even the well-to-do farmers stood in awe, as one who could cast some sort of spell to make their wells run dry and their cows give bloody milk, and who had more than once discovered a stolen horse, when three hairs dropped from the lost animals tail were brought to her. These hairs she tied together in a knot and laying them on a shovel lighted the ends,

and which-ever way two curling ends of the singed
hairs pointed, thither the thief had gone.   She had
a wonderful " charm string."   It was 203 feet long,
composed of shells, old coins, snake rattles and an
endless variety of buttons, each with a history, if
Barbara was to be credited.   This charm, when
coiled around the old woman, had a diameter of ten
feet or more, and weighed some 300 pounds, with
this she practiced her divination.   Her powers were
undisputed by the Scoopers, and were not altogether
discredited among the country folk, at least they
thought it not unwise to propitiate her from time to
time, with gifts, which, though given in the name of
charity, were a secret tribute to her powers.

More than one country maid, with whom the
course of true love did not run smoothly, or perchance, stood altogether still, had asked counsel or
help from old Barbara Fisher, with many misgivings,
it is true; but nevertheless they had gone there, as
a last resort, and had come away with assurances,
which were vague enough to leave Barbara's reputation unimpaired which-ever way events might turn.

Henry, after much reflection, decided that she,
alone was approachable; and yet he did not quite
see his way clear, as minister of the Presbyterian
church, to pay court to old Barbara by consulting
her as a fortune-teller.   Nevertheless he made up
his mind to visit her, and trust to the spur of the
moment to extricate him from any predicament in
which he might be placed.   It was easy to find her;
and there was no mistaking her, when he saw her.
She was about 80 years old, but still active and ap-

parently strong, though much bent and wrinkled. Her thin hair was as white as snow, and long, white hairs grew from her chin in such profusion as to give them almost the dignity of a beard. Her pale blue eyes were as bright and keen as a hawk's, and she fixed them so intently on her visitor that there was undeniable power in her gaze. There was a very great veneration for her among the scoopers, which was heightened by the fact that well dressed people came there to consult her, and paid her money for advice; and her powers were indisputable after farmer Brown had charged her with bewitching his dog so that it ran wildly about in a circle, suffering great agony, and she had refused to exorcise the spirit, until he had paid her an exorbitant sum of money. Whereupon the justice had fined her three dollars; this settled, in their minds, the fact that her power was beyond question. Every deformed, idiotic, tongue-tied or "liver-grown" child, (as the sickly little ones were called), in the whole region, was a testimony to Dame Fisher's secret powers. Of these she did not need to boast, there were plenty to do that in her behalf; she simply needed to look wise and be silent, while these things were laid at her door.

For the rest, they were such a miserable horde that Dame Fisher stood out in bold relief, and Dinsmore heard, on every hand, of her wonderful powers and of the potent sway which she exercised over the band.

He dressed himself in a shabby suit, which had been through many a tangled brier patch and laurel thicket along the trout brooks, and started off, one

afternoon, to seek the "witch-woman," feeling not
unlike the wayward King of Israel, when he set himself to seek the witch of Endor; and he had as little
idea of what the outcome of his visit would be.   The
autumn sunshine was still warm and the hazy atmos-
phere was full of dreamy suggestion, as he stood on
the brow of the hill that overlooked the little hamlet.
Here and there, some more industrious scooper was
plying his trade, at the door of his hut; but none of
them gave him any other greeting than a sullen glance
as he enquired the way to Barbara's hut, toward
which they gave him a nod of direction.   At the door
of her hut sat the old woman, sunning herself, with
her idle hands folded in her lap, and her keen eyes
blinking in the sun.   On the door of her hut there
were nailed two bats, with outstretched wings, and
in the middle of the floor, lay coiled the mighty
"charm string;" in one corner was a brass caldron
and on the walls hung charms and amulets and
branches of withered herbs.

She had a sense of the surroundings appropriate to
her calling and had enhanced her reputation, not a
little, by these stage properties.

On a shelf in the other corner was a large folio,
bound in boards, with its heavy covers secured by
brass clasps, into which none ever looked but herself.
This was her "Wonder Book," over 300 years old,
written by a great Magician who was her ancestor,
many generations back.   And those who had caught
a glimpse of it in the old beldame's hands declared
that it was written in great black letters of a strange
character, and the first letter of the pages in blood.

On the way over, Henry had been pondering how he should open his conversation, and here he was face to face with her and without any idea of how he was to explain the object of his visit.

"Is this Dame Fisher?" he asked with some embarrassment.

"Aye, so they call me. What do you want?" asked the old beldame, eyeing him suspiciously.

"I was passing this way and had heard of you often, my good Dame, and I felt as if I would like to know you," he answered.

"I am not used to be called 'good Dame;' and I have no time to waste on them that comes to gape at me, with no good reason for it" answered the old woman, looking keenly at him.

Dinsmore smiled, as he replied to this thrust;

"There are not many women like you, Dame Fisher; and I wanted to be able to say that I knew you, and also ask you to tell me something about yourself. I like to know the story of those who are my neighbors; and I feel an interest in every one of them."

"And be there so little business for such as you, that you have time on your hands to gossip about every old woman that lives within five miles of your meetin'-house" said the old woman; and her keen look said, as plainly as words, "You have not fooled the old witch-woman with a suit of shabby clothes."

Dinsmore laughed outright.

"Then you know me, Dame Fisher, as well as I know you. Ah! well, there is no use trying to outwit you, I see that, so I may as well talk to you about your parish and ask you what I can do, with your help, for the good of your people."

This tribute thawed the heart of the old dame a trifle, and she was less inclined to stand on guard against this cheery, young fellow who seated himself down so comfortably and seemed inclined to recognize her as the leader of this community.

"You have plenty to do, without bindin' your hands with such thriftless folk as ours. We do well enough as we are; if other folks mind their business."

"Ah! well, I don't want to meddle with your people, Dame Fisher; but there are a host of little children about here. They can't all be bred to the scooper's trade; some of them must go out into the world and look for work, and they will stand but a poor chance if they can't read or write. You have got some grand-children here yourself, haven't you?"

"Yes I have that, five little ones that would stand but a poor show for their bread and butter, with my Barbara's drunken husband, if I didn't help them, out of my own purse. Yes, yes the children must live, and after us, what are they to do? That's what I often ask Barbara, what will you do when I'm dead and gone?"

"Then let me try, with a Sunday School, over at farmer Brown's, with his daughter Fanny for teacher, and let the children learn to read and write," said Dinsmore.

"There ain't much use of it, as I can see" answered the old woman, drearily. "They ain't got no clothes; and you can't get farmer Brown to be

havin' scooper's brats—that's what they calls 'em—
hangin' round his place."

"That's my look-out," said Dinsmore, "If you
say that the children may be taught, I will see to it
that they get taught. Won't you show me your
charm-string, Dame Fisher, I have heard so much
about it that I want you to tell me how it is made."

The old woman took him into the hut and was
soon in the midst of a voluble tale of the wonders of
the charm-string, and when and how each token was
gotten and added to the treasure. She let the young
minister gaze on the covers of the "Wonder-Book"
also, but denied him even the most transient peep
between the lids. As Henry was about to leave,
after inspecting the wonders of the cabin and listening to Barbara descant upon them, he renewed the
subject of the school.

"I am going to see Fanny Brown" he said "and,
on Sunday afternoon, I will bring some picture books
and readers, and will come over here to gather some
of the children for a school in farmer Brown's barn,
and your four grand-children will surely come, and
such others as you can persuade to come with them."

"I'll see what I can do" she answered. Then, as
Dinsmore slipped a quarter into her hand to buy some
sugar and tea, she said "I can't take your money,
without telling your fortune."

"And I can't let you tell my fortune; for, you
know, we ministers believe that God not only made
but takes care of us all, and that He only can know
what will happen to us."

"Oh! yes, I know all about that preacher's talk;

but I took you for a sensible young man, and a kind-hearted one too," she said.

"Oh! well, Dame Fisher, may be you will think better of me, when the children begin to learn, in the Sunday School," said Dinsmore, laughing kindly.

"I don't know about that," said the old woman; "but I can't take this quarter, without telling a fortune for it; for its unlucky to have dead money," and the old woman eyed the shining silver, as it lay in her open hand, with a pathetic look of regret. And then without further parley, she continued, "I was sittin' in the centre of my charm-string, last evening, for I felt in my bones the kind of ache I always have when a stranger is comin'; and I fell asleep and dreamed, that there I was a sittin' at my door and a young man came and wanted to see me and wanted to know about something strange and new, and he didn't ask his fortune and so it came to me, all the quicker. He had a long, long life-line in his palm, and very soon across his life line there was a love-line, very deep and strong. And I dreamed of two crows and that means black will mate with black and I dreamed of a robin and a wren and that means that the tall will marry the small, and the one who laughs little will marry the one who laughs plenty for both; and he is tired already of a lonely life, and he wants some one to talk to, and some one to share his troubles, and some one to make him merry, and she is near at hand, and is waitin' until he tells her what he wants, and then she'll want to do as he wishes." Henry grew confused, under the old witch-wife's keen eye, as she drew a picture, for which he could supply the living counterpart and wondered how in her isolated life, she came to know so much, or whether after all it were only a shrewd guess. At all events he did not dare try to find out and stood before her like a child in the dark, afraid to move hand or foot, for fear, as the children put it, something would catch him. "It was a pretty dream, and though I am an old, lone witch-woman, it made me remember the time when I was young, and my dim eyes could laugh, as well as my lips, and they were waitin' for some one to make them dance. The pretty girl, I saw in my dream, was a kind young lady too, and was good to the poor, and would be a help to a man, and make him feel kind to the poor and sick. She stood at the door and smiled on the lad as he went down the steps of her father's house; and he looked back, when he got to the bottom of the steps, and she smiled again; and the young lad smiled all the way down the gravel path; and my 'Wonder Book' says the first smile that a maiden gives puts a wedge in the centre of a young man's heart, and the second smile that a maiden gives fastens the wedge in its place; but the third smile is right in his eyes and drives the wedge home and splits his heart in two." Dinsmore's face grew red, as the old woman sketched, with all too true an outline for his comfort, his parting with Mary Lowther, but three days ago, as he left the Judge's house.

"But there is no truth in dreams, Dame Fisher," he said.

"And yet the preacher's tell us about Pharaoh's dreams" answered the old woman.

"Well some dreams come true because God wished, by them, to tell men something that they needed to know and they would believe it if it came to them by dreams, sooner than in any other way," he replied.

"And so do I believe most in what comes to me by dreams; and my dream will come true, and when it does come true, then Barbara Fisher will earn another silver piece" said the old woman, with a sly twinkle in her eye.

"My dream, Dame Fisher, is of a tidy group of little ones, that are left uncared for now, gathered in a school, and learning to be good men and women. You will help me to see that my dream comes true," said Dinsmore.

"I will help you" said the old woman "but my dream needs no help from any one; it comes true of itself."

Dinsmore let her have the last word, a satisfaction which is said to be an inexorable demand of her sex, and in this case he did not feel inclined to dispute it. He went his way, in the autumn afternoon, with the dreamy air floating around him, and he was not ten paces from the old woman's door, before his thoughts were astray from the Sunday School in farmer Brown's barn, and the judge's front door was in his mind's eye, as clear as an actual vision, and Mary Lowther's dancing eye led him on and Mary Lowther's catching laughter rang in his ears, and—ah! well it is a waste of words to go on telling how, step by step, he trod the "primrose path." It will suffice to say that he was near half a mile beyond farmer Brown's gate, before he remembered that his mission to Dame Fisher had been, not to have his fortune told, but to organize a Sunday School for the forsaken children of the scooper's dell. Shame-facedly he retraced his steps, castigating himself with the lash of conscience as faithfully as ever did anchorite with the thongs, when he had been lured away from his devotions by thoughts that would intrude like uninvited guests.

But the lash did not preclude a smile or two, as he retraced that penitential half mile.

Arrived at farmer Browns he gave them an account of his visit to old Barbara; and it was as the old "witch-woman" said, the thrifty farmer was averse to having the "scooper cubs git the run o' his place." But by dint of persuasion Dinsmore won his permission to turn the big barn into a Sunday School room, and imparted to Fanny Brown some of his hopeful enthusiasm as to the result. And she undertook the task which he proposed for her, and suggested that they ask Mary Lowther to come down and lead the singing and tell the children some stories. "You know Mary has taught the infant class, and she's just splendid at tellin' Bible stories. I know that our children'll walk all the way to the village, any day, just to be in Mary's class."

"I don't know about asking Miss Lowther, if she has the infant class" said Dinsmore, who was not yet healed of the smart that old Barbara had inflicted, and thought that the old witch-woman would see visions and dream dreams of a more pointed character still, if, with her hawk-eyes, she saw him coming with Mary Lowther, to farmer Brown's, next Sunday afternoon.

"Oh! Law" said Fanny "you needn't be afraid to ask her; she'll come. She loves to work; and don't mind a walk either; and she has her pony and phaeton, if she wants to ride. And I heard her say, when you first come, that she'd be bound if she didn't do all she knew how to help the new minister along. So you can just depend on her the same's if you had already asked her."

Dinsmore accepted Mrs. Brown's invitation to stay and "take a sup with them," and, after supper, the young pastor was asked to lead family prayers for them, and declining farmer Brown's invitation to drive him home, thinking that he would rather be alone on the way, to think over his Sunday School plans, betook himself home, in the autumn moonlight. The Sunday School plans were soon settled to his satisfaction. These naturally led him to think of Mary Lowther and her place in the proposed scheme, and the thought of her naturally led him— ah! well led him naturally and sweetly, through the soft moonlight, all the way home.

Do not let us prejudge him as sentimental and an easy prey to light fancies, he had been driven to think of her; on every hand her name had been spoken, or the picture of her had been drawn and set before him, and the thought of her crept, softly and sweetly, into his imagination, even as circumstances, not of his seeking, were making them allies in every good work. No we cannot blame him; we may pity him if we choose; but he might not be grateful for our pity.

CHAPTER VIII.

ON the next evening, after prayer-meeting, Henry asked Mary Lowther to aid them in their proposed scheme for the improvement of the neglected children of Scooper's Hollow. "I should certainly be ashamed to say no after the talk that you gave us, in prayer-meeting" she answered, with a merry, little laugh. "Are you testing my faith by my works?"

"Oh! no" he replied with more confusion than the occasion warranted. "I was talking over the plan with Miss Fanny Brown and she suggested your name."

"Well I will come, and very gladly too" said Mary.

Then Dinsmore felt that he ought to offer to pilot her there, and yet he did not feel quite clear in his mind as to the best way of doing so; and, while he was fumbling for a convenient phrase, she said brightly: "I suppose you will be there, Mr. Dinsmore, and, if you like to walk, I shall ask your escort."

"Indeed I would much prefer it," answered Dinsmore, leaving the young lady to guess whether his preference was for the walk, or for her company; but so it is that we do not always say what we mean, any more than we always mean what we say.

The prayer-meeting had been one of more than

usual interest. Dinsmore was making an effort to enlist some of the people in what he called the conference quarter. He had arranged the prayer-meeting on rather a novel plan. They occupied an hour, from half past seven to half past eight. But the prayer-meeting proper did not begin until a quarter before eight. For the first quarter of an hour, he was not in the desk, but walked round among the pews shaking hands with one another and talking aloud with them, asking them questions, principally about the subject of the prayer-meeting, which he always announced the week before and again at the Sunday service. The subject for this evening was "sweetness and light." The large number of his hearers were a silent audience, which he trusted were receptive of what he strove to teach them, but certainly were not able to impart anything of that which they received. These, ordinarily, spoke in sepulchral whispers, or sat altogether silent; but, by dint of persistent effort, Dinsmore broke up this propensity to whisper. To some he would appeal for suggestions or questions which they would like him to take up; and sometimes he gained apt and homely responses.

Mrs. Livingston always answered to the point and Mary Lowther too was active among the younger girls, some of whom only giggled when Dinsmore addressed them. Deacon Shelton was all too apt to fall into a lengthened homily, which sounded ominously like an abstract of one of his father's sermons, and it gave Dinsmore not a little trouble to curb the loquacious Deacon.

But old Deacon Gilder could be relied on, always, to speak pithily and to the point, albeit much inclined in his talk to ride his two hobbies, a crusade against rum and tobacco; but never did he do this in his prayers, which were real, earnest and direct, as to a person with whom he was talking familiarly, but reverently. He strove very faithfully with the young pastor against the occasional segar with which Dinsmore would quiet his nerves, after a hard day's work, but, as yet, without avail; so the old man pitied him and loved him, and trusted to the persistency which he purposed to use in winning his pastor to better ways.

Hugh McDonald the white-haired, rosy-cheeked Scotchman was sure to have some quaint and homely saying, to the point, and all the better put, for the Scottish words that, here and there, cropped out in his richly accented utterance. Sometimes their very pithiness would provoke a smile, as when he prayed " Oh Lord prevent us, that we do not learn to ape the devil and strut aboot the warld as if we were somebody."

Then too from Deacon Shrake there sometimes came just as quaint bits of strange mental processes; but not always so full of pith or wisdom, as when the subject of family worship was under consideration, the week before, Dinsmore was dismayed to hear his sapient announcement " I believe there be warrant o' scriptur' for holdin' that the chief sin of the five foolish virgins was that they did not maintain family worship."

But, with all these drawbacks, Henry felt that

there was this compensation in his plan, that, after some fashion or other, each, according to his ability, was set to thinking upon the subject that was to be presented to them.

On this evening he had asked Mrs. Livingston, as he stood by her side, in the aisle

"What can you tell me about the sweetness that comes from light, Mother Livingston."

"Well, I ain't no hand at talkin' in meetin' and least of all tryin' to teach my minister; but I du know that there is nothin' like light for keepin' milk-pans sweet, and there is no use tryin' any other way than settin' them in the sun. Stove heat won't do it, so as you don't give 'em a sunnin' from time to time—Mebbe folks get sour the same way."

"How is it about the butter, must that be made in the light?" said Dinsmore, smiling, as others did, at the homely wit of the old woman.

"Well no; on the contrary, you want to keep sweet butter in the dark. But mebbe churnin is more like afflictions, and when we're beat about then we show whether there is any good in us or not."

"I guess that is pretty near the truth of it Mrs. Livingston—The word that we use for trouble, tribulations, comes from a Latin word *tribulum*, a threshing flail, and tells us that troubles thresh the chaff from the wheat; and the same lesson is taught you by the churn that brings the butter from the cream."

"Du tell?" was the old dame's only comment.

"I like to know these homely illustrations of the truth. They make our every-day life preach to us —And what have you to say, Mr. McDonald, that will give me another homely figure for my talk on light, to-night " said Dinsmore to " Auld Hughie," as they called the Scotch Deacon, whose twinkling eye, as he listened to the talk between Mrs. Livingston and Henry, assured the young pastor that the canny Scot was wide awake on the subject.

"Aweel" answered McDonald, "I was grubbin' in my cellar, one day, makin' ready and clean for the roots to be put awa' for the winter, and I found a wee bit potato, puir thing, that was left alone, sin last spring; and it had made shift to sprout in the darkness and had grown up atween the box and the wall till it found the licht, at the window, and there it lay down its head on the window sill wi' twa green leaves on the top o' it, and a' the rest o' it was but the wraith o' a potato stem, wi' ne'er a leaf alang it. But it minded me o' the Lord's sayin' 'a bruised reed he winna brake;' and I took the puir thing out and plantit it in the garden, and surely it turned green; but it winna bear ony fruit. And isna that like mony a puir sickly soul, Mister Dinsmore."

"Indeed you're right, Mr. McDonald; and that is one thing that I want to put before you to-night;" and, with that, Dinsmore turned to the desk and gave out a hymn.

Mary Lowther played the melodeon and led the singing in a way that put sweetness and light into that part of the service. After a prayer by Deacon Gilder, sweet and simple in its heart-felt recognition of the mercy that had given us the power of seeing and such a wealth of beauty to reward our sight, he plead for those who could not see; and Miss Anna

Smith, whose gentle face was pathetic in its sweet content, when you knew that those soft eyes were only turned toward you in courtesy, but knew neither day nor night, sighed softly to herself as the tears trickled through her lids.

Then Dinsmore talked to them, for fifteen minutes, on the text " The light is sweet and a pleasant thing it is to behold the sun" Eccl. 11, 7.

" It is a fashionable phrase 'sweetness and light' with which some have beguiled themselves into thinking that they have found a new philosophy or religion; but it is as old as the very beginning of the religion of the Bible, and the truth is to be sought, not in the twilight of human reason, but from Him who is light. Here is the true light, and it is for every man that comes into the world.

" Its clear shining enlightens the whole nature, giving light to the reason or understanding, and to the conscience, and to the heart."

He then made use of some of the homely illustrations that had been furnished him by his quarter-hour talk; and closed by making the broad distinction between the philosopher's doctrine and the doctrine of the Bible.

" With them the doctrine is that light and sweetness shall be sought for its own sake and for the benefit of those who seek it; but the urgent teaching of the Bible is that we must seek it, in order to give it away. It cannot be kept, any more than the sun can keep from shining; to have light we must give light."

Then he told them of his plan to reach the children

of the outcast Scoopers, and that, after he had gotten this plan in working order, he should need clothes and books and some money with which to start the school, and this, with what help he needed in the way of teachers, was to be their share of the work.

After this, what answer could Mary Lowther make to his request but a cheerful assent?

On the next sabbath afternoon, directly after dinner, Dinsmore called at the Judge's house and found Mary ready for the walk. There was a fine touch of womanly delicacy in the plain and simple dress which Miss Lowther wore. Dinsmore recognized the feeling that prompted her to this plainness of attire and felt how fine and true her woman's instinct was, when, even in such a trifle as this, she regarded the feelings of those whom she sought to reach. He could reason out the laws and grounds of Christian conduct, and analyze the Christian character and the motives that should govern conduct; but, after all, there were lessons that he could learn, and, on every hand, he was beginning to see that living truth was to be sought in human hearts, and not in books.

They went out of the village and on, over the hill, in the glorious autumn sunshine, and the enchanted ground and the princess, and all the fairy tale seemed as though it were indeed come true.

But the way was not trod in the silent reflection which had marked his lonely ride up through "the Barrens."

He began to tell Mary Lowther something of his inner history, his hopes, his fears, his dreams and how, in some measure, he was realizing them, and as she listened entering into all his plans (for she was a dear, good girl) there was borne in upon his heart the emphatic teaching of old mother Livingston, that, "of all men, a minister needed someone to talk to."

As they came up over the hill, where the road forks, and the one branch leads off over the hill to Pleasant Pond and the other winds down through Scooper's Hollow, past Hard-Scrabble (as the Scooper's hamlet was called), there, at the fork of the road, was old Barbara Fisher with nine of the unkempt, ragged scooper brats. They looked thoroughly scared, and, like a pack of wild rabbits, ready to take to the woods, at the slightest approach of the strangers. Barbara, apparently, had been taxed to the utmost in fetching them hither, and it seemed very doubtful whether she had not reached the limit of her influence to move them farther, by entreaty or threats. They huddled close to her, it is true, like a frightened covey of partridges, and as many as could do so clutched tight hold of her scanty skirts, and those who could not get hold of her, held fast to those who had a grip of her garments, so that, if the strain of a sudden fright had been put upon them, her well-worn skirts would have been torn to shreds. But while they clung to her, as their sole defence, it might be another matter when she tried to deliver them over bodily to the enemy. In such a crisis Dinsmore and Mary might have to hunt their Sunday School through the copses of Scooper's Hollow.

Mary Lowther took in the situation at a glance, and asked Dinsmore to walk on, up the hill road, to farmer Browns, and "Remember Lot's wife" she said "and do not look back."

She carried a satchel, slung over her shoulder with a strap, and out of it, she drew a parcel of tea for old Barbara, being careful to hold the bag so low that the children could catch a glimpse of some cookies, doughnuts and ginger-snaps within.

"I have brought you some tea, Aunt Barbara," she said, smiling pleasantly on the children. "And is this little Barbara, for whom I dressed the dolly, when she was sick," and she patted the head of a little flaxen-haired child, who had the blue-eyes of old Barbara, which had descended to the second generation. "Thank you kindly, my pretty lady" said the old woman. "Aye that is Barbara. Curtsey to the lady, you ill-mannered hussy" she said, giving the child a cuff, which produced a certain semblance of obeisance. "Ah but they're an ill-mannered set of young uns", she continued; "and they're no ways worth your takin' all the trouble to come here to teach 'em; for what they learn from the pretty lady, on one day, they'll forget before she comes again. But it'll bring you good luck, one way or another, this tramping out, of a Sunday afternoon, to do a good turn to the Scooper's children."

If Mary Lowther guessed the old woman's hidden meaning, she did not show it by any outward sign; she probably had not the slightest inkling of it.

All her thought and address were needed to secure the leadership of this covey of wild game, and get them into farmer Brown's big barn. She was glad

that it was the barn and not the parlor, for before
the terrors of the horse-hair furniture and the splen-
dors of the gorgeous carpet they would have flown,
when their steps were on the sill. Into the barn she
might hope to lead them, perhaps some of them had
been there before, on a foraging tour for fresh eggs;
but this may be doing them injustice.

"We are going to have a kind of children's party
over in the barn" she said to Barbara, not looking
at the others. "I am going to tell you some stories,
and sing for you, and teach you to sing a little with
me, if you will. Then we will have a little feast with
these cookies and doughnuts," and she opened her
bag and showed them the tempting contents, and it
was evident that the appeal was not in vain. Little
Barbara lifted her eyes to Mary's, as she bent over
the child, took a long, searching look right into her
eyes; then, with childish decision, let go her grand-
mother's skirt and put her hand in that of the pretty,
young lady, who had dressed the doll for her when
she was sick. And Mary was repaid for that unre-
membered act of kindness done on an impulse of
compassion, when old Barbara begged at her father's
door, in the name of her sick grand-child. The
next time that the old woman came, the doll was
ready. The Judge had laughed at her for being so
easily "gulled by the old witch-woman's lies;" but,
all the same, he kissed his girl and blessed her for
her kind heart, if he did make merry over her too
easy credulity. Now it would be her turn to boast
over him, that she had felt the touch of reality in
the pathos of the old witch-woman's voice, when she

told the tale of her little grand-child's sickness, which
it turned out was true.

She turned to go, with little Barbara holding her
hand tightly; then, looking back, said to the rest of
the pack of urchins "Barbara and I will have a very
nice time together; but it will be ever so much nicer
to have all of you come along. Here's plenty for all."

"Go long with you, you foolish brats" urged old
Barbara, flinging them from her. "Don't you know
when you've got a good thing?"

Thus urged, in both directions, the majority of the
children timidly followed Mary, who began to sing
to Barbara, as they went along, and then fell into
chat with her about the doll, asking, particularly
after her health and the state of each piece of her
small wardrobe. And as the others heard Barbara
begin to prattle vigorously, they drew nearer and
some ventured so far as to enter a contradiction to
the little girl's statements in regard to this doll,
which had been a famous character among the children of the settlement, being the only whole doll that
had ever been known in Hard-scrabble, to say nothing of the wonderful clothes in which it was arrayed.
As the spirit of contradiction drew one and another
into the controversy, or led them to mention scenes
and incidents connected with the doll and her wardrobe which Barbara omitted, Mary took advantage
of this to learn the names of each new combatant
that entered the list, and, before they had reached
the barn, knew the names of more than half of her
covey; and little Barbara would have followed her
anywhere.

As she went off leading the flock, like the famous Pied Piper, Old Barbara watched her and muttered " Aye, she has the beguilin' tongue o' them, when they're young and pretty. But, bless her pretty heart! she was kind to me when little Bab was sick. She shall have all the good luck that I can help her to; and she'll lose none of it by comin' over the hill with that fine young lad, every Sunday afternoon, to teach the Scooper's brats."

Arrived at the barn they found a very primitive arrangement but, on that account, the most suitable to ensure them success. There was a table, with the pail of water and tumbler that seems to be an essential feature of every gathering in a country schoolhouse, whether secular or religious. Behind the table were two wooden bent-back chairs and, on one side, was Miss Fanny Brown's little portable melodeon. The seats had been lifted from two carry-alls and set on the floor, and these, with some sheaves of straw, formed the benches for the children. All this had an easy, natural look that did not over-awe the wild flock; they eyed the melodeon askance but it was not a formidable looking monster. Besides, the barn doors were left open and escape was easy, as none of the enemy were in the rear.

Overhead the sweet hay hung out from the mows and the quiet, sedate farm-horses peered out from their stalls at this unwonted invasion of their Sabbath rest, and from the nearest stall, a soft-eyed cow watched curiously the proceedings, dividing her attention between the Sunday School programme and a staggering calf that whisked about the stall in the

most uncomfortable way, now solemnly eyeing the
children, and then, making a frisky rush around the
heels of its mother, as though seized with an idea
sudden and imperative; and with every repetition of
the obstreperous conduct, the cow gave a deep low
of remonstrance or warning.   All this interested the
children very much.   They were akin to these dumb
creatures, and had a feeling of assurance in their
presence.

At the first notes of the melodeon the horses pricked
up their ears, the calf went frisking around the stall
with tail erect and an old hen, who had been laying
an egg in the mow, came fluttering down, with a tremendous cackling, and ran out of the barn, while the
old cow came in with a fine lowing bass; all this
made the children laugh and set them entirely at ease.

Dinsmore told them the story of Joseph, and then
handed them over to Mary Lowther, who sang for
them a bright, lively tune, with a simple refrain.
This she tried to teach them, but there was not a
peep or mutter from any of them when it came to
their turn to join in the refrain, save only from little
Bab.   She had given herself over to the pretty lady,
heart and soul, and so she set herself firmly on her
little square feet and shouted lustily, all out of tune,
but with plenty of pluck in her singing.

She was rewarded with Mary's hearty comment
"Well done, my brave Bab.   The first cooky shall
be yours, for that;" and Bab was as proud as a
prima donna.

The cookies were distributed, and then Dinsmore
tried to teach them a text of scripture, and made a

short prayer, a portion of the service which was
wholly unappreciated by these little ones.

"What's he adoin' Bab? He's shut his eyes, and
so hes the young ladies; let's cut," whispered Bab's
next-door neighbor, appealing to her as an authority.
"You set still" answered Bab "she knows what she's
about. When they wakes up, they's goin' to give
us dough-nuts."

"Why don't he talk with his eyes open?" queried
another who had listened eagerly to this whispered
conference, and was a little overawed by the unusual
exhibition.

"I dunno" answered Bab "unless he's thinkin.
Granny mostly shets her eyes, when she thinks.
Mebbe he's askin' our fortunes."

But they were not left long to ponder; for Dinsmore's prayer was very short and simple.

"I wonder if he'll get what he wants," thought
Bab to herself, as she looked up into the hay, to see
whether there was any one hidden up there.

As Mary distributed the doughnuts Bab pulled her
down and whispered in her ear "who's up in the
mow?"

The question was so earnest and direct that Mary
turned, with a start, to see what the child meant.

"Why no one Bab, did you see any one?" she
said.

"No maam" answered Bab "but he was talkin' to
the mow."

"What do you mean child? Who was talking to
the mow?" asked Mary, utterly at a loss.

"Why him, your young man, when he shut his

eyes," answered Bab, pointing to Dinsmore. Mary
flushed slightly, as she answered "I will get him to
tell you about it."

"Mr. Dinsmore," she said, as she came back from
her round "the children do not understand, what you
were doing when you prayed. Bab asked me who
you were talking to in the hay-mow, when you shut
your eyes."

So the exercises in the barn were concluded with
what Dinsmore felt to be, one of the hardest tasks
which he was ever set to do, to explain to these children what was the nature and ground of our belief in
prayer.

But there was this comfort and pleasure in it, he
was answering an enquiry, they were interested in
hearing the answer, he was telling them truths which
they had never heard before. There was something
very inspiriting in all this, it was sowing in virgin
soil. They listened with keen attention, with wonder and the simple faith that has never heard the
mooting of a doubt. Then when they had sung, or
rather Mary had sung to them, another hymn, she
said,

"Now you can go children; but next Sunday afternoon we want you to come here; and we will have
some pretty picture books and begin to teach you to
read. Good bye now, until next Sunday afternoon;
and then bring some more of your playmates with
you."

At first it seemed as though it would be no less
hard to get rid of them than it was to persuade them
to come. They lingered in their seats apparently

afraid to move, and then, as if moved by one sudden impulse they jumped out of their seats, and made a wild rush for the door and out into the field and down the road; all except little Bab. She stood her ground bravely, standing alone in the middle of the barn floor, with her flushed face and a scared look in her blue eyes wide and wild; irresolute she looked for a moment toward the door where her companions were gone, and then turned and ran to Mary and hid her face in the folds of her dress.

"Must I go away now? Can't I walk down to the forks, hold of your hand" she pleaded, plaintively.

"Why surely you can, Bab, and right glad I will be to have you; and, every Sunday I shall expect you to meet me there and we will walk up here holding hands, and down again holding hands; and we shall be great friends."

"I will," said Bab; and there was no doubt about it, after that.

As Dinsmore and Mary went home, after parting with Bab, and talked over the opening of the Scooper Sunday School, they were very well content with the first afternoon's work. They had secured the confidence, and in some degree, the interest of the children; and they both felt that they had one stout missionary in the person of the doughty, little Bab.

"Isn't she a brave little lass?" said Mary, who was won by Bab, quite as thoroughly as Bab had been won to her. "My heart always warms to a trusting child. Of all the winsome ways of child-hood none touches me more to the quick than that open, hearty confidence. It makes us friends at once."

"Yes," said Dinsmore, crediting, in his mind, as much to the winsome ways of Mary as to those of the child. "Yes, they win us quickly and firmly. And, as I think of our afternoon's work, the beautiful phrase of the prophet comes to me, 'A little child shall lead them.' This will be true perhaps, of this outcast band, these Ishmaelites that none can befriend; I have felt that it was hopeless; I could not go among them and do anything but excite their suspicion, and what I could not do, and you could not do, perhaps, that little child is going to do. And so I not only love such a child and feel drawn to her, but I have a reverence for a child, as a sort of priest of God; in its simplicity, owning a power which we, with riper years have lost, to appeal directly to the higher side of human nature and enlist in behalf of better things, hearts that are sodden to every other influence.

"That child can win the other children of the hamlet, and, more than this, the fathers and mothers to think better of us and our scheme than we could do, by the most earnest argument with them. They will believe her and trust her statement that we mean them well, when they would put a sinister interpretation on anything we might say. It was a grand missionary work when you secured Bab, and through Bab, old Barbara."

Then Mary remembered the unconsidered trifle which won the victory, of which Dinsmore knew nothing, and she thought what a mighty truth lay in

the Apostle's words "do good unto all men as we
have opportunity." How small the opportunity,
which she had embraced; how wide-reaching its consequences had been. It seemed as if that doll were
to be an important factor in the evangelizing of
Scooper's Hollow.

CHAPTER IX.

THE following week Dinsmore was called outside the bounds of his hillside parish, to the Fall meeting of Presbytery at Tonanda.

Dr. Bainbridge's elder brought his six-seated mountain wagon and picked up Dinsmore on the way, and to their party were added Henry Wurtz, pastor of Plainville, whose predominating quality was conscientiousness, and Nathan Wood the Dominie of Weymouth, who had perhaps a less imperative conscience and a large capacity for humor, and, later on, they picked up Father Search, as he was called, who, having no fixed parish, made the whole country his parish and worked here and there, as opportunity offered, in season and out of season. He was an ardent temperance lecturer, and had spoken to enormous audiences all over the country, and, in the course of a period of labor, extensive both as to time and place, had met with many singular and some very stirring experiences. He was a fine raconteur, with that genuine gift at story-telling that does not suffer the tale to flag for want of the proper touches to round it off. He was therefore a good companion for a long drive. Very small of stature, with a long, white beard, an incisive eye and mode of speech, he held his hearers, as did the Ancient Mariner. He had but just returned from a tour in the lower counties, and was full of these his last, but by no means least, stirring experiences.

While laboring in White County he had heard of a lumbering village called Buck's Nest where the rough and ready men of the woods, who drank whiskey like milk, had expressed a wish to see "the little, white-bearded scoundrel who was goin' round the country black-guardin' a man for takin' his sup." This was the invitation that sounded sweetest in his ears, for he was sure of speaking to the purpose, under such conditions.

He was full of his experiences, and Dr. Bainbridge took occasion, at once, to draw his fire.

"How did you fare in your crusade at Buck's-Nest, Father Search?" he asked, as soon as the little man was fairly seated.

He stroked his long white beard, his keen eyes glistened, and there was a smile playing under his white mustache that assured those who knew the symptoms that they were to be treated to something racy.

"Well, Brother Bainbridge," began the little man, eyeing the Doctor keenly, "I don't know how you will measure the success, for your lines have fallen in such pleasant places, and you have such a span of horses, and an elegant fur-trimmed coat, and Brussels carpets on your floors, and a silk-dressed congregation, that perhaps you may not think such an experience of much account, for I converted nothing but poor, rough lumber-men; yet I regard it as one of the triumphs of my life."

The Doctor smiled; he was used to these excursions of Father Search's; and they did not wound him.

"I suppose they have the same immortal souls, the same sins, sorrows, temptations, under their homespun, that are to be found in the hearts of my silkclad people," he answered. "If there is any difference you have discovered it, not I, Father Search."

The little man glared at him for a moment, and resumed "I have not; and I am glad to hear you set yourself right on the question, Brother Bainbridge." To which the Doctor's only answer was a smile; and the little man went on—"Well, when I heard how badly they wanted to see me, I regarded that as a distinct call of God to give them the chance, and down I went, without further notice. It was the night that a public meeting was called in the schoolhouse to take means to prevent Father Search from speaking in that settlement. The room was packed and there was a pretty strong current of feeling, and it was all one way. It is not often in a man's life that he has an opportunity of listening to such a hearty and unanimous opinion of himself as I heard that night. But there was no one there that could make a speech to the crowd, and, after two or three had gotten up, and cursed me in pretty tame sort of speech, there was nothing more to be had in the way of a speech to keep the pot boiling. So I called out 'Boys give me a chance and I'll give you a talk on Search, I know him, like a book, and I'll tell you all about him.' The cry was raised 'give the little sucker a chance'—'Hand him over' shouted a tall fellow in front, and, the aisles being jammed, they picked me up bodily and passed me along from one to the other, and the last man set me on the desk; then there was a cheer and cries of 'Go it little un'!' 'Light onto him,' 'Give him rats.' When the noise lulled a bit, I began. You want me to tell you about Thomas F. Search, boys. I will begin by saying that I have an opinion of that man so mean, so small, so contemptible that I don't regard him as worth five minutes talk. Here came shouts of 'Go on'— 'Drive ahead.' Well, if you want to hear about him, here goes. You may know a man best by the business he goes into. It takes a fine pattern of a man to be a lumber-man. He must know how to swing the axe with a sturdy blow, to make the chips fly clean and clear, to leave a smooth and even cut on the lumber he fells. He must be able and willing to live a rough life and not growl at the hard fare that he has to eat. He must be a clear-headed, sure-footed, brave-hearted man to drive logs, to go out on a jam and know where to cut and when to stand his ground. He must have all his wits about him. It takes a fine pattern of a man to be a lumberman. Then they cheered me finely. But what about this Search. He is not to be named in the same breath with such a man. What is his business? Running round the country, sticking his nose in other people's business, telling these splendid fellows that they must not have their dram of whiskey to comfort them on a cold day, to cheer them up when they are tired, to make them sociable when a few of them are gathered for a little frolic. What do you say to such a man as that? I leave you to imagine the howls of derision and the curses, which were their answer to this.

"And what in the world, my friends, can this man mean by making himself this kind of a public nuisance? I suppose he must have some reason for it. Perhaps he has heard a story of some brave fellow, clear of head and strong of limb, going out on one of the lumber jams to break it up and, though he had been for many a long day the leader of the gang that drove the logs, yet this time he was lost, and the story ran that the reason was that he had taken a drop too much. (You see this happened only two weeks ago.) Then I went on and pictured the widow and five little children left penniless, to mourn that the husband and father, the bread-winner was gone, only because he had taken that drop too much. I tell you, brethren, there was scarcely a dry eye in that room, and those who were not weeping looked as scared as if a thunder-bolt had struck the school-house. Then I went on 'Well, if old Search hears such stories and believes that they're true, no wonder he carries on so; but we know better.' 'It is true, every cruel word of it is true' wailed a woman from the farther end of the room. I tell you, Brethren, that woman's voice made my blood run cold.

"Is that true? I asked of a great, stalwart fellow in front, who had been loudest in cursing me. 'Yes, stranger' he said solemnly, 'that's gospel truth.' Well I heard it and I came down here to find out all about it, and I have a subscription that I have been collecting for his widow; and I'm Father Search; now what are you going to do about it?

"God bless you! said a dozen or more voices, and, Brethren, before I left the school-house, every man there had signed the pledge, and that settlement is a temperance town to-day" and the little man's eyes gleamed as he said it.

"Well, my brother" said Dr. Bainbridge, "I congratulate you. That is more than I can do with my people clad in silks and satins."

As they rode on, up the banks of the winding river, now slowly climbing a hill that overlooked fertile flatlands and again passing through groves of oak and chestnut they came to a field where three fine chestnut trees had been left standing, and their spreading branches bending down low were laden from top to bottom with the open burrs full of the merry brown nuts. One of the party (which one was, ever after, matter of dispute) suggested that they should call a halt, fill their pockets with the abundant fruit and provide a perpetual feast for the rest of the drive. No sooner said than done; and soon sticks and stones were flying and the showers of nuts were falling.

But good Henry Wurtz, alone of all the party, lingered on the outside of the fence. With firm but gentle remonstrance he recalled his erring brethren, and bid them remember that the fruit was not theirs to gather. But, when, at some more effective cast of a club, there fell a golden shower of nuts, then he broke the restraints of conscience, bounded over the fence, and soon had his pockets as full as any of the others. But scarce had the good brother been fairly trapped into the felonious business, when a shout came from the far-away farm house down the hillside, and up came the angry farmer.

"What are ye doin', stealin' my nuts?" he shouted as he hurried on toward the group.

"There!" said the good brother, dolorously, "what did I tell you brethren? This is nothing less than robbery."

"My good man," said Dr. Bainbridge, "we did not mean to trespass on your rights. There was such an abundance of chestnut trees all along the road, that we thought they could not be gathered and that to fill our pockets from this one was no harm; but we will cheerfully hand you over all that we have gathered, and apologize for the trespass on your land."

"Well, who be ye, anyway? I can't quite make you out" said the farmer, mollified by the Doctor's quiet tone.

"We are Presbyterian Ministers on the way to Presbytery meeting" said the Doctor quizzically; while poor Henry Wurtz groaned inly, at the thought of how his cloth was degraded, and fingered a tract in his pocket; but was ashamed to hand it to the farmer under such circumstances.

"Well, it is as you say," said the farmer. "We don't gather one half o' the chestnuts on the place and you're heartily welcome to all you've got, and there's no harm done at all. I only felt like makin' a fuss because I had given these three trees to my little gal, becus they was easy to git at; and she hes the money fur her own, that she kin make by sellin' of the nuts. That was all; but 'tain't no count; for the boys kin go to the woods and make it up to her; and I'm sure you're welcome to all you kin get." He would not listen to their proposal to disgorge the nuts, nor take any payment. But Dinsmore went round to each one and collected a quarter and putting them in a hollow of the tree, laid a stone over the hole and told the farmer to tell his little girl to look there for a part of her crop of chestnuts. The farmer urged them to come back to the house and wait for dinner, but this they could not do; and so they parted, with mutual good will, and the ministers were merry over their adventure; all save the good brother Henry. His conscience forbade him to enjoy the nuts, which the rest ate with relish, nor were his pangs of conscience appeased by Dr. Bainbridge and Dinsmore, who twitted him over the affair.

"We went into it with clear consciences albeit they may have been blinded by our desire" said the Doctor; "but you let your desires get the better of your awakened convictions."

"And I made full amends, by the payment of tenfold the value of the nuts that we had taken," said Dinsmore.

"Ah! brethren you may make light of it; but we have sinned in this matter, all of us; and I have grace given me to see and repent of it," said Henry Wurtz, dolefully; seeming to derive small comfort from his repentance, while the others were very jolly sinners indeed. And so they journeyed on, cracking the nuts and their jokes.

At the Presbytery meeting, beside the routine of

business, there was a very warm and earnest debate on the appropriation from the Home Missionary fund toward the salary of Father Whiton, whose ministry of many years to the outlying village of Smugtown had produced no result other than to gather a dozen or more sleepy auditors. There was no life in the place, nor was there ever likely to be, and the maintenance of a church organization there seemed a fruitless waste of money that might be used to establish, in some growing Western town, a church that would be living and would become self sustaining. This was the view that Dinsmore took, as a member of the Committee, and on him devolved the duty to make the motion that Smugtown should cease to be as a church and be annexed to Father Whiton's charge as a preaching station, leaving the people to remunerate the preacher according to their estimate of his ability and appreciation of his services.

But the old man was inclined to do battle for " the bruised reed " as he called this feeble parish; and pleaded that his necessities were such that he needed this supplement to his salary.

Now Father Whiton's wife was reported to be well to the fore in the matter of this world's goods. The old man was tall and florid, with scant locks that were snow-white, and of very deliberate speech, in a low monotone, and had a curious fashion of cocking his head on one side, closing his left eye, and hardly opening his lips as he murmured his speech.

His feeble, deliberate mode of speaking was irritating in the extreme to the nervous, little temperance lecturer, who was alive in every fibre; and it was a call to battle for Father Search whenever his fellow patriarch of the Presbytery rose to his feet. When therefore the old man pleaded slowly and faintly for his perishing little flock in tones that seemed to reflect their dying condition, his traditional foe grew restless, and watched for the point of attack.

"I leave the question therefore with you, my brethren," said Father Whiton; "believing that you will recognize the spiritual need of the church and that you will not altogether ignore my own temporal necessities."

"Did I understand the brother to refer to his own necessities, with that new carriage-robe that covered his lap, that glistening new buggy in which he rode, and that high-stepping nag that brought him over to Presbytery," said the keen, little Father Search. "If necessities was the word that he used, I think it about time that he shall give us his definition of the term."

"These trifles which the brother refers to are the property of my wife; but, brethren, she has her limits, and, when these are reached, I have thought it prudent to refrain from urging little matters of daily necessity upon her attention," he said it slowly, and with a pathetic spreading out of the palms, and Dinsmore was touched at his helpless position. He knew what merciless raillery from Father Search such a situation would invite, and he wanted to shield the old man. "We'll endeavor to lose the old lady's grip on the purse-string" Father Search muttered; but before he could uncross his legs, Dinsmore was on his feet, and, having the floor, moved that this question be referred with power to the Committee on Home Missions, having in his mind a plan to soften the blow to the old minister. Father Search made an effort to debate the question, but Dinsmore held him firmly to the point and carried his motion, with one dissenting vote.

CHAPTER X.

"I HEAR that the summer boarders hev' begun to come to the hotel," said Mother Livingston, as Dinsmore sat on her porch, one fine evening.

"Yes! there is a young fellow here who, I am afraid, is far gone in consumption; his cough is not so bad, but he is wasted, and his hands have that transparency that seems to me a very bad sign."

Then there was a pause.

"I didn't know anything about the young man," resumed Mrs. Livingston, "but on Sunday I saw a bunnit in the congregation that I know'd wa'n't made outside of the city; and Wednesday evenin' after prayer-meetin', where I couldn't get because my rheumatiz' was so bad, Adaline Morse, the milliner, dropped in, and I asked her ' whose was that bunnit;' and she said she seen it at prayer meetin', and kept her eye on it as it went out, and sort a-lingered along and saw that she was a summer boarder at the hotel."

The old lady did not add that the wearer of the bonnet had waited for Dinsmore to escort her from the prayer-meeting; nor did he volunteer the unnecessary information.

"Oh! that was Mrs. Keene," he said. Again there was a pause.

"Is she goin' to spend some time here?" queried the old lady.

"I believe so," was the laconic reply.

"Any of her folks with her?" persisted Mrs. Livingston.

"No one, but herself," his answers were so brief that, but for the tone of his voice, they would have been curt.

"Is she a married woman, or single?" asked Mrs. Livingston.

"She is married or has been, at least;" he stumbled over this sentence.

"She's a widow, then, I suppose," said his tormentor, for by this time she seemed so.

"Well, no. That is I don't exactly know, but I believe she is not living with her husband."

"Humph!" was Mrs. Livingston's reply to this, which incited Henry to further explanation.

"She seems to be a very lovely woman, and has shown a great interest in my work here, and I am sure whatever her history is, that she is not to blame; for a husband who could be untrue or unkind to such a woman must be a brute." He paused; here he was, after only a week's acquaintance, acting as champion and defender of this charming *divorcée.*

To this warm defence, Mother Livingston's rejoinder was "Of course there is generally more fault on one side than on the other, sometimes it's wholly on one side; but more times it's about equal. Is she goin' to work in the church, while she's with us?"

"I do not know" answered Henry. "I presume that she will" he added, though it seemed rather incongruous the idea of this brilliant, witty, well-read, fascinating woman teaching in the Sunday School, or indeed doing any other work than that which she was now doing so well, namely encouraging and entertaining the pastor by her bright talk about books and society, both American and foreign, giving him a rest from the routine work of his country parish.

"Well! as she is going to be one of us while she's here, I think I'll make it my business to call on her," said the old lady.

As he walked homeward Dinsmore pondered upon the outcome of such an interview, but it was not his province to help or hinder it. He hoped that his name would not be brought into the conversation of this ill-assorted couple; for he dreaded the thought of the impression of his character which Mother Livingston might impart to Mrs. Keene; nor did it please him to think of what Mrs. Keene might say of him to this shrewd old "mother in Israel."

There was much that enlisted his interest in Mrs. Keene. She had told old Mrs. Hollis something of her life's sad story, and Mrs. Hollis had re-told it to Dinsmore. It seemed so out of place that one as young and gifted as she, with such an earnest and tender nature should be left, with the grave responsibility of her twelve year old boy, to face life alone. If death had robbed her of her natural guardian and protector, that would have been sad enough; but she had to bear the bitterness and reproach of desertion. She seemed, too, so capable of loving, so worthy of being loved.

"I cannot tell you Mr. Dinsmore," she said to him

one day, and her eyes filled with tears, "how I long
for some one to counsel me in regard to my boy. I
want him to be a man true and noble, scorning mean-
ness of every kind, manly and brave; but how can a
weak woman so guide and mould a boy's nature,
that he shall be what a man ought to be."

"There is nothing that tells on a boy's character
like a mother's influence if she be such a mother" he
was about to say—"as you;" but he thought better
of it and concluded "as some of the noblest and best
of men have born witness have moulded all their
lives."

"That may be true in early life, then I will admit
that the mother's influence is formative; but as the
boy grows toward manhood he shirks his mother's
influence and needs the firm, strong hand, the wiser
counsel of a man, from whom he is content to learn
the lesson of how to be a man. If my lot in life
were cast here, I should have no fear, for I could
turn to my pastor, whom next to a boy's own father,
one may naturally look to as willing to exercise a
sort of paternal control. Could you not write me a
set of rules by which, when I am among strangers,
with no one to look to, I might guide my boy to be
such a man as you are." She leaned toward him,
her voice, low and soft, was a very pathetic plea,
enforced by her moistened eyes; and, in the intensity of her feeling, she laid her hand gently on his
arm. She watched the effect of this upon the young
pastor. He did not move, nor was there the slightest sign that he was conscious of her touch.

Dinsmore was absorbed in thinking of her hapless

position, and anxious to be of real use to her, he was also too much embarrassed by her allusion to himself to have the fitting answer ready at the moment; and yet he felt her touch and acknowledged it by a certain thrill, which made it harder still to make a suitable reply to her appeal.

"As the responsibilities of life are laid upon us, wisdom and grace are given us to meet them," he said, taking refuge in a vague generality.

"Ah! yes, wisdom, if we only know how to apply it to each case as it arises," she answered in a sad and dreary voice.

There was a brief silence. She toyed with the leaves of the book that lay in her lap and watched Dinsmore as he sat with his eyes fixed on the line of blue hills that bounded the southern horizon.

He started as she leaned forward and picked a thread from his coat sleeve; he remembered how much meaning some attribute to such an action on a woman's part.

"I wonder how you would solve the problem of life as it lies between the covers of this book; how much you would find true, how much false, and how much a matter of indifference? I have thought of you, all along, as I read," she continued.

"I am quite sure that very little would seem a matter of indifference," he answered, "unless it were so untrue to life that it was unworthy of notice. To me things rank themselves always as true or false; if they make any impression on me."

Then she sketched the outline of the story for him; one of those pictures of love, so called, which is but

the basest counterfeit of the affections; and closed
her analysis of the story with the question "How do
you think we would have worked out that situation?"

"Unless I had lost all my senses, I would never
have gotten myself in any such situation. I abhor a
man who looks on women as subjects of conquest;
and regards them as able to take care of themselves,
putting them on the defensive. Every true gentleman ought to make a woman feel that in his company,
under any circumstances, she is safe. There was a
time when gentlemen regarded themselves as the de-
fenders of women," he spoke rapidly and with earnestness of tone.

She smiled and commended the chivalrous tone
which he assumed. "But was it always so, my young
knight-errant? I have heard that those young stu-
dents in the city's schools are ' sad dogs;' that they
work havoc with the hearts of the girls, and do not
despise any game that comes within their range.
They make some of their conquests over the counters
of the shops—make a clean breast of it. I know
how kind you are to these country girls. There is
that little Mary Lowther; you have generously spared
her, and I commend you for it. If she had only had
some advantages of good society, she would be
charming game, quite worth your while. She has
pretty, rustic manners, she is intelligent and well
read, she seems like a sincere, good girl, with a sweet
disposition."

Under this *résumé* of Mary Lowther's character
Dinsmore winced; he was ill at ease, and would have
resented it, if there had been anything that he could

9

have laid hold upon. Mrs. Keene watched him and a pleased little smile nestled in the corners of her mouth.

"I am not going to let you break that pure, little heart, while I am on hand," she continued. "But no, I will not do you the injustice to assume that you will cease to be merciful, as you have been. But tell me, truly, have you always been so kind to women as you are now?" and she laughed lightly, and waited for his answer.

He was all on edge; but he did not want to let her see how angry he was.

"I have never looked on women from the point of view that you assume that all men take. It may be that it is a common one; but in my set of acquaintances there was no one that took such a view. I may have been unusually fortunate; and yet I must say that my experience is that such rakes as that story pictures, are not common among American gentlemen; and, when they are found out, they are given the cold shoulder."

She smiled again at the hot words with which he scorned the picture which the realistic Russian had drawn of human nature.

"You cannot always live in Arcady," she said; "some call will come to a 'wider field of usefulness.' I think that is the usual term for a larger salary, is it not? When some city churchmen wander up this way and hear you preach, you will be called away to be in nearer touch with the great world, and may see men and women from another point of view."

He rose to go to his study. The two-seated buck-

board belonging to Judge Lowther was coming along
the Main Street, with the brisk pace at which the
pair of Morgan horses always stepped, with Mary
Lowther in the back seat. She was coming to take
Mrs. Keene for a drive; who had brought a letter of
introduction from her counsel in the city to Judge
Lowther.

He had called upon her more than once, and she
had fascinated him with her gracious manner and her
easy conversation.

"Upon my honor, Mary" he had said, in his pom-
pous fashion, after his first call, "there is a woman
who might well beguile a man of sober years to think
on matrimony, for the second, or even the third
time."

And when this first visit had been followed up by
a second and a third, within a fortnight, the interested observers of village life and conduct, sometimes
called gossips, had begun to whisper that the Judge
was "keeping company with the city widow."

At all events, he had insisted upon having her there
to tea, on the score of courtesy to the "learned
counsel" who had commended her to his kind offices.
Moreover he had offered her the use of his horses,
and Mary's services as cicerone, to show her something of the beauties of their drives over the hills
and through the valleys surrounding Clintonville.

It was the first of these engagements to drive that
Mary Lowther was coming to fulfil; and it cut short
this conversation.

Mrs. Keene rose to meet her as she jumped from
the buckboard and came bounding up the steps of

the house, her eyes aglow and her cheeks flushed
with the fresh, mountain air.

No one could resist her smile nor fail to answer
with anything less than a genial smile to her laughing eye.

Dinsmore did not wait to see the meeting of these
two; but retired to his study. His windows com-
manded a view of the Main Street of the village, for
a half mile or more. He stood at the window and
watched them as they drove away; there was a va-
cant seat in the buckboard. He might have been
in it just as well as not; but, if he had been, would
it have been a comfortable seat?

When they were out of sight he turned to begin
work on his sermon for the coming Sabbath. He
had already chosen the text and made some notes
from which to write. The text was " For love is of
God and cannot fail."

He sat musing, with his head resting in his hand.
He read over the text, and then there floated before
his mind the image of Mrs. Keene and Mary Lowther; and he wondered how each of them would look
at the proposition of the text. He reviewed his talk
with Mrs. Keene. How out of touch all her thoughts
of love were with the opening clause of his text.
Such love as she recognized was certainly not of God.

In her view love was of man, on his lowest side.
How was it with Mary Lowther? It was strange;
he had known her much longer, they had been as-
sociated in community of interest, in work that was
a bond between them, but they had never spoken of
love; and yet with Mrs. Keene, after a week's ac-

quaintance, he had been led into a discussion that implied an intimacy between them far closer than he would care to acknowledge, even to himself.

She had touched upon questions of a delicate nature, with an ease and fluency that startled him.

He spent more time in trying to solve the question whether he had led her into this style of conversation or whether she had led him, than he did upon his sermon. When the afternoon was waning he had nothing, as the result of his cogitations, but an empty sheet of paper, an unsolved riddle, and an uneasy consciousness that he had been led into the meshes of a net.

CHAPTER XI.

A S the Morgan horses rattled a long the main street, Mary directed the driver to turn down the road to Pleasant Pond. "It is one of our prettiest drives" she said to Mrs. Keene "and a favorite of mine because the road runs along the ridge and, on either side, the hollows are so picturesque, Scooper's Hollow with its rude hamlet, and on the other side the Willowemoc like a silver thread, here and there, among the dark firs."

"I have heard Mr. Dinsmore talk of Scooper's Hollow. He has a very interesting mission there I think" said Mrs. Keene, smiling as she saw Mary's color rise.

"Yes, it is very interesting; one feels that such teaching is sowing on virgin soil," added Mary.

"Yes, indeed, that is what I fancied Mr. Dinsmore felt. A young man is apt to find that sort of sowing, ploughing, and reaping wholly to his taste," and she laughed softly, but not sweetly, Mary thought. "But what will the harvest be" Mrs. Keene added, singing the refrain of the popular hymn, in a light bantering way, like an air from the opera.

Mary did not know what to answer; it grated on her and perplexed her. She was on the point of saying "A harvest of souls;" and yet instinctively felt

134

that this would bring out a further remark from Mrs. Keene that would have the form of sincerity and the spirit of banter.

She was silent for a moment and then launched into a description of their first experience with the Scooper Children.

Mrs. Keene listened with an amused smile.

"How delightful," she said as Mary finished the rapid and somewhat confused account, "It is really a romance, like gathering a posy of wild flowers. Do you know, I should like above all things, to meet this old witch woman and let her tell me some of her tales. Fortune has not smiled on me;" her voice grew soft and tender; "I have made one dear friend since I have come to your beautiful mountain village. I am better here than I was in the noisy, gay world. The nearness to nature has made my heart simpler and truer, I hope; and the quiet of this simple village, has healed the wounds which I have gotten in the battle of life. I think this has made me appreciate how good and true Mr. Dinsmore is. I lean on him more and more every day. But, my dear, minister though he be, he is still a man and we cannot come too near one another without danger to us both. As a young girl, you cannot appreciate this as I do; but a woman that knows the world, knows that between a man and woman there cannot be too close a friendship without danger to one, perhaps to both. I have begun to feel that I must be careful in my association with Mr. Dinsmore; of all women, one in my position needs a woman friend."

She paused for a reply; but Mary was at a loss

what to answer. "Won't you let me call you my
friend?" she said, and laid her hand on Mary's. "I
could pour out my heart to you, and know that you
would sympathize with me."

"I could do nothing for you, Mrs. Keene," Mary
answered, confused and yet flattered that this woman
of the world should lean on her. "I have lived the
quiet, simple life of a country girl, in this little village, and have neither the wisdom of age nor of experience."

"Ah! my child, it is not that sort of help I need;
but that of a heart fresh and young as yours is, the
help of truth and goodness, the contact with a heart
and life unspotted by the world. I come to you as
I come to your mountain home, with its air pure and
untainted with the miasma of the town." She leaned
her head on Mary's shoulder. "Child, let me love
you, and love me;" her eyes looked full of unshed
tears, and Mary felt that she would give that wounded,
weary heart all the love she asked for.

They drove on for half a mile in silence, Mrs.
Keene leaning still on Mary's shoulder and her eyes,
in dreamy reverie, resting on the lovely landscape,
as it lay on either side of them glorified with the
June sunlight.

"Your life runs in a soft, even current" she said
as she sat upright again "and yet it would be monotonous enough if you had only these plain people
about you. You must find much of your diversion
among books and with your music, do you not?"

"Oh! yes, I am occupied, more or less, every day
with reading and practising: but, after all, Mrs.

Keene these dull people are not without interest when you come to know their inner life. There are not so many of them, but the story of their lives is very much like that of others in the world, I think."

"Ah! you have been taking lessons from Mr. Dinsmore; that is his favorite theme."

How Mary hated herself as the color flew to her face. "I suppose he has made me see it more clearly" she said, "but I think, even before he came, I felt it in some degree."

"He has a wonderful way of enlisting one's feelings in what interests him. He has fairly captured me and made me feel as if this 'Hillside Parish' as he calls it, was of more importance than any other parish in the country. If he can lay hold of a stranger's heart in this way, I suppose he can make you, who live here, enthusiasts in his work."

"Indeed, I am" answered Mary. "There is nothing I love better than to work with him. He is so full of life and real earnestness; he has so many new ideas, and whatever he undertakes he is sure to carry through. He is so gentle and so strong; makes you see what he wants you to do, and it seems so well worth doing."

She paused as she noted the smile on Mrs. Keene's lips. She could not tell whether it was one of pleasure or amusement; but it checked the free flow of her speech.

"You do him barely justice Miss Mary," Mrs. Keene added, after a short pause, "He is all that you say, and more too, for he is a highly cultured man, of fine mind, well read, and able to hold his

own in a very much higher sphere than the one which
he now occupies.   But my dear, he is not the safest
of spiritual advisers.   He is too handsome, too sympathetic, too engaging in every way for us poor
women.   I think too that he is susceptible.   We must
keep him within bounds; you and I can teach him
some things of which he may stand in need;" and she
laughed and patted Mary playfully on the shoulder.

It was very discomfiting to Mary to be forced into
this partnership.   It placed her in a relation to her
pastor which she was loath to occupy.   She resented
it in thought, but did not know with what words to
voice this resentment.

"I always think of Mr. Dinsmore as our minister,
and cannot imagine myself trying to teach him" she
said.

"Do you?" laughed Mrs. Keene.   "Ah! little
woman, men are men, whether in homespun or
broadcloth; and we are women, and sooner or later
we find each other out, even through the thickest
disguises."

"I do not want to believe, and I do not believe,
at all, that Mr. Dinsmore thinks of anything before
his work" broke in Mary, after a moment's pause,
in which she seemed to be mustering strength to
speak her mind boldly.   "If you knew him as I know
him, Mrs. Keene, in the work of the parish, you would
not think so."

Mrs. Keene smiled.   "I must admit, my dear,
that I do not know him as you know him.   That
could not be unless I were, like you, a fresh young
nature unspotted by the world.   But, my dear girl,

he is, after all said and done, a marriageable young
man, and he knows it."

On their way home, they stopped to visit Old Barbara Fisher. The old dame greeted Mary with a
smile; but when Mrs. Keene stepped forward, her
small, blue eyes shrank and glittered like a snake's
in the intensity with which she looked into Mrs.
Keene's eyes. She gave no answer to her greeting,
and under her fixed and silent gaze, Mrs. Keene was
uneasy, and soon ready to leave.

After his vain attempt at sermonizing, Dinsmore
came out on the balcony and watched, in listless
mood, the road down which the buckboard had disappeared. On the steps below he saw Sidney Keene.
The handsome little fellow, like himself, had been
left behind. He too had spent the last quarter of
an hour sitting on the steps looking down the road.
But his gaze was not so fixed as Dinsmore's, for,
from time to time, he looked up the road, in undefined
hope that he might see something suggestive of what
to do.

Presently he ran down the steps, jumped on the
gate, and swung to and fro vigorously, making a few
sounds, half war-cry, half hurrah, such as none but
a boy can make, and no one else would attempt.
They meant nothing except that he was a boy off
duty and ready for anything that should turn up;
and they broke the oppressive silence better than
whistling.

Suddenly, as if a bright thought had struck him,
he threw open the gate and ran down the street,
yelling like a young Indian. Dinsmore leaned over

the balcony to see what had fired his enthusiasm; there was not a sign of man or beast on the broad street, lying still under the June sunshine. It was simply the intensity of physical action finding vent; there was nothing else to do, so he did that. A dog ran out from under a porch on the other side of the street. Sidney picked up a stone and threw it at the dog and then bent over as he watched the stone, with his eyes and mouth screwed up, as though he was afraid that he might hit the dog. He had thrown the stone because he and the dog and the stone were there; but he did not want to hit the dog. He was glad that the stone missed, but delighted that it fell so near as to send the dog on a gallop up the street. As the dog disappeared around the first corner, he turned and looked intently up into a tree. There was nothing there, but there might be. Then he whistled with a long, shrill note, then, with a yell, broke into a run, and rushing into the yard banging the gate behind him, sat down on the steps again. He had done something, he was, for the time being, content.

As Dinsmore watched him, it recalled so strongly the physical demand of boyhood for activity, that he too felt that he must be on the move, and leaning over the balcony, he called to Sidney that he was ready to fulfil his promise to take him trout-fishing, if he wanted to go. There was no other answer to this proposition than a yell of delight, as he came, like a whirlwind, up the stairs.

They walked off the genuine and fictitious activity by the time they had gotten over the North Mountain to the Willowemoc, the Indian's "Noisy Water;" well named, as it tumbled around and down the mountain's base.

As they came out of the stream near the North settlement with a nice string of trout, and struck the road to Clintonville, they were in sight of the North grave-yard, on a little plateau skirted by the brawling stream, the long stretch of country road on the other side, and the North Mountain rising above the sea of hemlocks that skirt its base. There is a low stone wall around it, and at the entrance a sliding-gate, hung on two posts with a beam above, such as the farmers use at the entrance to their fields or barn-yards.

The big gate was padlocked, but, beside it, is an open stile, leaving the yard free to passers on foot to come or go. Dinsmore and Sidney went in, and sat down to rest.

Far down on the water, at the foot of the hill, the foam drifted lazily around the bend of the stream, as clouds and distant objects seem to move; for, as if in courtesy to the dead that rested on its banks, the "Noisy Water" grew still as it rounded the rocky base of the grave-yard hill; and the white foam, with its dreamy motion, seemed the counterpart of the clouds that floated still above it.

There were only two shafts, one over the grave of a soldier who died in the din of 1864; another, inscribed simply "Toothaker," surrounded by a curb of cut granite. On this curb, Dinsmore and Sidney seated themselves.

Dinsmore looked at the shaft in the centre of this

plot and thought if there had been a "ch" in the last syllable, one might proclaim a pilgrimage to this spot where lies the evil genius that puts in the mouths of men the grumbling misery that steals their patience.   But the headstones round about showed that it was merely the grave of an old patriarch, who rested here, surrounded by his children, grand-children, and great-grand-children.

He had been a minister of the gospel, and had transmitted his name to many descendants.   The other side of the shaft revealed him as the Rev. Benjamin Toothaker, dying at the ripe age of seventy-two years.   He had been the mortuary poet for the numerous households of his descendants.

On one side of the tablets of this family were usually inscribed simply " Husband," " Father," " Wife," or " Mother;" which mixed the genealogy, from Dinsmore's point of view.

But on the reverse of the " Toothaker " headstones there was, during the time covered by the old ministers abiding in the flesh, some simple verse.   One of these, a variation of the famous " Stop careless friend as you pass by," read—

> " Friend pass this spot at a slow pace
>   And view where I am laid to rest,
> Far from the anxious care and toil
>   Which once my soul oppressed."

Another could lay claim to originality—

> " Dear Mother has gone, she has gone to her rest
>   Her trials on earth are all o'er
> We have smoothed her grey locks, the last kisses prest
>   She needeth our care no more."

Then the good old minister, who for two generations had gone in and out among them, baptized, married, and buried the people, was taken. There was doubtless a great gathering and sore lamentation as they bore him tenderly to the grave-yard among the hills. But there was no one to write an epitaph for him and, after his departure, no verses on the tombs of his descendants.

The rest of the graves had no inscription other than the names. One was marked only by a stake, on which was nailed a cedar board, and on this, in large letters, was written with lead pencil (as gardeners mark their planted seeds) "William Bradford," a good old Mayflower name. There was an American Flag on this and on several other graves, and the withered flowers of Decoration Day lay scattered about.

There were many graves which had no stone, save those of which the soil was full, which made a melancholy rattle on the coffin's of those buried in this "God's Acre."

Among the branches of the Toothaker family was one full row of Perkins; whose favorite device was a hand in bas-relief, with the thumb and three fingers tightly folded, and a preternaturally long index finger pointing upward—sometimes with the legend "Heaven is my home;" sometimes the hand alone, leaving the rest to the imagination of the passer by, which was more economical.

As Dinsmore sat reading the inscriptions, or watching the drifting foam down on the stream, or the cloud shadows chasing one another across the distant hill, Sidney suddenly asked "What are those grave-stones, Mr. Dinsmore?"

"They are the graves of Perkins" he answered, absently.

"Why do they bury them here" asked the boy in a wondering tone.

"Because they died," replied Dinsmore; as he read some more of the inscriptions.

"What are Perkins?" asked the boy in a perplexed tone; and then before Dinsmore could reply, "Oh! they are people" he said, spelling out the name of one Eli Perkins.

He had mistaken them for some nondescript, whether of the animal or vegetable kingdom Dinsmore did not enquire. "How much of a history like that of the world of living men" he thought "one can gather from a country grave-yard, reading between the lines on the grave-stones, matching dates and names, as the children do in their zigzag puzzle; putting together the picture that has been cut into pieces. I wonder how nearly I have matched this picture of times gone-by."

Then they picked up their string of trout and set out on their homeward way.

CHAPTER XII.

DURING the next week, the young Pastor was initiated into one of the important ceremonies of the village, namely the funeral of one of his parishioners.

Everybody went to a funeral in this little village; the Academy was closed, and the scholars were expected to use the half-holiday in attendance at the service; an expectation not always fully realized in nutting time, or when the trout were biting.

The coffin was placed in the centre of the parlor; on a side table was an array of gloves, the scarf of white linen for the minister and long bands of crape called "weepers" for the undertaker and pall-bearers. There were six pall-bearers, who took their places on either side of the coffin, and acted as ushers for the company. For the more prominent persons of the village society and for the immediate friends of the family, kid gloves were provided; for the humbler class of attendants, the gloves were black cotton, and it was a nice point to decide who were entitled to kids.

As Dinsmore entered the room Tim Mitchell came forward, his face beaming with satisfaction, holding in his hands a pair of two-button kids for "the Dominie" and the white linen scarf, which he adjusted

10   145

with the peremptory air of one who knows exactly how it should be done.

Dinsmore took his seat near the head of the coffin by a small table on which was a bible, a hymn-book, and a glass of water. The crowd outside pressed close to the windows; for it was the new Dominie's first funeral.

Eli Hilton who knew well the customs of Clintonville, and was a sort of leader in good society, was the first to enter and view the corpse. As he came into the room he took off his hat with his left hand, and with his right smoothed down his hair, answered the whispered enquiry of Tim Mitchell, "What is your size?" received his kid gloves, walked up to the coffin, gazed upon the face of the corpse, drew down the corners of his mouth and closed his eyes tightly, and then passed out to the plot in front of the house.

"It's as beautiful a corpse as I ever saw" he said as the crowd outside waited for his verdict. "You oughtn't to miss the chance of seein' it."

One after another filed in, and observing the same order of coming and going, each making some wry face as they looked on the face of the dead girl, returned to the lawn in front of the house and talked politics or swapped horses and heifers, until it was time "to lift."

In former times, as they left the house, they passed by a table on which were set out cold meats, bread and butter and liquors, where each took a glass of his favorite toddy; but now, as one old man said to Dinsmore, with some bitterness "Temperance has done for funerals."

The service was brief and simple. Dinsmore made a prayer, the choir sang a hymn, he read the XIVth chapter of St. John's Gospel, and commented briefly on the first four verses.

"It was a middlin' short service, it seems to me," said Deacon Shrake, whose bargain for a yearling heifer was interrupted by the announcement that it was "time to lift." "It was short" answered Deacon Shelton, "but we must remember that Julia was quite a young gal, and had been a church member not over six months. Of course on some of us older ones the Dominie will hev more to say. There is a natural propriety to be observed in all these things which those of us thet hev experience understand."

This silenced Deacon Shrake, but did not console him for the loss of his bargain.

Tim Mitchell marshalled the procession promptly, as one who knows he is in command and what is expected of him. Dinsmore with his white scarf and long, crape "weeper" was in the lead; after him came the six bearers whose "weepers" reached to their waists; then came the coffin, covered with the black, velvet pall, carried by the four under-bearers; then the family and the friends, arranged by Tim, with peremptory order: he snibbed them into file with a nod of his head or a touch of his hand, and no one dared move except at his prompting. Through the village they walked their horses decorously, but, once out of the village bounds, they rattled along at a good, round pace; for Tim was a busy man.

When they came to the North burying-ground, where the Snyder's family plot was, the black bier, a simple shelf of wood on four legs, was brought by the friends of the family who had volunteered to dig the grave, as was the universal custom.

After the brief prayer at the grave, everyone stood around and watched in silence while the friends filled in the stony soil, set a rough stone at the head and foot, rounded up the soil over the grave and replaced the sod, packing it down with the backs of their spades; and then planted the black bier over the new-made grave to await the next who might need it.

To Dinsmore it was a most melancholy scene; needlessly harrowing, he thought, to those who stood there as mourners; and yet they seemed to find a grim kind of consolation in this dreary ceremony.

"Have you seen Mrs. Snyder since Julia Ann's funeral" said Mrs. Livingston to Dinsmore, two or three days later. "I tried to talk to Anna but 'twant no use. She's got the notion into her head that 'twas harder for her to lose Julia than 'twould be for any one else to lose their darter. Of course she was the only gal in the family; but there's been others where 'twas the same," and the old lady sighed as she remembered the day when, with her own hands, she stitched the shroud and laid out her own and only daughter. "No! 'taint no use talkin' to any one when they get the notion that what they suffer is more'n others suffer in the same afflictions: I guess we're all built on nigh the same pattern."

"I have seen her once, but could not talk with her," said Dinsmore. "She sat cold and numbed with her grief, and with a stony gaze, looking straight before her; she did not seem to hear one word that I said."

"You'd better go see her soon again. If she don't get moved out o' that rut she's in, I wouldn't answer for her life; let alone her reason."

So Dinsmore betook him to the little house, set back from the roadside about one hundred feet. Along the straight path bordered with box, which had a funereal aspect and odor, were the flower beds planted and tended by Julia Snyder, a delicate girl as pale as one of her snowdrops, but as sunny at heart as one of her daffodils. She had faded away gently, and, three days before her twenty-second birthday, had died. She passed away with a tender smile on her lips as her mother held her hand, trusting and believing, without a shadow on her soul.

Dinsmore had thought it an ideal parting from this life to enter on the new and higher life.

But it had left the blackness of darkness in the mother's heart. "It's all right for you Mr. Dinsmore; you're the preacher, and it's your business to talk about God's being good and Julia's bein' happy; but she wan't your daughter, and you don't know nothing about that side of the matter. I could ha' borne it if she'd been took young; but here she was just growed up to be a comfort to me; she was a help every way; she was all that made my life happy, and I say it ain't fair to leave me to get so wrapt up in her and to take her right away—no warnin' giv and nothin' left to me. I don't call that fair. I wouldn't do it to my worst enemy."

"His ways are not our ways and His thoughts are

not our thoughts," replied Dinsmore solemnly, to this tirade.

"No, they are not" she replied hotly, "That's just what I say, I would be ashamed to look anyone in the face that I had treated that way."

"Mrs. Snyder," said Dinsmore, quietly, "let me tell you a story of another mother whose sorrow was very much like yours, and whose story will perhaps throw some light upon your own case. There was a young mother in Ireland with a daughter about sixteen years old, and three younger boys. They had lived on the same little farm year after year, and their means had grown narrower and their lives more sordid and hopeless, and they were now at a point where starvation stared them in the face. Her father had often urged her to emigrate to America; but she was afraid of the new and untried country, and, ruled by this fear, she was more ready to let her children almost starve than move to the undiscovered country. One day, her father came to the house and took away her one, only, darling daughter and carried her off to the far country where there was bread enough and to spare for them all, that he might make her feel that there was a home for her there, where her daughter was; and when, at last, driven by want from her old home, she started for the unknown land, she found that she did go forth with courage, because her daughter had gone before her and was there to welcome her. Do you think that father was cruel?"

Dinsmore waited anxiously for her answer.

"I think he might ha' taken them both together" she answered, fiercely.

" But she was not ready to go " he said, gently ; " and what would have become of the little boys ?" he added.

To this she made no answer, but relapsed into her cold, sullen, indifference.

That evening he was at Judge Lowther's to tea, and, after supper, told Mary of his talk with Mrs. Snyder, and its fruitless result. " Will you see her to-morrow, Miss Mary," he said in a hopeless tone, as though at his wits end, and having no suggestion to make other than that Mary should see her.

" I cannot do anything to help her, if you cannot, Mr. Dinsmore " Mary said. But Dinsmore thought that she could. So on the next morning Mary went to see her and found her in the same dull, hopeless state which Dinsmore had described—and felt appalled before a grief so dumb; so drowsy, unimpassioned, hopeless a woe.

" Have you looked over Julia's things to see whether there were any that she wanted given away?" said Mary, scarce knowing what she said.

" No! I haven't had courage to touch anything belonging to her, nor even to go to her room; but it seems as if I'd dare go if you'd go along with me Miss Lowther."

So Mary put her arm around her and led her up stairs to the dainty little room, which though simple and plain in its furniture, showed the marks of natural refinement and delicacy. She sat Mrs. Snyder down, and, with a feeling of awe, opened the bureau drawers and looked on the neat and orderly arrangement which had been made by the hands now lying under the stony soil.

As she opened the box in which the handkerchiefs were daintily folded, there lay a letter from Julia to her mother. She looked at it for a moment and her heart beat fast; it was like a message from the other world, this unopened letter.

She hesitated but for a moment and then took it to Mrs. Snyder, but she looked at it in a dazed, helpless way, as it lay in her lap.

"Who is it from?" she asked.

"It is from Julia to you," Mary whispered, in an awed voice.

"A letter, already, from Julia; and she gone only two days?"

Mary feared that her mind had given way; but then to her great relief she saw the tears slowly rise to Mrs. Snyder's eyes and drop, one by one, upon the letter lying in her lap. "It was like her" she said, "It was just like Julia to do that. Read it to me Mary. I can't see to read it myself."

Nor could Mary until, by a strong effort, she checked her rising tears, with the thought that it was for this that she had come here. She could not minister to this stricken heart, nor could Mr. Dinsmore, but her ears would be open to the voice of her darling. So she sat on the floor at Mrs. Snyder's feet, with her face turned from her, and read her daughter's letter.

It was written in a clear hand, without a tremor, and told her mother, first; that she knew how near the end was and that she faced it without any fear; that after she was gone there were some things her mother could do for her, and then she detailed the gifts among her little circle of friends, and others to the poor, which she would like her mother to give in her name. "And will you take them yourself, mother; for it will do you good to talk with those that love me, after I am gone. And remember, mother, whether on earth or in heaven, I am forever and ever,

Your loving daughter

Julia."

When the letter was ended, Mary's restraint gave way and she burst into almost hysterical sobbing. Mrs. Snyder lifted her up and took her in her arms.

"Don't take on so, poor child. I oughtn't to hev let you read it to me. Don't cry so, Julia ain't taken away from me. She's my own daughter yet; that's what she says 'on earth or in heaven, your own lovin' daughter.' Why, child, I see it now. I couldn't see it before, but I see it now—I know it, and want to set right about the things she wants me to do. If you'll help me to sort some of the things, so as to be sure that I get them all right; 'twill do us both good, I'm sure."

But there was little need of sorting; for a slip of paper pinned to each article told for whom it was intended.

As Mary left the house and bade Mrs. Snyder good-bye, the cold, set look was gone from her face; it was soft and loving, and there came to Mary's mind the words "the peace that passeth understanding;" this must be what was meant.

That night, at prayer meeting, Mary understood what lay on the young pastor's heart so heavily, as he seemed to strive in prayer for hearts that were burdened with sorrow greater than they could bear.

She saw his look of surprise, when, after the meeting, Mrs. Snyder came to him and said briefly " I see it now Mr. Dinsmore, as I didn't see it when you were talking to me."

He walked home with Mary Lowther, who told him of the scene when she read Julia's letter; and while Mary dwelt on the sweetness of heart and mind shown by the dead girl, he credited the living messenger with much of the result, though she seemed unconscious that she had borne any important part in healing this broken heart.

On his return to the hotel, Mrs. Keene met him and tried to enlist him in a discussion of the book that lay in her lap, then rallied him upon being so distraught; but could not recall him from the memory of that scene which Mary had so graphically but simply described to him, where it seemed, almost, that one had risen from the dead to tell of what lay beyond this life.

CHAPTER XIII

M RS. KEENE filled so large a part in the village gossip, and her name was linked, now with Judge Lowther's, and, again by others, with the young minister's; and there were so many conflicting opinions regarding her, that Mrs. Livingston made up her mind that it was her duty to call and see for herself what kind of a woman this was, who might become her pastor's wife. So, donning the black satin dress and the black mits, which were reserved for grand occasions, and carefully adjusting the poke bonnet, she made her way slowly up the village street, halting from time to time to take a look at one or another neighbor's yard and note their flower beds, or to pass the time-o' day with them, and, at last, found herself at the hotel.

Enquiring for Mrs. Keene, she found that she was out for a drive, but Mrs. Hollis was at home, and the panting old lady sat herself down, partly to get her breath, and partly to hear from Mrs. Hollis her impression of this grand lady.

"Good-day, Mrs. Hollis! After walkin' down street and up them steps I really haven't breath enough left to ask after your health. How ever folks live in houses with high stoops, beats me to know."

"If you'd asked after my sickness I could ha' told

155

you more about it, Mrs. Livingston. My health's been gone so long that I most forget how it feels to be healthy."

" Do you keep your appetite to eat?"

" Well, I never hed no appetite to boast of: but I do take some comfort still in corn-beef and cabbage, if I can have mince pie for dessert, to round it off. I notice my failin' mostly in that I can't bear sour bread. It turns my stummick upside-down. I was tellin' Mrs. Joyce to-day that I can't stand her bread, no longer. She flared up in a minit; but I told her it wan't no use her gettin' mad, for that only proved the bread was sour."

" Sour bread is more'n you're called on to stand, Mrs. Hollis, specially at your time o' life."

" I ain't so old as some folks take me for, Mrs. Livingston, and can git up a flight o' stairs without losing all the wind in my body; but I allus was springy in the tread."

" The most poorly of us hes somethin' to be thankful for, if we only know to find it out " said Mrs. Livingston; then shifting from ground that was getting dangerous, "I dropped in to see Mrs. Keene, seein' that she was attendin' our church, quite regular. Hev you made any acquaintance with her, Mrs. Hollis?"

" Why, I may say Mrs. Livingston, we are quite intimate; she bein' a stranger here, I felt bound to enquire who she was and where she come from; and hevin' no one else to turn to, I went straight to her. I am bound to say she acted like a perfect lady. She's been unfortunate in her marriage, through no

fault of hers, and now she's free from a perfect brute;
how she came alive out of his hands is more than I
can tell: but through it all she acted like a perfect
angel. I've advised her, as the safest course for her,
to marry some good man who can protect her and
her little boy: and there's only one man in the village fit to call her wife. Amelia Ann don't agree
with me; but that's no reason to make me alter my
mind. I'm bound to make that match if I can. She
reads books way ahead of anything that is writ in
English, and reads poetry too; and what's more she
understands it. She's just cut out for a minister's
wife, by her winnin' ways. Why, when she's a'talkin'
to you, you know there ain't no body in the world
she'd rather talk to, and she knows just what you
want to talk about. I tell you she'd make sech a
minister's wife as has never been seen in the country;
and, poor thing, after all she's gone through with,
she deserves just sech a man as Mister Dinsmore;"
the old lady paused to take breath.

"Well, I'm real grieved she's not to home," answered Mrs. Livingston. "I shall surely call again,
hopin' to find her in. And I'll say good-afternoon,
Mrs. Hollis."

"You'll be pleased Mrs. Livingston" answered the
old lady; and despite her "springy tread" she bade
the old dame good-bye at the top of the stairs.

On her way home, dame Livingston stopped to
look at no flower-beds or pass the time-o' day with
her neighbors. Steadily she plodded her way homeward, pondering. What she had heard, even from
the enthusiastic admirers of Mrs. Keene, by no means

assured her that either Mr. Dinsmore or the parish would be benefited by having this lady installed as the pastor's wife. She was more than ever determined to get her own impressions, from a personal interview.

She let but one afternoon pass before, arraying herself again in her company dress, she trudged up the Main Street to the Inn. And, this time, fortune favored her, for she found Mrs. Keene sitting on the balcony. Passing into the parlor, and seating herself on the sofa she waited until she had gotten her breath and then, finding Mrs. Joyce, asked her to tell Mrs. Keene that she had come to call on her.

As Mrs. Keene came into the darkened parlor, from the bright sunshine, she looked round, for a minute, before she discovered Mrs. Livingston, nestled on the sofa in the darkest corner of the room.

This gave the old lady a chance to see her at close range, without the glamour of Sunday dress and that city "bunnit." Her dress was of white muslin, with a red sash at her waist, a little bow of red ribbon in front and on the sleeves. Her light, auburn hair was coiled in a simple Grecian knot, low down on the back of her head. Her figure was slight and girlish, and her agile movement contributed to make her look ten years younger than she was. It was only when one got a nearer view of her face, and talked to her, that one could form a truer estimate.

From the dark corner, where she was passing her crooked fore-finger across her lips, Mrs. Livingston set her down as "giddy."

As the old lady arose, Mrs. Keene hurried across

the room to meet her, with outstretched hands and a smiling welcome.

"I cannot tell you how much I feel complimented by your calling on me Mrs. Livingston. It was rather my place to have asked you to let me call and see you."

"That's not our way with strangers, Mrs. Keene. We like to make them welcome to our village and so, as I did not find you home day before yesterday when I called, I came again to-day; that you might not think us neglectful."

"Why, my dear Mrs. Livingston," said Mrs. Keene seating herself on the sofa beside the old lady and laying her hand on her arm, "I am so sorry that I did not know of your call, so as to have saved you this walk in the hot sun. I should have returned your call right away; but I did not receive your card."

"And no wonder you didn't, for I have never fell into that new-fangled way of goin' round leavin' cards to let folks know that I've called. I've allus held that the best card to leave was a good shake of the right-hand. There are only four folks in the village that use those cards any way; and they never use 'em on me. I've allus supposed that they come to see me, and, if I wan't to home, they'd come an-other day when I was; and I never could see how leavin' a card makes out a visit."

Mrs. Keene did not deem it worth while to enter into the defence of the customs of society with this downright old lady, who sat, comfortably blinking at her, and stroking her lips with her crooked fore-finger; which had the same disconcerting effect on

Mrs. Keene that it had on every one, who saw it for the first time.

"Do you expect to stop some time in the village" enquired Mrs. Livingston?

"I cannot tell how long I shall be here. I came for rest and change of scene after six months of trouble that had quite broken me down."

"It seems to ha' done you good already, for you look now as if you were in the best o' health."

"There are some troubles of the heart that do not show on the face, Mrs. Livingston."

"Yes, but I thought there was allus a sort o' bright, protrudin' eye that went along with heart-disease. I don't think your eyes have that look," and the old lady scanned her keenly, as she passed her forefinger to and fro across her lips.

"I do not mean heart disease, Mrs. Livingston. I mean sorrow of heart, trials and troubles that wear out life and make it seem not worth living."

"Yes, we all of us have our troubles. Some of 'em we make, some we borrow, and some are sent to us. I never knowed anyone to die of 'em though. I've seen a many that felt they was goin' to die; but they didn't. They lived right on, and a'most killed those that had to live with 'em. Besides religion, I think the best cure for these is to try to help some-one else, who is in worse trouble than you are. That seems to fetch you right out of the rut and give you more of a lift than you give to them."

As this did not meet Mrs. Keene's case, from her point of view, at least, she made no answer to the dame's homily.

"Are you a professor?"

Mrs. Livingston shot the question at her, after a moment's pause, so briefly and quickly that she answered with some confusion—"No, I have never taught; having never needed to earn my living."

The old lady smiled. "I didn't mean it that way. Are you a professin' member!"

"Oh! I beg your pardon. No, I am not a communicant of the Church, though I am a regular attendant."

"Yes, I saw you there whenever I was out, and when I wasn't others hev told me of your bein' out, and at prayer-meetin' too. It might do you good if you was to become a professin' member. It helps some folks very much; others it don't seem to do no good to; but that I hold is their own fault."

"You must congratulate yourselves on having secured such a man for your pastor. Mr. Dinsmore is such an interesting preacher that one does not care to miss his services."

"He seems to be gettin' his place among the people," Mrs. Livingston answered. "To be sure we miss our old Dominie yet, especially in seasons of trouble. You know young folks don't take no account of trouble, Mrs. Keene. As we get along in life and hev had our own, we can understand those of other folks. Mr. Dinsmore knows of course, the right texts to use in cases of affliction, and his remarks on Julia Snyder was very affectin'. Some said that they was ruther short, but I told 'em they was full o' gospel peth; and long enough, seein' how hot the weather was and the corpse three days old.

11

And then, there was an awful big crowd to see the
corpse, and it was the fust time Mr. Dinsmore was
scarfed; and everythin' seemed to point to a short
service.   Our Old Dominie, I don't suppose, was
generally considered so good a preacher as Mr. Dinsmore, but he knowed us through and through—hed
baptized most the whole congregation; seen 'em
through teethin', measles and chicken-pox; married
'em and buried one or more out o' every family in
the village.   When he come to talk to you in affliction, maybe he couldn't handle texts as good as Mr.
Dinsmore; but he knowed us clean through, and
could tell us, without any texts, just what we needed
to hear.   I suppose you hev found it so in your
afflictions, Mrs. Keene, that a young minister ain't
nowhere alongside o' one that's old and full of experience."   The old lady paused for a reply.

"My troubles were of a kind, Mrs. Livingston,
that led me to seek relief not in the counsel of ministers, but in the courts of law."

"That's hard lines for a woman, but if our old
Dominie hed been livin', so as you could ha' gone to
him, I'll be bound he'd ha' fetched you through
without leavin' you in the clutches o' the lawyers.
Be you goin' to work in our church while you're with
us, Mrs. Keene?"

"I do not know, Mrs. Livingston, whether I can
find anything suited to me in the way of work.   I
should have been delighted to have gone out to that
Sunday school in Scooper's Hollow.   There is something charming in the idea of taking hold of minds
that are almost savage in their ignorance and watch-

ing them as they begin to develop; but I stopped there the other day, with Miss Lowther, and that old witch Barbara glared at me with such an evil eye, that I do not want to go near the place."

"You'd get no harm from Barbara, Mrs. Keene. She's round the village a good deal, and whatever folks may say about her bein' a witch, she's the best of the whole lot; and, if you're kind to her young ones, she'll do you a good turn. The old woman does more than the whole lot of those drunken lazy men to keep them Scoopers in some sort of order. But if you don't take to work with the Scoopers, I was thinkin', from what Mrs. Hollis said of your readin' o' furrin books and poetry and such like, you'd be just the one to take a Bible Class o' young women. You see, as the girls git older, they want a little higher schoolin', than those who hev been brought up in the village is apt to give 'em."

Mrs. Keene smiled, as she thought of the "furrin books" as subjects for Bible Class study. "Well, we will see about it Mrs. Livingston, and I will ask Mr. Dinsmore what he thinks of my fitness for a Bible Class teacher. They tell me that you have such a charming home Mrs. Livingston, so cosy and full of comfort, and that no one ever forgets the first day they taste your chicken-pie; that your garden is full of those dear old-fashioned flowers, which are so much sweeter than these new things with long names. May I come to see you, some time soon? and when you know me better I shall hope for an invitation to supper with you."

"Sakes alive! how folks do talk. 'Taint nothin'

to raise primroses and daffodils and lilacs and sweet-peas, and marigolds, and 'taint nothin' to make a chicken-pie, when you've got the chickens and hev been taught, from a girl, to roll puff-paste. I'd expect you to come to see me, or I wouldn't ha' called on you; and you're welcome to supper, any day, only so I know it the day before, so as to hev a chicken killed. I like to let 'em lie one whole day before puttin' 'em into pie. Suppose we make it day after to-morrow. We take supper at six. And I'll bid you good-afternoon, Mrs. Keene, hopin' as your health will allow you to come down, to-morrow afternoon;" and, without more ado, the old lady sailed out of the room, nodding her head to Mrs. Keene's acceptance of her invitation, and acknowledging it with a series of low grunts.

When she was gone Mrs. Keene sat down on the sofa and burst into a merry, ringing laugh.

On her way down the street, Mrs. Livingston, by turns, knitted her forehead or smiled shrewdly, and nodded her head; at times emphasizing her thoughts with a low, aspirated grunt.

CHAPTER XIV.

SOCIALLY considered it had been a dull year for Clintonville. Neither wedding, fair nor festival had broken its monotony. During the winter, owing to the lack of a pastor's wife to superintend them, there had been no church sociables and the missionary sewing society had suspended. In fact Julia Snyder's funeral had been the one social event of the year. Eli Hilton, the well-to-do village bachelor, whose failure to marry was one of the unsolved problems of life in Clintonville, declared that "unless some one else died or got married he was agoin' to do it himself;" uncertain, it seemed, whether to choose a wedding or a funeral.

He was sauntering past the hotel waiting for the stage-coach, as was his wont, summer and winter, in rain or shine; for being well to the fore in worldly goods, and having no other occupation, he made it his business to inspect every new-comer to the village and gather the outside gossip which the stage-coach brought.

There were very few strangers, or old inhabitants, who escaped the sort of customs inspection of which he was the self-appointed officer.

Dinsmore had accosted him, as he was strolling by, with the inquiry, "why have you changed your seat from the front pew in church to the very last ?"

"Well! Dominie, I didn't care to sit quite so close to the mouth of the cannon," he replied, with a twinkle in his eye.

"I can't see that it makes much difference whether you are near or far away."

"It seems a little easier back there. I can see how it strikes some o' them in front; and it don't seem to come so straight at me, Dominic. I'm more comfortable back there."

Eli was reputed to be something of a free-thinker, and this might account for his preference for a long range. Dinsmore did not pursue the subject.

Then he uttered his protest against the dull monotony of life in Clintonville, and wound up with the suggestion of a donation party for Dinsmore.

It required some persuasion on Dinsmore's part to divert this compliment from himself to Mr. Forrester, but he was finally successful; for Eli, who prided himself on the breadth and liberality of his opinions, was impartial in all relations of life. He meted out his attentions, measure for measure, among the village belles, so that if he was reported to be "keeping company" with one of them he would, during the next week, equalize matters by the same amount of expenditure on another; he voted in alternate years, with conscientious regularity, for the candidates of each political party; he had a pew in both the Episcopal and Presbyterian churches and was scrupulous in dividing his attendance, and his contribution of 25 cents per week, between the two churches.

Dinsmore persuaded him that age and priority of service entitled Mr. Forrester to be considered first, and thus diverted the threatened function from himself to the old rector.

He had been honored by one such gathering, on a much smaller scale, and without the donation feature, and that festivity had been enough to make him eschew such honors, until the memory of that party at Farmer Brown's had been softened by time.

The families of the West Settlement had been invited by the hospitable farmer to meet their new Pastor at a "Sociable."

To Dinsmore this seemed a sad misnomer; for, when he was ushered into the parlor, there sat the farmers' wives and daughters, on the stiff horse-hair chairs and sofas which were pushed back tight against the wall. They sat in silence staring in front of them, with their hands placidly folded in the lap of their black alpaca dresses, or when those more accustomed to the ways of Clintonville society broke the silence, it was in a subdued whisper.

The men were gathered in a knot at the lower end of the hall. Their Sunday clothes gave a Sabbatarian character to the meeting, and they could not shake off the feeling that it was a church service, or at least a funeral. Their starched shirt fronts were veritable straight-jackets, their cuffs were gyves upon their wrists; they were in thrall body and soul; and looked out from their white shirt collars with a meek and penitential air.

Farmer Brown met Dinsmore at the front door, took his hat from him and, with a jerk of the thumb, invited him to enter the formidable precincts of the parlor; but did not offer to lead the way.

As Dinsmore walked into the room every voice was hushed, even the faintest whisper ceased, and all eyes were fastened on the young pastor. The old Dominie would have gone round the room and, with pleasant nod and handshake, would have asked after the welfare of parents, children and grandchildren; what would the new Dominie do? Mrs. Brown straightened herself in her chair, prepared to answer any question that might be addressed to her. Fannie Brown would have liked to step right forward and give the young pastor a hearty shake of the hand, and welcome him to their house; but she knew that this would bring upon her the united frowns of the matrons of the whole settlement, and the reputation of being a saucy, forward girl; and the conventions of good society in Clintonville restrained her from even a smile, and kept her eyes demurely on the carpet at her feet.

Dinsmore stood for a moment in the glare of the kerosene lamp on the centre table, and two tallow candles on the mantel-shelf, and looked for his hostess. The men in the hall had crowded to the door to see what would become of him. In the dim light of the kitchen he saw a cluster of faces at that door, where a number of the young men and girls had retreated and were having a good time, on the bare floor and wooden chairs.

The row of farmers' wives in black alpaca or dark serge dresses round the wall with their hands folded in their laps and the throng at the two doors of the room, reminded him so strongly of the gathering and conduct of the people at a funeral, and there was the open melodeon with a Moody and Sankey hymn-book on the rack, that his first impulse was to shut his eyes, fold his hands and say "let us pray."

He caught sight of Mrs. Brown at the farther end of the room, and walked quickly over to her. "I'm awful glad you could come, Mr. Dinsmore."

"Thank you Mrs. Brown," and he shook hands with her.

There was a sigh of relief, some of the women looked at each other in a meaning way, one or two smiled, their young pastor had done the proper thing; their minds were relieved; on the main point of etiquette he was all right, it only remained now to be seen what order he would observe in speaking to the others, and what time he would devote to each one; whether he would remember those who had been or were now sick, and whether he would inquire for the children by name, and get the names attached to the proper families.

There was almost a question of principle in this latter point; for some families were wont to indulge in names gotten from books of poetry or call their children after leading men or women, while others adhered, on principle, to names taken from the Bible, and even these they tried to choose not at random, but with conscientious regard to their meaning.

It was a serious blunder therefore, to forget that farmer Hilton's oldest boy was Adonijah, or confound his name with Deacon Shrake's son, whom he had called Extra Harry Lincoln Shrake.

Therefore the whole room listened while Dinsmore went the round, with Mrs. Brown by his side as chaperon; for, after the handsome way in which he had come right up and spoken to her, she would not leave him in the lurch. Not only did she recall to him the name but often some of the family points of each guest, as he made the round, thus saving him from more than one pitfall.

As he passed around a hum of conversation arose; those to whom he had spoken fell into talk with their neighbors, those who were awaiting him were silent.

When the circuit was completed, there was a sudden relief of restraint; every one talked freely.

Fannie Brown came forward and asked him which was his favorite hymn, and when he hesitated to make choice of the many good things in the Moody and Sankey books, she chose three herself, and having distributed the books, sat down at the melodeon and led the company, supported by a muffled bass from the hall and the kitchen.

The announcement that supper was ready in the kitchen brought another hush upon the company, for, in Clintonville society there was observed a certain becoming gravity when they were summoned to the serious business of eating.

As soon as the announcement was made all conversation ceased, a self-restraint of manner was apparent, and an absence of anything like unseemly haste to go to, or even turn toward the kitchen door. The hostess was expected to go round to each guest and with some pleasant quip or more serious invitation urge their flagging steps toward the loaded table in the kitchen. "I hope you ain't left all your appetite to home Mrs. Shrake."

"Well if I had, Mrs. Brown, I expect I'd git it again, when I see your biscuits."

"Of course Mrs. Smith you'll not find chicken pie like your'n, but sech as it is, you're welcome to it."

"Law Miss Brown how you do take on, my husband makes me real jealous when he tells me about that pie o' your'n he tasted, when he was helpin' raise your barn."

"If you can stand my butter Miss Pelton, I hope you'll make yourself to home at the supper-table."

"It's the first time I ever heard a word said agin your butter; but, comin' from yourself, I suppose you ken stand it."

With more familiar friends there was greater freedom.

"Law sakes! Amanda, I've seen you eat in this house, till I was fairly amazed to see what you could hold. Now, you go and show the rest on 'em that there ain't nothin' wrong with them vittles."

Such appeals were met with a smile and shake of the head, and sometimes with a "Law! how Miss Brown does take on," and the subject of appeal would bridle and march into the kitchen. The young pastor was led by Mrs. Brown to the head of the table, and asked to say grace.

Then decorum required that all should stand around, and with great solemnity, view the feast. It was in order at this time to make whispered comments loud enough for the hostess to hear on the golden color of the butter, the lightness of the biscuit, the puffiness of the paste on the chicken pie, the size and splendor of the turkey.

It was then in order for the hostess to invite them to begin the feast with some pleasantry.

"If you set such store by them biscuit, Miss Jones, I don't see why you don't find out whether they taste as good as they looks."

"I say Mr. Brown, you're wanted in here to carve this turkey. Why don't you men in the hall step right in and help yourselves first, and the women afterward."

This brought the men straggling in shamefacedly.

They clustered in the far corner and eyed with fixed gaze, in unbroken silence, the women on the other side of the room or Farmer Brown as he carved the great turkey.

Hiram Shrake, the deacon's oldest boy looked stiffly out from his white shirt front at pretty Sue Pelton, standing demurely on the other side of the room with her eyes downcast. Was that the girl that he had chased across the meadow this afternoon, when she dared him to catch her and kiss her if he could. She had outrun him; but he could catch her now. He shivered to think what the effect on the company would be if he did it, and claimed the forfeit, then and there.

The silence was such that you could hear the fat sizzle as the Farmer cut off great, generous slices.

But when this preliminary work was gotten through with, and they were all seated and helped, and had begun to eat, then the more genial and homely surroundings of the kitchen, the absence of the horse-hair furniture, ingrain carpets and mantel ornaments began to tell on the spirits of the company, and the "Sociable" closed in a way to justify its name.

The donation party to Mr. Forrester was a different kind of entertainment, a combined festival and fair. The old minister's powers did not extend to the consumption of all the good things with which his host of friends were sure to testify their goodwill.

It would not please them to think these good things were turned over to fill the larder of the inn; and so they made an arrangement to consume them on the spot, and, that the old rector might benefit by this arrangement, the attendants at the donation party were expected to take their supper there and pay for it. Articles too bulky, not cooked, or otherwise, unsuitable for the supper were auctioned off to the highest bidder, and the proceeds of these sales were handed to Mr. Forrester.

An odd consequence of this method was, that, sometimes, a farmer's wife who had brought a great pound cake which was left over from the supper, would find her husband loyally bidding a fine price for his wife's cake, and in the end it would be knocked down to him at about twice its value, and they would carry it home again, not quite sure in mind whether they had been gainers or losers by the transaction.

There was none of that awkward stiffness which had made Dinsmore shrink from having the honor conferred on him.

It was a brisk, cool Fall evening and every one

came into the warm room with blood astir and nerves keyed up, by the bracing, frosty air. Mr. Forrester knew them all well, many of them from the cradle. Fred Hutton was there, and he wore starched shirts every day of the year. Judge Lowther and Mary were among the guests, and Mother Livingston. These were all people who received callers in their parlors, ate in dining-rooms, with carpeted floors, and used the kitchen only for cooking.

Mrs. Hollis came gasping downstairs, Amelia Ann wore a pale blue silk, and Mrs. Keene came to see the novel sight of a donation party.

Eli Hilton, who felt that the party owed its existence to him, came in, a little late, with his mother on his arm, wearing for the only time in her life a black silk dress, the first and, as she declared, the last that she ever would buy. "It cost a terrible sight" she whispered to mother Livingston. She saw the old lady's eyes on her, the minute she entered the room, and the crooked forefinger began to play across the old lady's lips. Mrs. Hilton was sure that it must seem a sinful waste, in the eyes of Mrs. Livingston, for a woman, at her time of life, to buy such a dress as that. So she made her way over to the sofa on which the old dame sat hunched up in the corner, and without more ado burst out with the confession on the one subject uppermost in her mind.

"Yes! it did cost a terrible sight; but you see, Eli, he knowed that, about twelve years ago come Christmas, I had made up my mind to have a real silk dress; and I had the samples in the house, I was trying them for spots with water, and for fadin' with a hot iron. You see I knowed it would need to be turned in time, and the seams would have to be pressed, and I wanted to be sure which kind would stand the iron.

"Well! the very night I had made up my mind which sample I'd buy from, our barn burned down. As soon as I saw the fire I said 'there goes my black silk.' Well I spose Eli has heard me tell that story forty times since then; and the last time I told it he says, 'I guess you better quit telling that tale, mother; and the only way I see to stop it, will be for you to get that dress.'

"Quick's a wink, I says its too late now, Eli—I'd look like an old fool in a black silk dress with hair as gray as mine is. He up and says 'I want the girls to know that the women folks o' my family can dress in silk if they choose to.' Well! you know, Mrs. Livingston I had set my heart on Eli's getting a good wife before I'm gone; then the dress will answer for me to wear at his weddin'; and I'm sure there's nothin' could be so suitable to lay me out in —I allus did fancy a corpse in black silk—It sets 'em off so; and they do look the perfect lady.—So, takin' it by and large, it didn't seem to me a useless waste," and then she paused for the old dame's reply.

The old dame passed her crooked finger to and fro, her eyes twinkled, and after a pause, she answered quietly, "I do think you've laid out use enough for that dress to make it worth while to buy it, if it didn't come higher than silk dresses usually do."

"What do you think o' the set o' it, Mrs. Livingston. It's city-made; I sent 'em my old alpaca tellin 'em I was a leetle fuller in figger than when that was made. That was all they had to go by, and I think they did wonderful. This is the fust time I've worn it out, and I feel a little strange to it. I've had it four weeks. I wear it Sunday mornings an hour, before church-time. I haven't had the face to wear it to church. Silk does rustle awful loud in a still church, and our pew, till last Sunday, was 'way front. I had thought of waitin' till the fust hymn was bein' sung, and, under cover o' that, gittin' into our pew; but then folks would ha' thought I had come late just to show off my dress. I don't see no other way than just to git used to it by wearin' it regular to home and then, some Sunday mornin', just walkin' off, careless like, to church tryin' to think to myself that I had forgot to change it till 'twas too late. I spose folks gits used to them, like they do to anything else; don't they Mrs. Livingston?"

"Yes," answered the old dame, with a gentle smile, "you'll get used to it Mrs. Hilton. I've known harder things than that to get used to."

As Mary Lowther came up to speak to Mrs. Livingston, Mrs. Hilton moved away, slowly, for the silk creaked when she moved fast; and she did not want it to become, too suddenly, the object of attention from the whole company.

She wanted to give Eli a word of warning; she felt that he would be reckless with his money, though no one else thought of him as a spendthrift. The supper would cost twenty-five cents, Eli would be sure to take two girls, to avoid suspicion; then there was his supper and her own, that would make one dollar; there was lemonade, which was extra, and there was no telling how much he would spend on this; there was a candy-stand besides.

She was too late. She found him at the candy-stand surrounded by a bevy of girls, and overheard him say, " Havin' a good time Miranda?"

"Oh! just splendid Eli!"

" Enjoying it are ye?"

"Oh! more'n enjoyin' it!"

" How'd ye like the lemonade?"

"Oh! it was splendid!"

" How's them gum-drops Sally Hill?"

"Oh! ain't they good! They're just awful nice."

"Which flavor did you take, rose or lemon?"

"Well I took rose 'cause they was so pretty in color, but I wish now I'd a' took lemon. They seem to last longer."

" Let me get you a paper of lemons and you can try first one then tother and see which you gets the most chaw out of."

At this sally there was a chorus of laughter. As Eli stepped out of the circle to buy the lemon drops, Mrs. Hilton laid her hand on his arm. " Ain't you goin' a little too far Eli? Remember them girls can chew gum-drops all night; and you ain't got no call to give 'em all they ask for."

"Well mother they enjoy it; and one dollar and fifty cents ain't nothin' to me, if I see a girl enjoyin' things."

With a sigh, she let him have his way, comforting

12

herself with the thought that this lavish expenditure might make the girls feel that Eli's wife would have pretty much anything in reason that she asked for.

Fred Hutton and Amelia Ann were standing watching the group. Eli stopped in passing, " Mealy I want you to come down and see a Lafayette Watch that I picked up for a mere song the last time I was in the city"; for Eli was a collector of antiques when they could be had at the price named for this one.

"Thank you Eli, your antiques always interest me; for they are generally as cheap as they are old, and I never feel that money has been thrown away on them," and Amelia smiled on Fred, who responded with a giggle.

" I know antiques always interest you Mealy; they are a sort of let up from Fred," and Eli had his turn to laugh.

"If you want to add some genuine antiques to your collection, Eli, you ought to look up your toys when you were a child," retorted Amelia, "They would grace the collection of any museum."

Eli laughed heartily, "So they would Mealy; but you ought not to try that joke on this generation of boys. Fred, it was thirty-six years, come Thanksgiving that she got off that joke on me, at Deacon Shelton's dinner. I felt sore about it then; but she's repeated it about every five years till the sting is out of it, and its only fun now." Miss Amelia flushed, drew her thin lips together tightly over her large prominent teeth, for a caustic answer; but Eli forestalled her, with a wicked twinkle in his eye and an elaborate bow as he said "Upon my word, Mealy;

you hold your own well, you don't look a year older than you did at that Thanksgiving dinner;" and he turned again to the gum-drop counter before Amelia could gasp out her reply.

Her eyes glowed, her cheek flushed with anger, Fred Hutton giggled.

"A nasty, sour, old bachelor is the meanest thing on earth" she said; then as she saw Fred's suppressed mirth; "except a giggling boy," she added. "Don't be a fool, Fred."

To which Fred's response was to burst out into open and irrepressible laughter.

Amelia turned away disgusted with men, and began to enlighten Mrs. Keene as to some of the people with comments which, if they had not the glitter, had at least the hardness of steel.

Judge Lowther joined them. "I have had an amusing afternoon on the bench" he said "It is not often that the stern duty of finding out and punishing the crimes of your fellow men are relieved by such a racy scene."

"Let us hear it Judge", said Mrs. Keene, turning towards him in an attitude of delighted attention.

"Pat Dunn a full-bearded, wild-eyed Irishman was before me on a charge of beating his wife with a shovel, with intent to kill her. He said that he had no money, and no counsel, and asked me to telegraph for the British Consul; 'For I belong to the kingdom of Great Britain,' he said with a strong accent on the Great. In the absence of Her Majesty's Consul I assigned him counsel, but he would have none of him, and preferred to defend himself. His wife burst into tears, when I told her to uncover her head and show the wounds. 'I don't want to show it; I don't want to do him harum,' 'The fine girl!' muttered Dunn, 'It's like her kind heart.' The next witness was John Bing the constable. 'Aren't you an informer of the corrupt police,' roared Dunn, in cross-examination. 'I am not' said Bing. 'Don't you know that I treated my wife right, and that in testifying against me, Sir, you are depriving a family of a good husband and father, that is supportin' them in fine style?' shouted Dunn. 'I do not' replied Bing. 'When you had me under arrest on another false charge didn't you try to beat a confession out o' me with your blackthorn?' 'I did not' replied Bing. 'Yes you did' roared Dunn, 'and you told me that you'd like to mash my fine nose as flat as your own mug.'

" Two more witnesses closed the case, and I asked Dunn how long he wanted to sum up. He said he would need two hours, and I gave him twenty minutes. He used up most of his time in denouncing the charge as a conspiracy against Her Majesty's subject. In one part of his harangue he said 'Man is fallen, gentlemen of the jury, and every man is at some time a brute. Man is frail and is prone to beat his wife. You should all sympathize with me, gentlemen, and join me in putting down this conspiracy. My wife fell down stairs, poor soul, and hurted herself severely, and you should spare her the suffering of seeing me disgraced, who never laid a hand to her.' The jury promptly convicted him. I asked his lawyer if had any objection to sentence being passed, he said he had not. Then I asked Dunn—

"'I have' he said, 'I demand a new trial. I do not consent to abide by this one. Give me a new trial, Judge, or I swear that I renounce allegiance to the United States, and will go back to the Crown of Great Britain.'

"All this in a fine rich brogue, which I cannot reproduce," and the Judge laughed heartily, as he recalled the scene.

"And what will be the punishment of such a brute?" asked Mrs. Keene.

"I haven't sentenced him" answered the Judge. "He may get three or five years at hard labor in the State's prison. But his wife begs hard for a light sentence."

"That is the old story; the patient, forbearing, long-suffering woman pleading for the man that has broken every vow he made to her," said Mrs. Keene.

"Yes, Yes," said the Judge, uneasily, "I agree with you Mrs. Keene."

"Only a woman can know what it is to have her natural protector turn into her foe. But this woman has some one to do her justice. It must be a grand thing to sit as a judge righting the wrongs of the weak and oppressed," and Mrs. Keene looked up into the Judge's face.

"Well, sometimes, I don't know about it always. Your judgment is sometimes reversed on appeal", said the judge, as he moved to speak to Mrs. Livingston, who had been watching him as he talked to Mrs. Keene.

It was a merry scene as the evening wore on. The three long tables in the dining-room of the Inn were filled with a jovial party; the hot supper, the lemonade and the gum-drops contributed to make their joy more unconfined.   They were not under the restraint of conventional rules, and none were afraid to give voice and laugh free swing, amid the merry din that filled the room.

Mr. Forrester moved about like a genial old spirit, stirring up mirth wherever he went, leaving many a blushing girl in his wake; for if his jokes had been effective, the whole party of young people would have been mated without more ado.

He expected one or more wedding-fees as the result of one of his donation parties; and he was not always disappointed.

He was a matrimonial promoter, little reason as he had for regarding it as a blessed estate.   In these ventures he got the fee and there his responsibility ended.

For the older people he had a pleasant word or jest, a story about the time when they too were young, and always a word of apology or defence for the boisterous merriment of the young people; so that every one united in pronouncing one of Mr. Forrester's donation parties, "a jolly lark."

CHAPTER XV

A BOUT ten days after Mr. Forrester's donation party, when life at Clintonville had settled down to its wonted routine, Dinsmore stood on the balcony waiting for the arrival of the stage. On his right was Mrs. Keene, with a fur wrap thrown over her shoulders, to his left Mrs. Hollis stood with a black cashmere shawl over her head and held tightly under her chin, which threw into bold relief her gaunt, pale face.

The October sunset glowed amber toward the West, streaked near the horizon with a deep orange red, and fading off toward the South into violet and gray, against which the " Barrens " were outlined in deep, misty purple.

The old coach loomed like a ship at sea, as it came lumbering over the crest of the hill, the passengers on top silhouetted against the violet gray sky.

As it drew nearer to the Inn some familiar look in the pose of one of these figures on the top made Dinsmore scrutinize it more closely, and as the stage drew up before the door, all doubt was dispelled, when there rang out, in clear, strong tones, like the herald at the head of an advancing army, " Hello! old Harry! *Pax vobiscum*, your Reverence."

It was Tom Whitlock, an old law chum of Dinsmore's in Judge Channing's office. He was a loyal son of Stentor, and his greeting was so loud and hearty that the village street seemed invaded by an army corps.

It rather disconcerted Dinsmore, but he hurried down to greet his old friend, and help him unload his traps his dog and gun and array of hunting gear; for Tom had come to try the partridge shooting and, armed with all the necessary outfit and a letter to Judge Lowther from Judge Channing, felt confident that he was secure of good sport, under ample protection. His foot was hardly on the ground before he opened on Dinsmore a battery of questions.

"I say, your Reverence, are there any birds in your parish? Do the farmers object to a man's hunting through their fields? Will a letter to Judge Lowther let me in for some sport? Who was that trim filly beside you on the balcony, not your wife, eh? Did she hire that old witch to stand on your other side, as a foil? Is there much game of that kind here, for an evening's sport or a rainy day's hunt? How go the girls of this rural parish?"

Tom could not modulate his voice to a prudent tone, even when he tried to do it, and Dinsmore's chief concern was to get him under cover.

"Get your traps together and come to your room, and I will tell you all I know," he said, as he picked up the gun-case and led the way.

The door was scarcely shut before Tom began again "Who is the trim filly? Not yet your wife?"

"Her name is Keene, she is a widow with one little boy," said Dinsmore.

"A widow!—Why man alive she is not a day over twenty, trig as a girl; and such a pose!" rattled on Tom.

"But widows were too much for Weller, and she has all the elements to make her as fatal as the worst of 'em. Look out, Harry, my boy, she is not to be trifled with, she knows the whole game, having played it to a check-mate; you only know the opening."

"I ought to revise my first statement; she is not exactly a widow; she has recently been divorced from her husband; who must have been a perfect brute."

"Oh! ho! worse and worse, a widow may have been softened by affliction; but a *divorcée* has simply played the game out to the end, with a cool head and a firm hand. Moreover, she has none of that sentimental regard for her previous partner which surrounds him with an impossible aureole of noble attributes; he is simply a blunder which she has committed and which she proposes to rectify in her next selection; or he is an impersonality merged into the sex male, and she will get even with the said sex male by taking to herself another, and making him live the life of a dog. My guileless friend, Heaven forefend you from the pitfalls with which your path is strewn."

"Nonsense, Tom! how you let your tongue run away with your brains. One would think I had announced to you my desperate infatuation with Mrs. Keene" interrupted Harry.

"Not infatuation, not so far or so bad as that; but I confess that I was startled by that expression

'brute of a husband.' Those little straws do suggest the quarter from which the wind blows, to a
man of the world."

"All right, Tom, when my common sense gives
out, I will draw on you at sight, for a check of
worldly wisdom."

"Then it will be too late. I want to keep the
balance in your favor," laughed Tom.

"But enough of this, *Verbum sat.* Have you any
flowers not bred in a conservatory, native to the
soil, wild, sweet, fragrant, blushing, unwooed. I
have a letter to Judge Lowther, has he any family?"

"Yes, one daughter."

"Her age?"

"I'm sure I don't know. I never asked her."

"At a guess, should you say twenty or forty," persisted Tom.

"Well, certainly nearer twenty than forty."

"Give me her points, size, color of hair, and eyes,
complexion, previous condition of servitude?"

"I'm sure I don't know what you mean by that
last."

"I mean, engaged or not, affections enlisted or
fancy free?"

"It is not part of my duty as a pastor to inquire
into these matters," answered Dinsmore.

"Well unless the black cloth has wrought a mighty
change on your mental composition, I don't believe
you knew the girl two weeks before you had your
opinion pretty well formed on this point."

"Let's go down to supper", answered Dinsmore.

"Let's hear what is Miss Lowther like," retorted

Whitlock. "You were fly enough with your information as to Mrs. Keene. Is Miss Lowther such a cipher that she is indescribable. What's the matter with her? Is she hump-backed, or an imbecile? Out with it."

"What nonsense, Tom, come to supper; after supper I have to go to Judge Lowther's and you can come along and present your letter, and see Miss Lowther for yourself."

"All right. But this mystery I will fathom, this riddle I will solve, if I have to give up my whole vacation to it."

At supper Whitlock's curiosity as to Mrs. Keene was set at rest by an introduction and a seat beside her, with Dinsmore at the head of the table, and Mrs. Hollis and Amelia Ann on the opposite side.

"So you are fresh from the great, gay city, Mr. Whitlock, and can tell us plain country-folk something of what is going on in the world;" and Mrs. Keene smiled as she saw Miss Amelia bridle at this.

"No, Mrs. Keene, I cannot lay claim to be in touch with anything in New York, but a lawyer's office," answered Whitlock.

"You must be a paragon of diligence, if day and night you hang over those musty law-books. Even a stroll along a city street, the men and women that one meets on a single block, are an education to us who are stagnating on these hill-tops. Thus much of society you must allow yourself even in going to and from your office."

"I remember the *bon mot* about knowing a woman

being equivalent to a liberal education; but passing them on the street, is hardly enough to educate one. It is merely tantalizing to pass a face, in which there seems great possibilities, that you will never be able to realize.   Don't you think so?"

"Yes, that may be one view to take of it, another might be the determination to find that face again and test its possibilities.   But if the crowd tantalizes you, perhaps you are come among us to take up some of these human possibilities seriatim try them one by one, as you find them scattered on the waysides?   If that is your mission, I will go about warning the young rustic maidens.   I am the guardian of these simple-hearted damsels.   I have warned another young man that he is not at liberty to break hearts without interference from me," and she gave Dinsmore a knowing smile.

Tom Whitlock laughed heartily, Dinsmore frowned slightly, and added, "Mr. Whitlock is here to spend a short vacation in his favorite pastime, partridge hunting."

"Against that I have nothing to say, especially if he brings the partridges to the Inn.   Did it ever strike you how strong the predatory instinct is in men.   They are always hunting something, pursuing, chasing, bringing down innocent creatures.   They call them 'game' and seem to think that gives them a right to hurt and kill or capture.   Women are not so."

"It is a survival of the primal instincts of man, when hunting was his only or chief means of subsistence," answered Dinsmore.

"It seems to me" broke in Whitlock "that there is merely a difference of method. Men hunt, and women net their game."

"Women are put on the defensive by men, and must have recourse to the only methods that are within their reach, finesse and tact," answered Mrs. Keene, warmly.

Whitlock burst out laughing; Mrs. Keene replied to the laugh with a touch of asperity in her tone, "Men do not care to hunt game that is too easily caught. What is that couplet about

> "' The toy so fiercely sought
> Hath lost its charm by being caught ; '

and it is true."

"Oh! yes, no question of it," replied Whitlock, still laughing. "But my remark was intended to apply not to the hunted ones, who, chased by a too eager pursuer, throw here and there a lure or pitfall in his way to make him halt, and turn, and so give them a breathing spell. I think, to an onlooker, such a game as that, well played, is very pretty sport; and I am always with the hare rather than the hound. But, unless my eyes have misled me, I have seen the game reversed, and the net laid with great care, caution and skill directly across the path where the supposed hunter was wont to stroll without any thought of hunting. If I am wrong, you can correct me Mrs. Keene. And so it seemed to me that the sport went on from both sides; but with different kinds of weapons."

"You need hardly appeal to me for correction, Mr.

Whitlock, you seem able to draw your own conclusions," answered Mrs. Keene.

"We all draw our conclusions," laughed Whitlock, "even if they are only snap shots. But I would like to have, from some woman competent to tell the truth on the subject, an answer to these two questions. Are there not more women flirts than men flirts? Are not women greater adepts at the art, especially in that most subtle phase of it viz: making the man believe that he is the only one? Can't you give me an answer Mrs. Keene?"

"Thank you, Mr. Whitlock; I must disclaim being 'competent to tell the truth on that subject,' as you are pleased to put it. It is one of those endless controversies, for which no answer will ever be found that will satisfy a majority of either sex."

"It is a horrid man's notion that women are always flirting with them," broke in Miss Amelia. "I can tell them, it isn't so half the times they think that it is."

"Thank you, Miss Hollis" said Tom, with the utmost gravity, and a deferential bow. "That is certainly an honest opinion on an important phase of the question, and I shall note it down for future use."

Dinsmore felt uneasy and made a move to go, while Tom was inclined to sit still and push the conversation to extremes. "If we are going to Judge Lowther's, we had better be moving," said Dinsmore.

"Why so? The Judge doesn't retire at early candle light, does he?" answered Tom.

"If you are going to Judge Lowther's you will find a chance to put your question to a simple girl bred in this country town, far from the wiles that are practised in society. She is a dear, sweet, good girl, and is under my special care and protection. If she had had advantages, she would have been a match for any of you, and could have held her own without any help from me."

"She is entirely safe, Mrs. Keene, if you have thrown your ægis over her" said Whitlock, in a tone that made Miss Amelia titter with delight. "I have tried to get a description of her from my friend Dinsmore; but I take it that he does not know Miss Lowther very well, from the meagre scraps that were all I could gather."

Mrs. Keene turned on Dinsmore, with an arch smile, and lifting her eyebrows, answered Whitlock, "Fairly well, I should say."

At this Dinsmore rose, determined to leave Tom alone rather than let him run on, who could tell whither.

Tom followed him. "She's a hollow one", he said, as they reached Dinsmore's room.

"You seemed to strike an unfortunate vein, with her," Dinsmore answered; "she didn't show her best side."

"She led the conversation; and I naturally let her keep the lead. I don't like her. We will fight whenever and wherever we meet; and she will lead off."

"Nonsense! she is not of the fighting kind; she is full of tact, and persuasive rather than combative," replied Dinsmore.

"She may persuade you; but she will make war on me: mark my words."

"Tom, Tom, you are, as you used to be, determined that men and things shall be as you think that they are. I tell you that you have seen only one side of Mrs. Keene's character."

"Which you think is the hard side; and I will return you the favor by telling you that she is letting you feel that her touch is as soft as velvet. Harry, don't let that woman net you."

"You are wise beyond the demands of the occasion, Tom. Mrs. Keene spreads no net for me; we are simply friends by virtue of her unfortunate position and my ministerial office."

"Parson Harry, beware ' weave a circle round her thrice, for she on honey-dew hath fed, and drunk the milk of Paradise.' She has been in it; she is out of it; she will be in it again; or my name is not ' Tom the witless,' as you used to call me."

"As no amount of discussion will settle this matter, but only leave each of us more firmly convinced that he is right, suppose we go up to Judge Lowthers," answered Dinsmore.

"I'm with you there," said Whitlock; "for I want to see whether you do or do not know that young woman, and also whether she is worth knowing."

"All right" said Dinsmore, "draw your own conclusions and then you are sure to be satisfied, whether they are right or wrong."

On their way up to the Judge's Dinsmore had to answer a running fire of questions from Tom on nearly every house that they passed. He was full of animal life and off on a vacation, and he seemed to think that this out-of-the-way village was teeming with romantic possibilities. Dinsmore laughed and humored his whim.

"That is Conan Hill's house, an old, unsuccessful man who has retired from everything because, at everything he tried, he lost money. He has two daughters, Sallie, the village belle and wit, Mary who married a young lawyer with brilliant prospects, who gave her a chance, for two years, to see the life of the city, and then died from drink, leaving her a widow, without means, to return to her father's house and remember her short-lived experience of the outside world."

"I want to know Sallie. I don't care for Mary; those two years have probably spoiled her," was Tom's comment.

The next house was Mother Livingston's. Dinsmore's description of her interested Whitlock. "You must take me down to see that old lady", he said.

"This next house is Newman Digg's. He is the criminal lawyer of this district. Uneducated except by his own efforts, a fine mathematician, a first-rate chess-player, an inveterate gourmand. In his cellar you will find at almost any time a dozen terrapin fattening for his table. He is a skilful engineer and when he goes to New York almost always drives the engine. I attended last summer a remarkable murder trial, where he was counsel for the defendant. The trial turned on evidence of motive for the murder. There was a note which the prosecution put in evidence showing that the accused owed the murdered man a sum which he could not pay.

13

"Just before recess Diggs asked permission to examine this note, preparatory to his cross-examination in the afternoon. He had a photographer in an adjoining room, had a photograph of the note made, had an expert penman on hand and some old paper of the same kind as the note. During the recess his penman made six facsimiles of the note, with a corner torn off exactly like the original. When the court reassembled after recess Diggs took up the cross-examination of the witness; asked him as to the note, whether he was sure that he had seen it and could identify it, handed him one of the fac-similes, asked him if that was the note, and, after he had carefully identified it, handed him out the remaining six, with the true note among them, and asked him triumphantly, whether he recognized them all."

"Well you have a truly skilful bar, with methods unapproached even by our city counsel. But what said the Judge to this most skilful style of practice?"

"He said 'Mr. Diggs, this is the most extraordinary conduct of a case that has ever fallen under my notice. Your connection with this case is terminated.'

"Diggs picked up his papers, smiling broadly, bowed to the Judge, left the court-room, sent a young lawyer in to take his place and directed the case outside of court. He had another case the consequences of which he could not dodge so easily. He defended and secured the acquittal of two noted counterfeiters, and they paid him his fee in counterfeit money. How he did denounce those fellows and consign them to the penitentiary from which he had freed them."

The next tale of village life was called forth when they passed Bill Bennett's house.

"I tell you what, Harry, you showed grit, if you are a parson," was Whitlock's comment on the story of Dinsmore's encounter with the smith.

"Thanks Tom; but I am not willing to accept a personal compliment at the expense of my profession. There is nothing in a minister's life to make a man a coward, or there ought not to be."

"All the same, we don't expect ministers to show as much physical courage as other men, and I think you showed a lot when you faced that angry maniac."

"I don't," answered Dinsmore, "it was mere reliance on the law that mind would triumph over matter, intelligence over brute force. I had every advantage on my side, as the result showed. And I'll bet you that the chaplains of our army showed as much physical courage as the surgeons, in caring for the wounded on the field of battle."

"I don't bet with parsons," replied Whitlock; "the odds are in their favor."

By this time the latch of Judge Lowther's gate saved Dinsmore the necessity of a retort.

CHAPTER XVI.

A S they walked up the gravel path Whitlock insisted upon Dinsmore's giving him the cue to his behavior.

"Shall I talk law to the Judge and love to the girl, or *vice versa*," he said.

"You must use your own judgment and knowledge of the world," retorted Dinsmore. "But do please remember that I am the pastor of these people, and hoe your own row and not drag me in. I don't think you quite appreciate the situation, Tom. We are not chums in a law school, out for a lark together."

"Oh! yes, your Reverence, I see the point and will make it plain hereafter that I am an uncircumcised heathen and you are a priest of the temple," laughed Whitlock, slapping Dinsmore on the back with a blow that almost staggered him. "I suppose the Judge is a sinner and Miss Lowther a saint. I flatter myself that I can adapt myself to both; with the Judge I am Channing's pupil, with Miss Lowther I am a disciple of her revered pastor. I think I see my way clear. I find myself in a new role, the pastor's friend; but I think I can fill it."

Dinsmore did not doubt that Tom could fill it, but thus far his method had tended to bring such a new element into his pastoral life that it was rather disconcerting. But Tom was too good and true a fellow to do intentional mischief, and he could say and do, without offence, what would make for most other men a host of enemies. He was thoroughly good at heart, and could laugh himself out of a predicament.

They were ushered into Judge Lowther's study, and found the Judge in an easy chair, before a blazing wood fire with his slippered feet on the fender, and a newspaper in his lap; he was listening to Mary playing on the piano in the next room.

As they came into the room, he held up his finger to silence Dinsmore's introduction of Whitlock. "Listen to that," he said. "Doesn't she play that reel with spirit. Upon my word, I feel as if I could dance to her touch."

Dinsmore introduced Tom, who presented his letter of introduction.

The Judge read it through, before taking any notice of either of them; slowly and carefully he conned every word, through his gold-rimmed spectacles, as though it were an important piece of evidence on which he was to render a decision. Then, with a wave of his hand, "Sit down, sit down; and how is Channing? Busy as ever, I suppose; and with a parcel of young fellows about him, whom he is hatching into lawyers. That was always his way. Ah! well, he and I were young, once. Is he as gray as I am?"

"He has plenty of white hair on his head; but we never think of him as an old man," said Tom. "He can work us all tired, and he is full of fun over our work and has plenty of good stories with which he illustrates his teaching of the law."

"Yes! that's Channing. He always had a story for everything.

"Mary," he called, "come here and let me introduce you to one of Channing's boys." And thus, without ceremony, was Tom Whitlock brought face to face with this mysterious Mary Lowther.

She came smiling into the room, amused at her father's abrupt summons, her face slightly flushed, and Tom Whitlock was more than ever at a loss to account for Dinsmore's reticence.

He laughed as Mary shook hands cordially with him, and she answered him with a merry laugh. They were friends before they had spoken.

"Mary, take Mr. Whitlock into the parlor and play him some music. I want to talk to Mr. Dinsmore about the enlargement of the church building. You young folks won't be interested in that."

"I won't let you say that, Father, I am as much interested in it and expect to work for it, in my way, as hard as you do in your way," retorted Mary.

"I know that, my lassie" answered the Judge. "We know that; and as soon as we know what we want to do and what it will cost and how the money is to be raised, we will call you into our counsels, and you will do good service; but Mr. Whitlock won't care to join in our council of war, and now we are going to discuss only the general plan which will not specially interest you, and so the Court decides that you shall play, and we will plan out work."

And so, without further parley, the company was divided, Whitlock and Mary in the parlor, Dinsmore and the Judge in the study; which arrangement suited Whitlock admirably.

The Judge figured and planned and sketched and made estimates for the extension of the church at the rear end; calculated the number of pews, the rental, what they could raise by subscription, and what they could borrow.

Since Dinsmore had come to the parish the demand for pews had increased, so that now they had a list of twenty names ready to take pews and not an unrented pew in the church.

Through their discussion ran the strains of one and another song that Mary played or sang.

Then the music ceased and the murmur of the voices in the other room, with here and there a word or two in a louder tone, would catch Dinsmore's ear and distract him from the matter in hand so that he answered one or two of the Judge's questions so much at random, that the old gentleman took him up with "What? What? What's that you say, Mr. Dinsmore?" and he was more at a loss from the fact that he did not know exactly what he had said? "I guess you were going over those figures in your mind and did not catch my remark," and the Judge reiterated it so plainly that Dinsmore was able to make intelligent reply.

Whitlock was getting along famously with Mary, and their frequent choruses of laughter were quite as disconcerting to Dinsmore as the fragments of their talk that floated through the door.

When the Judge had settled to his satisfaction the general plan for the enlargement of the church building and completed his list of possible subscribers, he proposed an adjournment to the parlor for a song from Mary.

"We always wind up the evening, before I settle down to my night work, with a Scotch song," he added, as they passed into the parlor.

"Come, Mary," he broke in on the *tête-à-tête* chat, "Give us ' Within a Mile of Edinboro Town,'" and added, turning to Whitlock, "my lassie has a right to sing the Scotch songs, for her mother was a McKenzie from Inverness."

"She certainly maintains her birthright to sing them," said Whitlock when the song was ended; and the Judge concluded, on the spot, that Whitlock was a sensible young fellow, and with a hearty handshake bade him make himself at home with them during his stay in Clintonville. "Drop in to supper with us when you feel like it."

"Then you will take me out to-morrow and introduce me to Farmer Brown, Miss Mary," said Whitlock, as they turned to leave the room.

"That's a good move," said the Judge. "Brown has a fine farm with some good covers, and, if you have his good-will, you can hunt anywhere you please about Pleasant Pond."

Whitlock had certainly done famously on so short an acquaintance, securing Mary as a guide to his hunting ground, and the freedom of the house from the Judge.

Dinsmore felt as though he were somehow left on

one side, like a foot-traveller stepping aside to let a merry party drive by.

As they walked back to the Inn Whitlock was full of enthusiasm on the subject of Mary Lowther.

"I tell you what, old fellow, you have let a jewel slip through your fingers, while you were conning the sliddery graces of Madame the forlorn and forsaken."

"You are off on that tack again, Tom. How often must I tell you that there is no other bond, present or prospective, between me and Mrs. Keene, than the pity which I feel, for a woman in her position and the help and counsel that I can give her about her boy."

"Yes I know; and how often must I warn you that pity is akin to love, and that your fatherly interest in that handsome boy may ripen into assuming the position permanently."

Dinsmore laughed, "Have it your own way."

"It is not my way at all. But no matter what becomes of the 'willing widder,' you have shown amazing obtusity, not to know that girl better. She's a mighty sweet girl, sensible, cultivated, no nonsense about her, and as jolly as she is pretty. Harry your cloth must have dulled your taste in women. You have chosen dross and let the gold slip through your fingers."

"Go on; don't mind me," said Dinsmore.

"That is exactly what I propose to do. You give me a free run. I propose to take it. To-morrow Miss Lowther drives me over to Farmer Brown's and gives me her blessing on my sport. One day shall intervene and, day after to-morrow, I will take the

Judge at his word and go there to supper. And after that the Gods shall guide me. But my next vacation will be spent in this region; and opportunity will not be lost on me. What are the Judge's means?"

"I know nothing about that" said Dinsmore. "He subscribes liberally to all charitable enterprises, but whether from his salary as a Judge or from an independent income, I don't know."

"That's a good sign" said Whitlock. "But after all a girl like that is a fortune to a man, if she brings not one cent of dowry. The Judge is awfully fond of her; would not be able to live without her; would accept any man as son-in-law that pleases his 'lassie;' would take him in and give him a chance at law practice. There's a future for a rising young lawyer. Harry you may count on us as your parishioners and staunch supporters. How immensely superior such a girl is to a city-bred, fashionable girl to whom life is no more than a show, more or less hollow. There's something so genuine about such a girl, fresh air, nature, reality, all that sort of thing. You feel it in every word and look, though you can't define it and say just where it lies."

"You have certainly made rapid strides in discovery on a short acquaintance, Tom," answered Dinsmore. "And you lay out a programme for Miss Lowther's future as if she had commissioned you to do it, merely requiring of you that you please yourself."

"All right, old fellow. You have been more than obtuse, absorbed no doubt in pastoral cares, not to see what a jewel that girl is. I have made a good start with the Judge; and I'm going to have a good

time with the 'lassie'—and I will not worry myself as to the outcome of it. Wish me joy and
success."

"That seems hardly necessary" answered Dinsmore. "You seem to enjoy it and feel sure of your
success."

"Then all I will ask of you is not to meddle,"
said Whitlock, with a laugh, as they bid one another
good-night.

Dinsmore went to his room with a sense of discomfort, as though something had gone wrong, and yet
he could not fix upon anything that should be a dis-
turbing element in his thoughts.

Whitlock was too outspoken and reckless in his
talk; but that did not compromise him; he was not
responsible for what he said or did.

The plans which Judge Lowther proposed were
reasonable and likely to succeed. It was surely an
omen of success that, after six months work, the
church needed to be enlarged, and that so prominent
a man as the Judge took so lively an interest in the
work.

But it would have added to the interest with which
they worked out the plans if Mary had been in at the
conference. She was ready with practical suggestions, always; and Dinsmore felt as if he must talk
it over with her before they concluded on what was
to be done and how they should do it.

It seemed, too, as if she would, in some way, injure
her influence as his helper in Sunday School work at
Scooper's Hollow if she took Whitlock out to Farmer
Brown's on a shooting excursion. There was some-

thing unsuitable in it, just what he could not say;
but the two missions seemed incongruous.

What an odd stick Tom was. How he blundered
along in life; and yet he seemed to make his way,
and people took him for what he was, a real good-
hearted, clever fellow.

Dinsmore liked him well, but did not see why other
people liked him so well.

He was altogether in a contrary frame of mind,
liking and disapproving, satisfied and unsatisfied,
feeling as if something had thoroughly unsettled him.

And what was it that unsettled him? The affairs
of his Hillside Parish were in a prosperous state.
His ministry was acceptable; the church was to be
enlarged; his ambition to awaken these people was
already being realized.

He told himself this comforting story; and ad-
mitted that it was true, but it did not assure him
that all was well.

CHAPTER XVII.

THE next morning, right after breakfast, Mary Lowther drove up to the hotel in her basket phaeton with the pair of Morgan horses. How well she handled the reins, how fresh and rosy the frosty air made her cheeks, and how bright the morning light shone in her eyes.

Whitlock was ready with gun and game-bag, "Brown Bess," his cocker spaniel jumped into the wagon and curled herself up at Mary's feet and seemed to smile at Mary, as she leaned over and stroked the silky head.

Mrs. Keene and Dinsmore stood on the balcony, and wished them good luck, to which Tom roared his thanks.

"They make a very pretty pair," she said turning to Dinsmore as they drove away. "*Quien Sabe?* It may be that your friend will bring down some unexpected game. It is all in the professional line, and the Judge would no doubt approve of a match which brought both him and Mary a partner;" she watched Dinsmore as she waited for his reply.

"Yes" he said absently, and with a slight rising inflection, that left one in doubt whether he intended to assent to, or question her statement.

"Your friends impetuous, headlong ways would

suit an unconventional girl like Mary very well. She has good sense enough to curb his excess of animal spirits, and yet has not been reared in surroundings that would make her take offence at his boisterous ways. He seems to be a well-meaning young fellow," she added, after a moments pause, which had not elicited any reply from Dinsmore.

"He is a noble, true-hearted, manly fellow. I wish there were more like him," said Dinsmore, decidedly.

"Then he would be a valuable addition to your parish," replied Mrs. Keene, in an almost derisive tone. "We will do our utmost to further this little romance."

Dinsmore made no answer, but stood absently looking at the line of distant hills radiant with autumn glory.

"How the leaves flutter down, with every breeze" said Mrs. Keene, as if in a reverie. "And every falling leaf reminds me that the time is drawing near when I must go back into the world. Go back alone with my boy, to face I know not what; to face it alone; to battle against prejudice and suspicion and evil tongues that will misrepresent everything I do or say. When I am gone may I write to you for counsel, Mr. Dinsmore; or will the affairs of your 'Hill-Side Parish' so fill your mind that there will be no place left for any one outside the bounds of it. You are a man, strong, self-reliant, sure of your place and power in the world, and I suppose cannot know how a woman would dread what I shall have to face.

"You have my hearty sympathy, Mrs. Keene; and if I can aid you in any way I want you to feel always that you can call upon me, and I shall be only too glad to do what I can," answered Dinsmore.

He turned to go to his study, Mrs. Keene walked to the far end of the balcony and stood there tapping her foot impatiently. The young minister did not seem to be in a responsive mood; his answer was cold and formal, lacking spontaneity, deliberate as though it were forced from him.

This boisterous young law-student was held responsible by her for Dinsmore's lack of heartiness. He was an upsetting element in the quiet life of their little circle; he had a tongue that could not be trusted, and his laugh was positively offensive. She doubted her ability to set him down; for what answer could one make to an inane and boisterous laugh.

In the evening Tom came home from his hunting, in fine spirits, and with his face all aglow from his walk through the evening air from Pleasant Pond.

He had had a fine day's sport and was in the best of spirits. He had killed five plump partridges, had not missed a single shot, and "Brown Bess" had behaved as only a well-bred dog knows how to do and delight his master's heart.

The ride out there—well nothing need be said on that subject, for Dinsmore knew what his opinion of Mary Lowther was, and nothing occurred to make him change it one whit.

"But, Harry, my boy, you have a fine parish. My gracious! I don't believe many parsons have such hunting and fishing. You're in luck."

"I never thought of it in that light before Tom, as one of my ministerial privileges; thank you for a new point of view."

"Then you have a lot of nice people about you. That Farmer Brown is a fine old fellow. He asked me to dinner and I tell you it was a royal good dinner. Such a turkey and such bread and butter a man don't get except on the soil where they were raised; and after dinner we had a good smoke, while the Farmer showed me his cattle. And that girl of his is a dandy. She put on a jockey cap and started over the field to show me a cover where there was a covey of quail, and the way she went over that rough ground pretty near winded me. She's a nice girl, with lots of good sense and full of fun. I laughed once at one of her stories until I fell off the fence. She took me over in the afternoon to see that picturesque old witch Barbara. Upon my word you're in luck with a mighty interesting parish. I thought you were buried in a hole, but there are people here; no doubt about it."

"You have made a general exploration and have all the delight of one who is on a voyage of discovery, Tom; but it is not altogether news to me," answered Dinsmore, smiling at his friend's enthusiasm.

"No! I suppose not, but it was new to me. They're quite stuck on you, Harry. Mrs. Brown regards you as a thorough gentleman, and Miss Fanny is one of your devoted followers. Mrs. Brown said that to see you come forward as you did at her 'Sociable' made her feel like a mother to you."

"And what did you say to this undeserved praise of your humble servant?" asked Dinsmore.

"Well to tell you the truth Harry, I burst out laughing and looked at Miss Fanny. She blushed, and I laughed louder; then Farmer Brown chimed in with a hearty laugh, and then we all laughed together."

"The usual conclusion that you reach, one way or another," answered Dinsmore.

"Take me down to Mrs. Livingston's to-night; will you?" asked Whitlock.

"I don't know whether I will or not," answered Dinsmore. "You're an uncertain quantity, Tom. But I suppose if I don't take you, that you will go there yourself; and perhaps I had better go and keep you in hand."

"You had better go, Harry; or I will ask Miss Lowther to take me there, and we might make mischief for you. I feel safe under your wing. I tell you what, I think it's awfully jolly, this role of the pastor's friend; it lets me in for lots of sport on the very best footing, both with the men and the maidens."

Dinsmore laughed. Tom's views of the perquisites of a pastor's life were certainly original.

At supper three of the partridges were served, a brace of them had been despatched to Judge Lowther, with Tom's compliments.

"Your escort was a *mascot* Mr. Whitlock," said Mrs. Keene, when she saw the fruit of Tom's day of sport.

"Or the good luck that you wished me, Mrs. Keene," replied Tom.

14

"Oh, no Mr. Whitlock, spells and charms of every kind are in the hands of the unwed maidens. They are always called on to christen ships and bring good luck of every kind. In the eyes of men we women lose all the power to charm when we have once been under the ban of matrimony."

"That is not because you have lost the power, but because you have devoted it to one interest; so that your spells are all reserved for advancing his prosperity. It is a kind of close partnership that excludes every one else."

"Is it so with men, or is this theory of absorption only applicable to women?" said Mrs. Keene.

"I am in no position to answer, Mrs. Keene; as I am not of the guild," answered Tom.

"A candidate for orders, a neophyte, perhaps. Are you ready for the vigils prescribed for knighthood?"

"That depends on who is to bestow the accolade?" answered Whitlock.

"We have already settled that," answered Mrs. Keene, turning to Dinsmore.

Dinsmore's reply was a laugh, not merry, almost constrained.

After supper Whitlock and Dinsmore strolled down to Mrs. Livingston's. The old dame met them cordially and Tom made himself thoroughly at home.

"Are you come to make quite a stay with us, Mr. Whitlock," said Mrs. Livingston, as she brought in a pitcher of cider and set it down beside a plate of Belle Flower apples, and a dish of roast chestnuts;

"if so we want you to be sociable and come to supper when you can."

"I haven't a long vacation, Mrs. Livingston; not more than ten days or two weeks; but I am coming here again for my Spring vacation. I think my friend Harry has a fine parish, lots of good hunting, good fishing, and kind people. I don't see what a man could ask more."

The old dame laughed. "That wa'nt included in the call, I guess. We calculate to give our pastor a donation party and make him and his friends feel at home among us; but we never did include the huntin' and fishin' as part of the salary of this church."

"I suppose not, Mrs. Livingston; but Deacon Hilton has a trout-pond where his father used to fish until he was paralyzed; and now no one casts a line over it but the parson. Now that shows a true regard for the pastor's good."

"Well fishin' seems more scriptural for a minister than shootin' does. The Apostles were fishermen; and I never mind seein' a minister at it, now. But a gun was always a fearful thing to me; and it don't seem the sort o' thing for a minister to be handlin'."

"I don't object to your views, Mrs. Livingston, for that leaves the whole field to me. I hope you won't read me out of your books because I persist in my gunning."

"Oh! no, I've nothing to say against your gunnin' all you want; but I'd hate to see it in the papers that the pastor o' Clintonville church was brought home dead, havin' shot himself while out gunnin' for birds."

Tom laughed "The item would not seem so bad if my name was in it," he said.

"Not ne'er so bad, except to your mother. If you'd a been my boy, I would ha' kept a gun out o' your hands altogether."

"Well I'll promise not to take your pastor out gunning or lead him into any mischief, while I am here. I had very good guides to the field. Miss Lowther drove me out to Farmer Brown's, and Miss Fannie Brown took me over the fields of her father's farm."

"I hope you'll be careful handlin' your gun and not shoot either of those girls" said the old dame, earnestly; "for there aren't two nicer girls in the country."

"You may rest easy on that score Mrs. Livingston; for my gun is never loaded going to or from the field. There is only one thing needed to make this an ideal place for a fortnight's sport, and that is for my friend Mr. Dinsmore to have a snug fireside of his own where he can welcome his friends" and Tom laughed, as he saw the twinkle in the old lady's eye.

"I've told him as much myself," she said, "but that's one of those things in which advice is thrown away, until there's no need of advice. It would add to his usefulness."

"He would be much more useful to me" said Tom. "What do you say to it, Harry", he added, turning to Dinsmore.

"What I may have to say is but half the question. The answer that I am to get, the person that is to give the answer; these are the important points", answered Dinsmore.

"He will come to his senses, Mrs. Livingston" said Tom. "I have known him long enough to be sure that he was not cut out for the life of a hermit. He is sound on the doctrine that it is not good for man to be alone."

"I'm sure the day for hermits is past" said Mrs. Livingston. "If there ever was any use in them, they're not fit for these times. I hope the Lord will guide Mr. Dinsmore for his own good and the good of the parish. Have you met Mrs. Keene at the Inn. I suppose you and she, bein' both from the city, would have a good deal to say to one another."

"Yes, I have met her, Mrs. Livingston, but she is from another part of the city than I. She knows more about society, and I more about a law student's life in the city," answered Tom.

"She's different from our folks," said the old dame. "It's rather hard to say exactly how; but she is different."

"Yes" said Tom "she is very different. She hardly seems to belong to the same race as Miss Lowther."

"Mary's a fine girl" said the old lady warmly. "I love her as well as if she was my own child. I don't believe anybody that knows Mary can help from lovin' her. But Mrs. Keene has a mighty takin' way with her. There's old Mrs. Hollis thinks the world of her, and Judge Lowther is almost makin' a fool of himself, for sech an old man. And Mary thinks more of her than she deserves. She can make a'most any one she chooses fond of her. I suppose you and she are quite friends?"

"Well, not exactly, Mrs. Livingston. Somehow

we don't get along as well as we ought to. I am afraid my rough ways do not suit her," answered Tom.

"I thought, from all I had heard, that she was rather used to rough ways in men. But perhaps she's had enough of it and would prefer something more easy like, now. You can't believe all you hear, nor more'n half o' what you see, or think you see. Do you know how much longer Mrs. Keene expects to stay here."

"She told me yesterday" said Dinsmore, "that the falling leaves reminded her of how soon she would have to go back to face the world alone."

"That sounds like her" said Mrs. Livingston; and Tom laughed aloud; "for she told me, last week, when she took supper with me, that she had a mind never to go back to the city, but always to live here, and try to become interested in charity work; and she wanted me to teach her to make broth and jelly for sick folks. I told her I'd teach her; but she did not appoint any time for the first lesson. I guess it's hard for her to make up her mind what she does want; or perhaps it's too easy, and she makes it up different, once a week."

"She has a hard problem before her, Mrs. Livingston," said Dinsmore; "and I think she deserves pity and counsel and help from every one who can give it to her."

"I don't know nothin' about problems, Mr. Dinsmore. She's got a plain duty before her, to think nothin' about gettin' married, and give herself to the bringin' up o' that fine boy o' hers. She's tried bein' a wife and wasn't a success at it. Now let her try to be a good mother, and she'll find that that's no problem; but a plain duty that Providence has laid out for her."

"I think she feels that, Mrs. Livingston; and it is on this very point that she seeks counsel and help," said Dinsmore.

"She didn't ask any counsel from me on that point " said the old Dame, "she wanted to know how she could work among the people here and make herself a useful woman in the community, and feel that her influence was something, and she would be missed when she left us, and would feel that she was not livin' a narrow, self-centred life, and a good bit more that I didn't understand very well. I must own, she talked well, and at the time, I thought she felt what she said."

"I am sure she does feel her responsibility and her lonely position, very keenly ", answered Dinsmore.

"Well it's not so much the feelin' as the stickin' to it that makes a woman useful and good for somethin' in this world. Our feelin's is apt to run away with us; but stickin' to it gives you no chance to run away."

Tom's only part in this conversation was to applaud Mrs. Livingston with laughter, which Dinsmore feared was boisterous enough to offend the old lady; but her hearty invitation to Tom to take supper with her showed that no offence was given.

"The old lady sees through Mrs. Keene's thin disguises ", said Tom, on the way home.

"I think she sees more than there is ", answered

Dinsmore. "What object would Mrs. Keene have in laying herself out to beguile a simple-hearted old country woman whom she may never in her life see again?"

"Well, for one thing, the instinct that she has for bagging all game small and big. In the second place she has not wholly made up her mind to shake off the rural dust from her dainty shoes. It was significant, her desire to be an influence in this community", said Tom, with a laugh.

"I know she feels that her life, thus far, is wasted; that she must get out of herself or she will grow morbid or go mad," said Dinsmore.

"And getting out of herself implies getting into somebody else. Confound her sentimental rot, she is no more morbid than I am. She's on the market for a husband, if she can get one; and if she can't, then to make love to every man she meets, just for the fun of it."

"What do you make out of her evident desire to make friends with women just as much, or more, than she does with men," asked Dinsmore in a decided tone, as though settling the controversy.

"Why it's as plain as the nib of your Reverence. She either gains a direct lead to a flirtation, as in the case of Miss Lowther and Mrs. Hollis, or it serves as a general cover to her, as in the case of Mrs. Livingston. There is nothing more important to a woman who is shady in repute, or who is in for general flirtation, than the friendship of reputable women. It is like charity, it covers a multitude of sins."

" How preposterous, Tom. To what flirtation does Mrs. Hollis' friendship lead the way," asked Dinsmore.

" With Miss Amèlie "; and Whitlock roared with laughter; Dinsmore could not help laughing too.

" Don't be a fool, Tom," he said.

" All right " said Tom; " I won't. But don't you."

" I'll try not " said Dinsmore.

" That's right " said Tom. " Be humble; I always have more hope of a fellow when he is not stuck on himself."

" You must despair of yourself, sometimes, I should think," said Dinsmore.

" No, Harry, my pride is on the surface. In the depths of my heart, I am a very humble fellow, especially with women," said Tom.

" Save the mark! then I don't even know humility when I see it," retorted Dinsmore.

" You are in the way of getting a lesson in it that will last you a life-time, if you don't look out;" and, with this parting shot, Tom went to his room.

CHAPTER XVIII.

"HAS your friend Mr. Whitlock already found us too dull, and gone back to his law-books?" was Mrs. Keene's greeting, as Dinsmore came to the table alone.

"No," answered Dinsmore, "he has gone to Judge Lowther's to supper."

"In furtherance of his pastime, the pursuit of game?" she replied. "He is an ardent hunter by day and night. He is quite thoroughly impressed with Miss Lowther's charms."

"Yes?" was Dinsmore's laconic reply.

"Oh! yes, indeed. There is no subject, not even quail or partridge or his paragon 'Brown Bess' that elicits such a flow of enthusiastic talk as the mention of Miss Lowther's name. Have you not found it so?"

"We do not discuss Miss Lowther; we talk more of old times," answered Dinsmore.

"That is quite as it should be. A man whose heart is becoming enlisted in a woman is shy of talking to other men; for fear, I suppose, that they will ridicule him. He seeks his confidants among women, sure that his ecstasies will pass current with them. Is that the true explanation of the undoubted fact?"

"I am sure I cannot tell you, Mrs. Keene. On these matters one ounce of experience is worth a pound of theory; and I have not had one minim of experience."

"Being in a game of chess does not always give the surest insight. The onlooker has sometimes the best chance to see into both sides of the game," persisted Mrs. Keene.

"Then I must disclaim even that vantage point. I did not know that there was any game being played," answered Dinsmore.

Miss Amelia, an interested listener up to this point, now joined in the conversation.

"I am sure no one can blame Mary for having a good time, when she has so few chances; and if a girl wants to make a good match she has certainly got to look outside of Clintonville."

"I do not blame, I commend her" said Mrs. Keene, sweetly. "She is a charming girl, and if she made a good match, as you call it, Miss Amelia, a few months in the city would polish her manners and make her a most attractive young married woman, who would not want for attention and admiration from the best sort of men."

"I wonder what Miss Lowther would say to the attractive programme which you sketch out for her" said Dinsmore, as he rose from the table. As he went to his room he wished that he could see and hear what was going on at Judge Lowther's.

And this is what he would have seen. As Whitlock came to the door Mary was bidding good-by to Sally Hill. As he passed into the hall, he overheard Sally say, in a whisper so loud that it seemed to be intended for him,

"Mary, is that another to be hung on your string?"

Mary's face flushed as she tried to silence Sally.

"No, I won't keep still, unless you promise me that you will behave yourself with him. Promise me that you will reform, and to-night will be the beginning of the reformation," and Sally looked roguishly toward Tom, and pinched Mary's cheek.

"I promise," said Mary. What else would check this wayward tongue. Sally kissed her good-by. "I will call to-morrow and hear you confess," she said, as she ran down the steps.

Mary turned away with a sigh of relief, trusting that Tom had heard nothing.

"And so you made the promise," were Tom's first words when they were seated in the parlor. Mary's face had not recovered its usual color and it gained a new accession. "Do you always promise as easily as that?" persisted Tom.

"Yes! when I am asked to promise what I know is best for me," replied Mary, gaining courage as she spoke.

"Who tells you what is best to promise?" retorted Tom.

"My own common sense," replied Mary.

"Do you allow that to be prompted by the person asking the promise," queried Tom, laughing.

"Yes! when I think they are competent to judge of the situation", replied Mary.

"Do you think Miss Sally Hill such a competent person?" he asked.

"Under the circumstances, I did not need any

prompting from her. I felt the propriety of her request as soon as she made it," answered Mary.

"May I venture then to ask what was the nature of her request. I ask it not out of idle curiosity, but for my own guidance," said Tom.

"Certainly you are at liberty to ask what you please, and I am free to answer as I see good," replied Mary, laughing.

"Do you lay that down as a general proposition, or as applying only to this particular case?" asked Tom, with a reckless sort of laugh.

"It is confined to this particular case; and as you did not immediately embrace my offer; but asked a question instead, you threw away your chance, and the offer is withdrawn."

"I will embrace any offer that you make Miss Lowther."

"Then you must not be so slow, another time. That one is withdrawn. What sort of sport did you have to-day."

"Not nearly so good as when you drove me out to the hunt. Can't I engage your services for to-morrow; you to have half the result of the day's sport."

"No I can't go out to-morrow. It is prayer-meeting night, and driving in the cold air makes me too sleepy", answered Mary.

"Now that is what I call a lame excuse. Then can I take you to prayer meeting," said Tom.

"You would be too sleepy, after a day's hunt, and might fall asleep and tumble off the seat into the aisle and disgrace me," said Mary, laughing. "And if you did not, I can't associate you and a prayer-meeting in my mind. You don't seem to belong there."

"I can assure you, Miss Lowther, that I have been very well brought up, little reason as you may have to suspect it. I have been to prayer-meetings very often. I know how to conduct myself with perfect propriety, to keep awake by artificial means, if nature asserts herself too strongly, and to acquit myself creditably even in singing the hymns. Just try me once," pleaded Tom, as though a prayer-meeting was something from which he could not bear to be excluded.

Mary laughed and promised to let him go to prayer-meeting with her, upon the pledge of most exemplary behavior on his part, especially in the matter of keeping awake and singing the hymns in a very discreet manner.

"Do you sing, Mr. Whitlock," she asked, when they had retired to the parlor, after supper, leaving the Judge, in the adjoining room, with his newspaper.

"Oh! No" said Tom, "I only sing in prayer-meeting."

Now the fact was that Tom had a first-rate baritone voice, which he had not cared to cultivate and of which he spoke in a disparaging tone. But there were a few songs, that suited both his voice and disposition, which he could deliver with a dash that made them very effective.

"Before I give my consent to your singing in prayer-meeting, I must insist on a rehearsal", said Mary.

"You have no hymn-book here," answered Tom, "and if you had, the surroundings are not solemn enough."

"Here is the hymn-book" said Mary, putting one on the rack of the piano; "and I will seat myself, with folded hands and eyes cast up to the ceiling." She seated herself accordingly, and Tom sat down to the piano, strummed a few chords, rustled the leaves of the hymn-book and then, with a reckless kind of accompaniment, rattled off, in a rich, full baritone "The Midship-mite."

"Bravo" cried the Judge, as he came stumbling in from the library, waving the newspaper; "Give us the 'Star Spangled Banner.'"

"May I sing in prayer-meeting, Miss Lowther?" asked Tom, as humbly as if he were on trial before the music committee of a church for the position of chorister.

"Not if you go rollicking through the hymns like that", answered Mary.

Then Tom turned to the piano and sang softly and sweetly, as if he were full of the spirit of devotion "Nearer my God to Thee;" for he had musical instinct, and could give a true rendering of hymn or song.

"Yes, you can sing in prayer-meeting", said Mary.

"Thank you," answered Tom, sedately, as though he had won in a prize competition, and the judge had awarded him the honor.

"He's a fine fellow, Mary; a fine fellow, I say" said the Judge as they bid Tom good-night. "I must remember that lad. I begrudge Channing such a young fellow in his office. He's full of life, he has lots of stuff in him; he can work; there's the making of a man and a lawyer in that young fellow. He's a good shot. He's a good companion. He's a good fellow;" and the Judge chuckled to himself and rubbed his hands together, and went back to his study, muttering to himself all kinds of pleasant things about Tom Whitlock.

And Mary said to herself that he was "a nice fellow, and lots of fun;" and so Tom was getting along famously in the Judge's household.

"I'm accepted, on probation," was Tom's greeting to Dinsmore, as he came into his room, on his return from Judge Lowther's.

"A rather doubtful sentence, the full meaning of which, I do not catch, off-hand. Accepted as what? On what probation?" answered Dinsmore.

"Accepted as cavalier to Miss Mary Lowther and chief psalm-singer to your Reverence. On probation as to my conduct, and sobriety in prayer-meeting, especially in the matter of remaining awake while you are preaching, and being discreet in my style of rendering the hymns which you assign to us" answered Tom, flinging himself on the lounge and lighting a cigar.

"Did the 'Widder' seem to miss me at supper," he asked, after he had given a few puffs and watched the rings of smoke as they floated upward. "There's a beauty", he said, as he watched a very perfect ring float toward the ceiling. "I've got that down pretty fine. I say, was I missed at supper?"

"You're always missed, Tom. You make a positive mark wherever you go, and your absence makes itself felt."

"That's not what I mean; was there a dreamy vacancy in the 'Widder's' eyes, a dreary sort of blank in her voice, a distraught manner, as if she was trying to recall a fleeting memory?"

"No!" answered Dinsmore. "I cannot truthfully say that I noted any of these symptoms. Perhaps she was skilfully concealing her feelings."

"I've no doubt of it. That's what she generally is doing", replied Tom. "Did she mention my name?"

"Yes" said Dinsmore, "and asked where you were."

"And you told her, I presume."

"Yes! I told her", replied Dinsmore.

"Well! what did she have to say then. You're as hard to draw as the cork of an old bottle of port," said Tom.

"What do you care what she said; when you think all that she says is merely for effect?" queried Dinsmore.

"I like to hear it. She's fun, if she is hollow. I like to hear her lay it on, and pretend to swallow the bait."

"You credit Mrs. Keene with far more finesse than she has. As you come to know her, you will see that her feelings are more real than pretended, and that she looks on life seriously and wants to know just what she ought to do, in her very trying situation," said Dinsmore, in a positive tone.

"Let us not renew that well-worn theme", said

15

Tom, " I like that Miss Lowther better every time I see her. It would not do for me, in the present, and prospective, very limited state of my resources, to see too much of her, unless you can assure me that the Judge is so fond of her, that he would let his affection extend to any one that was fond of her. Take her all in all, on a short acquaintance, I will say that I never met a nicer girl. She is every way nice, good enough looking to be very pretty to a man who was in love with her, jolly and sweet in manner and disposition; a kind of girl that a man wouldn't tire of. She'd wear well."

" Miss Lowther would feel much obliged for your good opinion, Tom ", laughed Dinsmore. " But it was always your way to think most of what your opinion of a girl was, rather than what she might think of you."

" Well! of course I do. That's the order of nature. If I don't like her, then a fig for what she thinks of me. The first consideration is ' Do I like her ? '; if I do, then, and only then, does it become a matter of interest to inquire 'Does she like me.' That's logic isn't it ?"

" Yes; that's your kind of logic."

" Well, my kind is the kind that suits my case. But I am not in disfavor with Miss Lowther, I can assure you," said Tom. " You shall see us sit side by side, to-morrow evening, in your prayer-meeting, and hear our voices sweetly blend in psalm and hymn. I'm going to do the whole figure as visiting friend of the parson. You'll find I have done you credit, when I get through. They'll like you none the worse for having such a fellow as me for your friend;" and Tom chuckled to himself.

"Age does not dim your shining light, Tom. When I feel that I am growing old and dull under my burdens here, I shall send for you to come up and renew our youth," answered Dinsmore.

"You will not need to send for me. I am your unbidden guest; who will return Spring and Fall for fish and bird; and incidentally to stir you up. When does the 'Widder' flit?"

"I don't know", answered Dinsmore, "she was asking the same question about you, last evening. I suppose she wants to time her leaving so as to have you for a travelling companion."

"The mischief she does," said Whitlock, sitting up on the lounge. "Is that honest or only some of your chaff?"

"She asked me about it, at supper," said Dinsmore.

"Well I hope you told her that railroad travelling made me nervous, and I had to smoke, all the while, to keep myself in decent trim, and that riding inside a coach made me sick, and I had to be on top to get air," said Tom.

"I told her nothing of the kind. There was no chance to do so, and if there had been, I should not have taken that responsibility. I left it for you to explain your personal peculiarities as a traveller" answered Dinsmore in a dreamy sort of tone, as though the subject was losing interest for him.

"Well that is the dickens of a situation for me," said Tom. "You seem to think nothing of it; but here am I booked to play cavalier to that woman for about six hours on the stage and four more on the cars, and reach the City about ten o'clock at night. See here, you are not to know the day when I leave; do you understand?"

"That's well enough, but if I mistake not, I will have nothing to do with it. Mrs. Keene will probably get her information directly from you," said Dinsmore.

"Well you have made a mess of it, Harry. To book me as escort to that woman; when you know how we always are at cross purposes," retorted Tom.

"I had nothing to do with it. You came here, at this particular juncture; Mrs. Keene was here; she is about to leave, and sees in you an eligible travelling companion, able and willing to look after a lady, as every nice gentleman should be."

"I hold you responsible for it," answered Tom, as he bid Dinsmore good-night.

His fears were confirmed when, at breakfast, Mrs. Keene turned to him, with one of her sweetest smiles, and said, "I was afraid that you had left us, Mr. Whitlock. How soon do you go?"

Dinsmore smiled as Tom caught his eye, and his answer to Mrs. Keene's question was more embarrassed than the occasion seemed to call for; "I really am not quite sure, Mrs. Keene. I shall try to choose a sunny day when I can ride on top of the coach. It is pretty cold for an outside passage; but I can't endure the inside of those stuffy old vehicles."

"I quite agree with you", said Mrs. Keene. "It is a stupid ride, inside. On the outside, in this glorious autumn weather, it is a treat. If the sun is shining and you are well wrapped up, this dry air, even on a cold day, is exhilarating and one does not suffer any harm."

"Even on a rainy day, I prefer the top of the coach ", said Tom, desperately, as Dinsmore trod on his foot under the table.

"So do I," answered Mrs. Keene, who, it seemed to Tom, was in an unusually complaisant mood this morning. "Wrap yourself in a water-proof, and then let the cool rain pour on your face. I like the wind and the rain and the sun, if you are only fixed to meet them."

Plainly on this tack there lay no escape for him; he thought of suggesting that he proposed to walk to Weston; but that was a twenty-five mile trudge; so he let the matter drop, trusting that something would turn up that would let him slip off unnoticed. He let the talk drift to other things and kept discreetly quiet.

"You were very shy and retiring this morning; an unwonted mood for you, Tom," said Dinsmore, as they stood on the balcony, after breakfast.

"Why didn't you sail in and help me?" asked Tom.

"What help could I give you? What business was it of mine to regulate when, how, or with whom you should travel to the city? I think you would make a pleasant escort for Mrs. Keene, you would get to know one another better and would form a truer estimate of each other," said Dinsmore.

"I like that," answered Tom. "I hold you responsible for this. You got me into it; and I'll get even with you for it."

"That's right", said Dinsmore; "hit the first head that bobs up, when you are disgruntled. You had better get your gun and work off some of your vengeance on the partridges. They have more to do with the situation than I have."

"All right" answered Tom. "I'm going to Pleasant Pond, and shall have a shot with Barbara and find out from her whether the fates decree that I have got to travel with the 'Widder' and her darling boy. In the evening I am to escort Miss Lowther to prayer-meeting under a positive engagement not to nod to your exhortations."

At prayer-meeting Tom kept his promise, loyally, to behave himself in a way to prove that the trust reposed in him was not misplaced.

He kept his eyes tightly shut during prayer time; he sang the hymns with a gentle solemnity, and his voice blended so nicely with Mary's that she found it a real pleasure to sing with him; he kept his eyes fastened on Dinsmore's face, from the beginning to the end of his talk, and only uncrossed his legs once, and did not beat a tattoo on the arm of the seat.

"How did I do?" he asked Mary, when the benediction was pronounced.

"You did very well indeed?" she answered gravely; and Tom was pleased with himself, and with her.

He waited while Mary went up to give Dinsmore a message from her father about the church plans; and then he and Mary walked down the village green, chatting and laughing merrily. Tom felt the rebound from prayer-meeting.

As Dinsmore followed them, at a short distance, he could overhear their merry talk, and, in the bright moonlight, see their buoyant steps.

What a lovable fellow Tom was; how quickly he could win his way, even with strangers. He was winning his way to Mary Lowther's heart.

Mary Lowther had become, in every way a part of the young minister's life; how much so he had not realized, until now that he saw the prize being borne off before his eyes.

Insensibly her picture was blended, in his mind, with all his future plans. They had worked together so often, and so well, that her help seemed indispensable to success in any of his undertakings.

He had never felt this before as he felt it now. But he began to ask himself, by what right had he quietly appropriated this girl to himself.

She had certainly never given him that right. She was his friend and helper, and nothing more.

From this it was but a step to question, was it right? And above all was it right, now, when his friend had felt, and shown, an interest in the girl which he himself had never shown.

What had he to offer her in comparison with what Tom could offer? He had not Tom's sunny, happy nature, his strong relish for humor, his flow of buoyant spirits, that tided him so lightly over the rocks or shoals of life.

Her life with Tom would be in a larger world, which she was, in every way, fitted to enjoy.

Her life with him would be a monotonous round, in this little mountain village.

Above all, she was probably as much interested in Tom as he was in her, for Tom was a fellow that a girl must like, even on a short acquaintance.

He had put himself in such a position that he must stand aside for his friend, and, if he were loyal at heart, do even more than this, he must speak a good word for him, when Mary or the Judge questioned him as to Tom's antecedents.

He thought of the many times when Mary's earnest talk over matters in which they were mutually interested, might have given him the chance to tell her of his love.

And then he reproached himself, as he remembered that it was in his work that she had shown an interest, not in himself; and what a mean advantage it would have been to interpret her nobler interest into this lower, personal one.

He walked very slowly down the village green, and listened to their voices as they died away in the distance.

As he came into the Inn Mrs. Keene sat in the parlor.

"Your friend Mr. Whitlock is a truant to-night," she said.

"Oh no," answered Dinsmore, "he was at prayer-meeting."

"Then he has slipped the leash, since prayer-meeting", she suggested.

"Yes, he has taken Miss Lowther home," he replied.

"After the penance, a sweet indulgence. What a charming pair they make," continued Mrs. Keene;

"and they are thoroughly interested in one another. It will be a nice thing for a girl as capable as Mary to have the advantage of city life. She will make a very attractive woman."

Dinsmore made no answer but to bid Mrs. Keene "Good-night;" as he turned away she shrugged her shoulders, lifted her eyebrows, and smiled, as she watched Dinsmore leave the room.

He looked pale, and was more tired than usual after a prayer-meeting.

When he went to his room, he did not light his lamp; but sat down by the window and looked out on the moonlight. Over and over again he retraced the line of thought that he had followed, on his way down from prayer-meeting; and with each repetition, he became more convinced that it was the right and generous course for him to take.

Now it remained to be seen whether he could do it in a generous way, and not with such envy as would rob his conduct of graciousness toward his friend.

But never until now did he realize how thoroughly the thought of Mary Lowther had woven itself into his heart and into his work.

He felt that he was now to learn the very lesson that he needed. He had been imagining that it was his work that was filling his heart and hopes; the sacred ministry to which he had devoted himself, that was leading him on; but now he is revealed to himself as one who was letting the love of this girl stand for devotion to his sacred mission.

He heard Tom's step, as he came down the village

street.   It was brisk and cheery, and he was whistling
like a lark.

Dinsmore's first instinct was to lock his door, as
though he had gone to bed.

But it was only for a moment.   He lit his lamp
and waited for Tom's coming.

"You look tired, Harry," was Tom's greeting.
"You can preach, old boy.   I didn't pinch myself
once to-night.   Do you want to go to bed?"

"No! I am not sleepy, Tom; but I am very tired."

"I am as fresh as a lark; but I suppose it does
make a difference whether you are filling pulpit or
pew.   It would wear me out to preach.   You're a
level-headed preacher, Harry.   There's no nonsense
in your sermons; they are straight from the shoulder."

"Nonsense is not a common quality of sermons,
Tom."

"No, but I have heard as sheer nonsense from a
pulpit desk as I ever heard anywhere in my life;
perfect rot."

"I have been more fortunate, Tom.   I think I
never heard anything quite so bad as you describe.
'The worst speak something good.   If all want sense
God takes a text and preacheth patience' so says
godly George Herbert.   You have commended me,
I must in fairness say a good word for you as a most
excellent hearer, and a great help in the singing."

"Oh; I can do the square thing by a friend, in
almost any circumstances," answered Tom.   "Just
take me on the right tack, and you'll find me on
deck, every time."

Dinsmore smiled kindly on him.   What a good

fellow he was, and, where service to a friend was in question, how loyally he rendered it.

He had looked so demure, almost docile, as he sat in prayer-meeting, like a dog in leash, that Dinsmore would hardly have recognized him in a strange place.

This was his loyal tribute of friendship; could he be as loyal to Tom?

"I tell you what it is, Harry, I don't want to do anything rashly, but if I had been as head-over-heels as some people think me, I believe I would have been engaged to Miss Lowther, to-night; that is, always supposing she would have followed scripture and said yea, yea. I don't believe she would have said nay, nay; although doubtless she would have cooled my ardor, by postponing matters or remanding me to the Judge for sentence. She certainly likes me; don't you think so?"

"As far as I can judge, she certainly does. Most girls do," answered Dinsmore.

"Did she ever say anything to you about me, Harry? Does she ever talk about me? What does she talk about to you, anyway? I can't think what such a jolly girl, so full of fun would say to a minister."

Dinsmore laughed, more heartily than he had since prayer-meeting. "What do you talk about with me, Tom? Perhaps other people wonder what such a jolly fellow, full of fun and sport, can find to talk about to a minister."

"Oh; but that's different. Girls are always sentimental with ministers, and talk about their feelings, and things just on the edge of love talk."

"Well, on that point I can satisfy your mind, at once. Miss Lowther does not talk sentiment nor anything verging in the least on 'love talk' as you call it. On the contrary her talk is about others than herself, and of the most practical kind."

"Harry, I can't make that girl out. She's as free with me, in one sense, as if I were a girl, or she a man; in another sense, she holds me at more than arm's length. We are jolly comrades, but I would not care to presume on that, one inch; and she can side-track a fellow as easily as turning a switch."

"You seem to know her pretty well, Tom. On that side, I suspect you know her better than I do."

"Did she ever talk about me Harry? What do you think my chances would be with such a girl?"

"I think your chances would be good with almost any girl, Tom. You are the kind that the girls like."

"There you're all out, Harry. If you and I were to start in after the same girl (which Heaven forbid!) you'd do me up on the first quarter. It's your pale, big-eyed chap, with a black moustache and wavy hair, that takes the girls; my light hair, blue eyes, and hopeless upper lip are not in it. They'll have their fun with me, but are ready to drop it any time that I say quits, sometimes sooner. If love's in the question they want something sort of tender. Now I could be awfully fond of a girl, and give her my head, if she wanted it; but I couldn't be tender. I'm not made that way," and Tom's face was fairly rueful.

"That humility of yours which I discredited, does

really seem to exist at the bottom of your heart. I
think however, that you need not take quite so low
a view of your powers to please, Tom."

"Oh; I can please 'em, every time; but I don't
believe they'll fall in love with me."

"You don't mean to say that it is your deliberate
wish to have women, as a rule, fall in love with you?"
and Dinsmore smiled at the thought of Tom pursued
by a host of these love-lorn ladies.

"Goodness alive; no; but I may want some woman to fall in love with me, sometime or other.
This Miss Lowther seems so different from most
girls, so jolly, as if I might suit her, if she only
thought so. I do not consider myself in love with
the girl. Hang it all! I don't know what has gotten
me into this vein. It must have been going to your
prayer-meeting that has made me soft. You understand, Harry, don't you, that I'm not in love with
the girl. I haven't been spooning with her; she
isn't that kind and I'm not that kind. I was only
suggesting, just as you might, what would be my
chances with Miss Lowther, if I concluded to try;
no man need be afraid to try, he'd be in luck if he
succeeded. But after all, that's the question, would
it be well to try? If I go in, I go in to win. Give
me a bit of pastoral counsel, Harry; would you advise me to try?" and Tom waited for Dinsmore's
answer, as if he really meant to abide by his counsel.

"If I were in your place, Tom, I should certainly
try to win that girl for my wife, if I thought there
was any chance for me;" and with this sentence,
spoken slowly and deliberately, Dinsmore felt that

he renounced all thought of Mary Lowther as his helpmeet in the work of his Hillside Parish.

"I shall follow your good advice, for it accords perfectly with my own views," said Tom, rising to go to bed; "and give me your blessing, in pushing it to a successful issue."

"Success to you, Tom, you were born under a lucky star; but remember that, entering on such a race, no man has the right to take the hunter's view, that Mrs. Keene accuses our sex of taking. In such a matter the woman is to be thought of first; and her happiness and peace of mind ought to be the first consideration."

"Mercy, Harry, don't preach to me like that. I'm not going to shoot the girl, if she refuses me; as it is more than likely that she will."

As Tom left the room with a jovial "Good-night," Dinsmore settled himself to review the situation.

In this first encounter with the buoyant, happy wooer of Mary Lowther, he had been successful, and Tom had left him without one thought that he had taken away one of his cherished hopes. It pleased him to think he had thus far mastered his selfishness.

Then came thoughts of what his life would be when he settled down to work alone; when he would have no one nearer than Mrs. Livingston to appreciate and share in his plans for his life work. And as he thought, it seemed to him that the burden was heavy and would grow heavier. The thought was like an east wind, gradually spreading the first thin vapor, which will cover the sky with a uniform, leaden gray.

At last wearied with the recurrent thought, he went to bed and fell into a restless sleep and dreamed it all over again, with a vividness that endowed it with reality, even after he was awake.

During the remainder of Tom's visit, Dinsmore spent his time, chiefly in making visits to the outlying settlements, and studiously avoided Judge Lowther's house.

Tom as studiously frequented the premises, and entertained Dinsmore, in the evenings, with the recital of the progress he was making in his suit with Mary, to all of which Dinsmore listened with patience, if not with enthusiasm.

"Yet after all," said Tom on the last day of his vacation, "I don't seem to have made the requisite progress. I haven't the proper sentimental gift. I'm not tender and persuasive; I'm there on a good footing; but somehow I'm only there. I don't know what's the matter; but I'd rather take a mad bull by the horns than propose to that girl."

Tom was going to drive down, that afternoon, with Farmer Brown, and thus avoid playing cavalier to Mrs. Keene.

"I've given the 'widder' the slip, any way," he said, gleefully. "And when I am gone, Harry, say a good word for me, will you?"

"To Mrs. Keene?" queried Dinsmore, "I am afraid her ears will not be open to any good word in your behalf."

"A plague on the 'widder.' She's deaf as an adder to any good word, for any one. But when I am gone (pathetic you see), speak gently of me to

Miss Mary. I'm coming back, next Spring, and then, perhaps I will dare to try my fortune. Break up the soil for me; there's a good fellow. I've had an awfully good time, Harry, and I'm glad I came. If any of my clients have a nice farm, with as good shooting and fishing, as nice girls, and as kind people as you have in your parish, I'll think I'm in luck. Good-bye, till next Spring," shouted Tom, as they drove off; and Dinsmore watched him, wondering whether he took away with him the heart of Mary Lowther.

CHAPTER XIX

T HE light came cold and gray through the green blinds of his room as Dinsmore turned uneasily and half opened his eyes, closing them quickly again for he thought that the dawn was just breaking. But, try as he would, he could not force himself to go to sleep. After a quarter of an hour's effort he recognized the fact that he was wide awake and could not help matters by lying longer in bed. He listened for the usual sounds of life astir about the Inn, but all was still; the very air seemed muffled as the gray light stole between the closed blinds.

When he had fought with wakefulness until resistance only proved how wide awake he was, he drew his watch from under his pillow and found that it was nearly eight o'clock.

He jumped out of bed, threw open his blinds and looked out on the leaden sky from which the snow had been falling all night until now it was nearly knee deep, on the level. The village street lay untrodden by any step of man or beast, with the spell of the snow upon it. In front of his window stood a load of tan-bark on a wagon where the teamster ' had left it, late last night, intending to take up his journey in the morning. The snow was nearly up to the hubs of the wagon, and the deep red color of the bark contrasted strongly with the snow that covered it. As he stood looking at the load, wondering how the teamster would reach his destination now, Bruno, the big Newfoundland dog belonging to the Inn, came bounding out, barking, dipping his muzzle into the snow and tossing it about.

What a change the silent, soft-falling flakes had made in the whole landscape. What a complete transformation of the relation of things. In the city the snow means only added dirt and discomfort; in the country it changes at once the whole mode of life.

It upsets the topography. From the barn, which is only a few steps away in summer, comes the lowing of the cattle, with a muffled, distant sound, as if they were in the far pasture. Now it has become a journey to reach them; for every step of the way must be shovelled.

How disconsolate and isolated the chickens are, afraid to leave their night's perch, unless indeed some venturesome Spring cock who has never seen snow, has been rash enough to fly forth and is now perched fearsomely on some fence or tree or shed, where an expedition must be sent to rescue him.

How it arouses the feeling that there is something to be done for each department of the farm-stead. It is as if the whole place were in a state of siege, and the garrison of each portion must be relieved.

At first there is a sense of exhilaration in this pressing demand for extra work, but, before long, it dwindles into the drudgery of every day; but, be-

fore the novelty is worn off, what prodigies of work
the first snow storm calls forth from man and boy on
an isolated farm.

What secrets the snow reveals. The hard earth
tells no tales to the country boy, but in the new-
fallen snow, he finds the track of rabbit, fox or bear.
With what wondering eyes he looks on these and
thrills with the thought of how lately the wild creatures have passed that way. No one knows this who
has not hung breathlessly over such traces of the
hidden life about us.

As the day wears on, the long-suffering oxen are
yoked to the big sled, and all hands that can be
mustered, start out, armed with shovels, to break
the road. Each farm house as they pass, hails them
as a rescuing party; they give the news of how the
inmates fare at one or another house, and new re-
cruits join their ranks.

At the head of the village, just beyond Judge
Lowther's house, there is a heavy cut, where the
main road passes over, and in part through, the
steep and narrow hill. Here the snow always drifts
and fills the cut full.

Through this it is impossible to break a road and
therefore it is always tunnelled, and, for weeks, all
travel is through the snow tunnel. The parties from
the West settlement and those from the village meet
here and tunnel from either end until they reach the
centre.

To be one of this tunnelling party was the ambition of every boy in the West settlement and in the
village; what excitement as they hear one another

in the tunnel and with what a yell the first boy breaks through.

But as yet there was no sign of all this active combat with the storm's silent forces, and Dinsmore looked out on the untrodden snow that made the village street so still, as though all sound had died.

He turned away from the gray scene to dress; the room was cold, the water in his pitcher was frozen, the bits of ice floating about in the basin numbed his finger tips, and made his morning bath decidedly uncomfortable.

At breakfast the long dining room looked dingy and comfortless in the cold, gray light. There was a poor fire and the room was chilly. The only occupant of the big table was Miss Amelia. A white, knitted nubia, with a crocheted, blue, shell border, thrown over her head and around her shoulders, and the gray light made her look blue and cold. Mrs. Hollis was in bed, afraid to expose herself to the chill dining-room on such a stormy morning. Mr. Forrester too was taking comfort in a prolonged nap, on this dismal day.

Tom Whitlock would have made the snow storm a merry scene, but he was gone, until next Spring, and Mrs. Keene had followed two days later; with Miss Amelia alone for company the snow storm was a dreary threnody.

Mrs. Joyce served the first buckwheat cakes and maple syrup of the season; but they did not dissipate the dull monotony of the persistent storm.

Dinsmore went back to his room, it was chill and uncomfortable; do what he would to feed the little stove with the birch wood chunks, he could not make it cheerful. It was Saturday and he worked, all the morning, at his sermon for the next day.

After dinner he lit a cigar, kindled up the fire anew, took a book and, seating himself before the fire, tried to feel comfortable and jolly. It kept on snowing hard, all day; it seemed as if the heavens were full of snow, and would never weary of dropping it softly and steadily over the earth.

From time to time Dinsmore rose from his seat before the fire and walked to the window.

It was not hard to be comfortable; with a bright fire, his cigar and the " Noctes Ambrosianæ " in his hands, he could easily find creature comfort; but it was not so easy to be jolly.

The steady onding of the storm weighed on his spirits.

The day wore on toward evening, and, through the winter twilight, the snow fell persistently, as if it was the destiny of the earth to be buried under the soft, white pall, gentle but resistless as the feet of the avenging gods that are shod with wool.

Dinsmore closed the shutters, lit his lamp, and tried to think his room cheery, and that the wintry waste was shut out.

He spent the evening in revising his sermon for to-morrow.

Sunday morning dawned cold and gray. The snow had ceased falling, but all the roads were blocked, and there would be no one at church outside the small congregation which the village would muster.

Even in the village the paths were only partly shovelled out; in the country they were busy still cutting paths to the stock, the barns and the fodder.

It promised to be a dreary kind of service.

The light came through the green blinds of the church, a dull uniform gray; the wet wood hissed in the stoves. Dinsmore took his place in the pulpit. The stamping of feet in the vestibule sounded like a troop of cavalry invading the church; the sexton stood ready with his broom to sweep the snow off of each comer.

The young people came laughing into church, and gathered around the stoves greeting one another in a louder tone than, on ordinary occasions, was fitting and decorous. The usual restraints were laid aside in face of the snow-storm, which obliterated the ordinary features of every day life.

Sally Hill was there to play the melodeon; but Abijah Shelton the deacon's son, was absent, from stress of circumstances, and so the big bass viol stood idly against the wall.

Newman Diggs, whose visits to church were few and far between, was there. On a day like this, he felt called upon to turn out, either on the theory of encouraging the pastor when there were few on hand, or because he felt that he could appropriate a larger share of the sermon to himself. He listened to a sermon always with the thought uppermost of what it would furnish in the way of controversy. At such times, when there was, perchance, not a single person between him and the minister the sermon was a sort of personal challenge to argument; and he could listen and fill his mind with points in contro-versy.

Mary Lowther came in, her cheeks red with the exertion of walking through the snow, her eyes glowing. As she took her seat she caught Dins-more's eye as he sat in the pulpit, and she smiled at him; almost nodded to him.

Every one spoke to her as she passed into the church, on every face she left a smile. As she took her seat, the light in the church did not seem so gray and cold, she had brought sunshine with her, the smile on the faces of those to whom she had spoken left a warmth upon them.

Sally Hill beckoned to Mary to come up and help her with the singing, as she was alone and must play the melodeon. As Mary's sympathetic voice rang through the empty church, it seemed to impart life to the service, and Dinsmore felt more interest in preaching to the small congregation, on this cold snowy day, than he had often felt when the sun shone bright and the church was full. "

It was a pleasant service; but when he went down to dinner in the dingy, chill dining-room of the Inn how cheerless it was.

He hurried through dinner and went up to his room; it was snowing again and he could not go out to any of the school-houses, for an afternoon service. Mr. Forrester came in to say that he would not hold any evening service, on such a stormy night.

How the hours lingered, as if they too were clogged by the snow. He was restless, and with no means of working off his restlessness. Once he thought of going down to take tea with Mrs. Livingston; but, on reflection, concluded that he was not in the mood to talk or to be talked to.

If he had been called to go out into the night and rescue some one fallen in the snow, that would have suited his mood.   He went out and walked up and down the balcony for a couple of hours.   Out in the storm it was invigorating; shut up in his narrow quarters it was oppressive.

CHAPTER XX.

DINSMORE woke up on Monday morning and, as he looked out, the same spirit of adventure was upon him, the feeling that possesses those who live in the country, in the presence of a snow storm.

There was no snow shovelling for him to do, no dumb creatures waiting on him to release them from their isolation.

He bethought him of old Barbara Fisher and little Bab, and determined to go out to see them. Two weeks ago the child's mother had died, and the father solaced his grief by keeping himself in a perpetual stupor with opium. Bab had gone to live with old Barbara.

How helpless they would be, the old woman and the little child alone, with the great, white desert all about them. He went to Mrs. Joyce and had her fill him a basket of stores, tea, bread and eggs, and some cookies for the child, and started out on his relief expedition.

The road to the North Settlement was unbroken, and as he tramped on in the deep snow, he found that it was no Summer stroll; he sank knee-deep, at every step, the perspiration stood in beads on his forehead, his breath came thick and hard, and the light basket of provisions became a heavy load.

He had often walked it in thirty minutes; it took him now an hour and a half to reach the point where the road forks to Scooper's Hollow.

He sat on the fence to rest and looked down on the little hamlet almost hidden under the snow. The stupid inhabitants had not shown energy enough to shovel a single path. Here and there a track, like that of wild animals, showed where one or another had stirred from his lair.

Dinsmore went down the untrodden road, and made his way toward Barbara's hut, at the far end of the hamlet.

No footstep had broken the snow there; it lay piled upon the roof and on the window sills until it shut out half the daylight; a drift before the door was nearly waist deep.

He struggled up to the door, and felt afraid to knock. When a childish treble answered to his knock "Come in," his heart gave a bound that made him appreciate how much the silence around the hut had filled him with the foreboding of death within.

As he came in from the broad daylight he could scarcely see, at first, in the dim light; but there, in the centre of her charm-string, with her wonder-book open in her lap, sat old Barbara.

She was bending over her book and, for a moment, did not notice Dinsmore. Then she slowly lifted her head and he saw, at once, that her eye was dull and her voice so husky that it was hardly audible.

Bab was bending over her with a picture book that she had gotten at their Sunday School. It was called "The Good Shepherd," and contained four or five pictures of the Shepherd finding the lost sheep, leading them to the fold, and carrying the lambs in his arms. This Bab was trying to show to Barbara, in place of the Wonder Book, which had no such story, and no bright pictures.

But Barbara's eyes were dim and she querulously murmured, "I cannot see the Good Shepherd, child."

"But there He is, Grannie, right there where my finger is pointing; I will show Him to you."

"It is no use, child."

Dinsmore took the Wonder Book from her lap and lifted the old woman up and laid her gently on her couch.

Her breath came in quick, short pants, and, unfamiliar as he was with wickness, he saw that she was stricken mortally.

He opened the cupboard and found a bottle of spirits and tried to give her some; but she was too feeble to swallow. He built up the fire and covered her over with whatever came to hand. Gradually he succeeded in giving her two or three spoonsful of the spirits, and, under its influence, she revived.

"Have you come for Bab?" was her first question.

"No, I came to see after you both and have brought you some food and tea and sugar in that basket," he replied.

"I can't eat nor drink. I'm going to die. I was settin' in my charm-string, tryin' to find out what was to become o' Bab, when I was gone, and to see if I could find out what would become o' me, too."

"Grannie's book hasn't no pictures like mine. I was tryin' to show her where the Shepherd was

carryin' the lambs.   Miss Mary said I was one o'
His lambs; but Grannie couldn't see it."

"Barbara, the Good Shepherd has sent me here
to-day, to tell you that I will take Bab, when you
are gone, and will see that she is well taught and
cared for.   I promise you that, Barbara."

"I believe you," answered the old woman.

"And now, Barbara, let me talk to you about
yourself.   I can tell you what the Good Shepherd
says about what will become of you when you die."

"Yes, Grannie, here's the picture.   See Him with
that lamb.   Oh! ain't it cute, the way his little head
is lyin' on the Shepherd's shoulder.   That's the
verse we learned last Sunday.   'He shall carry the
lambs in his arms and gadder 'em in his bosom.'
See Grannie," and she pushed the picture close to
the old woman's face.

"No, I can't see it Bab.   That's for you, child,
not for me.   I'm no lamb, I'm a tough, old ewe."
Bab turned away discouraged, and looked wistfully
at Dinsmore.

"Barbara the child is right.   In the sight of God,
we are all as little children.   The Lord Jesus, who
died to save us, wants you for one of his sheep, and
if you will trust his promise and believe him as you
believe me, then he says, 'This day shalt thou be
with me in Paradise.'"   While Dinsmore was talking,
Bab was slowly turning the pages of her book, scan-
ning each picture closely.   The last picture was one
in which the Shepherd was gathering all his flock
into the fold.

"There," she broke in on Dinsmore's talk, and

held up the book triumphantly, "There Grannie, is an old sheep, she looks tougher than you do, and the Shepherd is puttin' her into the fold along with the lambs."

"Does it say so Bab? Does it say that an old Grannie can be there with the lambs? Does it say that He cares for an old witch-woman? What does it say Bab? Tell it to me, child."

"I can't Grannie; we ain't got that far yet," and she looked wistfully at Dinsmore.

He leaned over and read softly to the child, who repeated the words after him in the clear, confident voice of a child who believes that it is telling an important piece of news. "In my father's house are many mansions. I go to prepare a place for you."

"Is that what it says, Bab?"

"Yes," answered the child proudly, smiling at Dinsmore, "That's what it says; and that's what the Good Shepherd is doin'; he's takin' 'em all in, lambs and old ones, and not leavin' one single one out in the cold;" and she nodded her head gravely, giving emphasis to her accurate description of the picture.

"I never went to church, and I never had a Bible in my hands, that I know of."

"No matter, Barbara, about what is past; that is gone; but are you now ready to believe the promise of the Lord Jesus?"

"Yes, if it's to me. Where's Bab?"

"Here I am Grannie; here," she said, as Barbara's eyes wandered, after resting on her face for a moment.

"Bab tell me again about the old sheep. What does he say to them?"

Dinsmore repeated it, softly over, and Bab in a loud voice "In my father's house are many mansions. I go to prepare a place for you."

As the words died away there was a whispered "Yes," or perhaps it was only a strong sigh; but, with it, the spirit of old Barbara returned to Him who gave it.

The shadow of death made the old face, all of a sudden, look gray and strange in that little hut, under the light from the leaden sky struggling in through the one small pane, and Bab turned with a scared face to Dinsmore.

"What's the matter with Grannie?" she asked.

"The Good Shepherd has taken her," answered Dinsmore. "Where's your hood and coat Bab?" As the child jumped down from his lap to get them he threw the sheet over the dead woman's face.

He tied the child's hood on and told her to put her arms around his neck, and he would give her a pig-a-back ride to Farmer Brown's.

"Shall I say good-bye to Grannie?"

"Yes you can call good-bye to her; but she can't answer you. The Good Shepherd has taken her to his fold."

"Good-bye! Grannie," shouted Bab, with all her might. "Give my love to the Good Shepherd;" and she clutched her picture book, as Dinsmore took her on his back.

It was not a long walk to Farmer Brown's, not more than three quarters of a mile; but, under present circumstances, Dinsmore found it a hard one. It had begun to snow again, all the way it was up hill, and in some places, the drifts were deep. Bab grew to be quite a heavy load, and he panted hard, long before he was at the Farmer's gate.

Once, as he stood still to get his breath, he felt Bab's arms loosen round his neck, and one little hand patted him softly on the cheek. The tears rose in Dinsmore's eyes. With the exception of this little token of encouragement, no word passed between them. Dinsmore was thinking how he could best fulfil his promise to care for Bab, and Bab was thinking that Dinsmore was the Good Shepherd and she was one of his lambs that he was carrying. "I guess if he ain't the Good Shepherd, he's a good deal like Him."

Miss Fannie Brown came to the door. "Why Mr. Dinsmore! what brings you here in this storm?"

"Grannie's gone into the fold; and I'm goin' with Mr. Dinsmore. Here's Grannie," continued Bab, opening her picture book and pointing with her cold, red, little fingers, so stiff that she could hardly turn the leaves, "there she is, that tough old ewe, in the corner of the fold."

Fannie burst out laughing; and Dinsmore, though he could not laugh, was forced into a sad smile, at the incongruous description which Bab gave, so earnestly and sincerely.

He explained to Fannie how he came to be there, and how it happened that he had Bab in charge.

"What a mercy that you went there, Mr. Dinsmore; but what a tramp you must have had. They have just come in from breaking the road, with two teams of oxen; and father said there were footsteps all the way from the village, and leading to the Hollow. It wasn't any Scooper he said that could take such a stride as that, in such deep snow; and he didn't believe there was a man among 'em that could have gotten through from the village, any way. They'll be back to dinner in half an hour; and you must stay, and father will drive you back to the village. Bab have you had any breakfast?"

"Yes mam, three crackers." Dinsmore had forgotten the cookies for the child.

"You poor child; come with me, and mother will give you something to eat."

"I promised old Barbara that I would take care of Bab," said Dinsmore, when Fannie Brown came back from the kitchen, leaving Bab there with her mother and a comfortable bowl of bread and milk. "I do not know exactly what to do with the child, on the spur of the moment."

"I would take her to Mary Lowther's, right away. Only two weeks ago, Mary said to me that she wanted to get Bab away from Hard-Scrabble; and, as soon as she was old enough to do anything about the house and learn, she was going to ask old Barbara to let her have the child and bring her up. If I were you, I'd take her right to Mary."

This suggestion accorded so exactly with Dinsmore's own views that he was prepared to adopt it, without any hesitation.

So, after dinner, Farmer Brown took the young pastor and his little charge into the village. Bab nestled close to him and kept her hand in his all the way, and Dinsmore felt loath to part with the child, so soon.

As he passed Tim Mitchell's he stopped, and sent him to prepare for Barbara's funeral.

As Mary Lowther sat looking out on the snow, which had kept her a prisoner for three days, except the expedition to church, she saw Farmer Brown's sleigh drive up to the door, and out of it sprang Dinsmore, and picking up Bab in his arms, carried her toward the house.

Mary ran down to the door to meet them. Her heart beat fast; she had scarcely spoken to Dinsmore for two weeks. He had seemed to avoid her, she fancied.

"Why, what is the matter, Mr. Dinsmore?" she asked, taking the child from his arms.

Bab's face glowed with intense satisfaction.

"I have brought the child to you," he said; "because Miss Fannie Brown told me that you wanted her; and I promised old Barbara, on her death bed, that I would take care of the child."

Mary carried Bab into the house and asked Dinsmore to follow; and having given the child in charge to the old nurse who had cared for herself as a baby, she returned to the parlor.

Dinsmore waited for her, his pulse beat with a tense, sharp stroke, so that he felt it throb in his neck. It was a long time since he had seen her to talk with her alone. He felt uncertain how to address her, what to say, what tone to use; they stood in a changed relation to one another.

17

And yet, when she came into the room, she was just as she had always been, the same natural, unconstrained, simple manner; the change had not affected her.

"What is it Mr. Dinsmore?" she asked. "How do you come here bringing Bab?"

He told her the story of his journey out to Scooper's Hollow, and the scene at the death-bed of the old witch-woman.

"Oh; you ought not to have gone out there in this storm, Mr. Dinsmore. If you felt that you must go, you should have sent word to us, and let us send you out there in the sleigh."

"But no sleigh could have gotten through, until the oxen had broken the road; and think what I accomplished by being with old Barbara when she died."

"Yes; but you ought not to go out, on these lonely roads, in such a storm," persisted Mary.

"Now that I am safely back with the child, the question arises how can I fulfil the promise that I made to old Barbara?"

"I will keep Bab. I have wanted to get the child under my care," answered Mary.

"That will be a very happy solution of the question," said Dinsmore; "as long as you live here."

"Well; we will always live here; that is until we die," replied Mary. "And I think Father would rather die than move away from Clintonville."

"Your father may live and die here, and yet that does not determine the question whether you may not find a home far from here," answered Dinsmore, with a ghastly attempt at a smile.

"I'm sure I don't know what you mean," replied Mary, thoroughly non-plussed; for this mood was one in which she had never before seen the young pastor.

"I mean that young ladies fortunes in life are not always regulated by their parents," answered Dinsmore, desperately.

"You look thoroughly tired out, Mr. Dinsmore. Won't you stay here to supper, and go and lie down and rest before supper. You ought not to overtax your strength so."

"I can't lie down. I am nervous and excited by the scene through which I have passed, and feel more like taking another long tramp."

"You can't do that. You would make yourself ill. You must not give way to such a feeling which is mere nervousness, and has no reason in it. You owe a duty to yourself and to us, to the church I mean, to take care of your health. You must not go out again," she paused suddenly, and her face flushed; she had grown so earnest that it seemed very much as if she were reading her pastor a lecture.

"If my work calls on me to go, ought I not to go? Can I let people die without the message of peace that I can bring to them, because I am afraid of my health. I have not held my work before me as I ought to have done. Other things have come between me and my duty. Ought I to hesitate when I am called by the sore need of those around me?"

Clearly he was not offended by her reproof, and Mary took up her parable again.

"You ought to answer a call of duty; but you can

do it in a way to spare your own health and strength. But now you have no call of duty. It is only your own restlessness that makes you try to invent one. Please don't go out again this evening, Mr. Dinsmore."

He had been pacing up and down the room; he seated himself quietly and said, "No; Miss Mary, I will not go."

How pale and tired he looked; and she was so glad that she had gotten this promise from him.

"What did you mean by your not holding your work before you as you ought to have done. Father said, the other day, that he never knew a man more enthusiastic over his profession or more devoted to his work than you. I believe that Mr. Whitlock has had something to do with your getting such a notion in your head. I'm glad he has gone home. Two or three times, when I would have had a chance to talk with you and father about the church plans, he was in the way."

"Yes, Tom had something to do with it," began Dinsmore.

"Well then, I wish he hadn't come here, and I hope he won't come back, next Spring," interrupted Mary.

"I don't think he will do any harm, next Spring," said Dinsmore slowly, as though he were measuring every word. "When I saw how much he was with you, and knew how well suited he was to make a woman care for him, and how happy a woman would be with such a noble fellow, I felt that it was to be my fate to see you taken away from me, and that I must learn to do my work alone. Then I began to fear, when I saw how this thought robbed my work of its zest, that I was mistaken in thinking that I loved my work for its own sake. Now you know what is in my heart. You know that I love you; I pray God, not better than my work as His minister."

He rose and stood before her, his eyes looked deep and dark and his voice quivered, so that every nerve in Mary's body tingled. She was sitting with her hands clasped tightly in her lap and her face bent down. Now she looked up at him; and he seemed like one of those "Sons of God," that wooed the daughters of men.

"Are you sure? Can I——" she was interrupted by the patter of little feet in the hall, and Bab ran into the room and perched herself on the sofa by Mary's side. As Dinsmore took his seat she gave each of them a hand.

Mary smiled on the child, Dinsmore looked preternaturally solemn.

"Say Good-night to Mr. Dinsmore," said Mary. "It is time for little girls to be in bed," and she led the child away.

Dinsmore paced up and down the room till she returned. It seemed to take a long while to hand the child over to a nurse and tell her to put her to bed. Mary's step in the hall, the rustle of her dress made him draw his breath quickly; and he stood waiting for her as she came in the door.

"And so you are really mine?" he said as he took her in his arms and kissed her, over and over again.

"Stop," she said. "I have not said so; and you give me no chance to say what I want to say so much."

So he stopped and gave her the chance; but let us not intrude, nor betray confidence by telling what she said.

Then they rose to go to Judge Lowther's study, Dinsmore with fear and trembling, Mary with easy confidence; but he was Mary's father.

As they came into the study, she took Dinsmore's hand and they walked up to the Judge, who looked up over his spectacles, startled at their unusual attitude, for he never remembered to have seen them walking about the house hand in hand.

"Well; what is it, Mary?" he said.

Dinsmore answered him. "I have come to ask your consent to my——"

The Judge interrupted, rising to his feet, "With all my heart," he said; "but bless me; I thought it was the other young man, Mary."

"You were mistaken, Father," she began.

"I see I was; never made a worse blunder in my life; but I'm glad I was mistaken." Then he shook Dinsmore warmly by the hand. "Either one would have suited me," he added. "But Mary was entitled to a choice; and I am sure she has made no mistake, this time. You mustn't take her away from me, you know. I can't stand that. We will build you a wing, opposite this study of mine, for a study. This is the way I would suggest," and the Judge sat down, with a sheet of paper, and sketched out a plan for a study on the south side of the house.

After supper Dinsmore and Mary sat in the parlor, reviewing the past and forecasting the future; and now the love of this girl and the work of his ministry seemed no longer in conflict.

"Promise me, Mr. Dins——"

"What?" he interrupted—

"Promise me, Harry," she said, after a moment's hesitation, "that you will go straight to bed, as soon as you get home. After such a day you ought to rest."

"After such a day I can rest, whether I sleep or wake; and I shall have plenty to dream about. And so I will go straight to bed."

As he passed Mother Livingston's he felt like stopping to tell the old Dame that he had followed her wise counsel; but he was under promise, and so he went straight home and to bed.

On the next day they laid old Barbara to rest, in the graveyard of the North Settlement.

At the service, held in the school-house, Farmer Brown's family, one or two of the nearest neighbors and Mary Lowther, were the only attendants. A few of the Scoopers lingered around the door and followed the little procession to the grave-yard, to see what they were going to do with old Barbara.

The storm had ceased and the sun shone brightly, as they stood around the open grave.

The white snow and the hard, red clay mingled with each other as they fell upon the coffin. The little group of Christian people bowed their heads, as the young pastor recited the benediction for "those who die in the Lord." The gaunt, dirty, ill-clad Scoopers stood apart watching the scene with a solemn, stupid curiosity.

To Dinsmore it was the ingathering of the first fruits of their mission in Scooper's Hollow, the first time that any of them had received Christian burial; and again he was reminded of the words "and a little child shall lead them."

It was Bab whose voice had led old Barbara, as she was passing out of this world, into the fold of the Good Shepherd. He bowed his head over Barbara's grave, and prayed God to give him the heart of a little child.

L'ENVOI.

AGAIN it was Spring on these hills over which the bleak Winter winds had whistled and where the Winter snows had lain so hard and fast, that it seemed as if they never would thaw out.

Dinsmore came down the village street, late in the evening, with lagging steps. He had spent a good part of the day on his feet, over in the North Settlement. He came into the village, just as the old coach drove up, and waited for the mail. Now, as twilight was falling, he turned his steps homeward.

He saw the glow of the fire from his study windows; and as he came up the gravel path, the study door swung open. He went in and flung himself in the easy chair in front of the crackling wood fire; for there was chill enough in the evening air to make a blazing hearth seem cheery.

"Bab run and get Mr. Dinsmore's slippers for him;" and the little pattering feet flew willingly on the errand.

"You are tired, Harry, you look pale, and fagged out. You must not work so hard in this enervating Spring weather," and she laid her hand on his shoulder, and leaned over and kissed him on the forehead.

"That sets me on my feet, Mary," he said as he brightened up, in answer to her smile. "Yes, I am dead tired; but not weary. It is the kind of tire that sleep will cure. I have had a good day. I have done lots of tramping and plenty of talking; but it has been to some purpose. Seven of the Hard Scrabble people have promised me to come to a service in the school-house, next Sunday afternoon; five women and two men. I think they feel that we gave old Barbara a burial like one of our own people, and that such decent conduct on our part deserves their approbation. I think we ought to take Bab with us, and let them see that we have neither killed and eaten the child, nor sold her into slavery."

Mary laughed. "You always had the most unbounded faith in Bab's missionary powers. You're a funny man, Harry; you stick to a notion so fast."

"I stuck to the notion of getting Mary Lowther for a wife. Was that funny?"

"Yes; that was the funniest of all your doings. But that did not take you very long; and what do you think of that transaction, now that you have had a month in which to test it."

"I would like to do it over a dozen times."

"Thank you sir. Once is enough for me."

"There's a letter from Tom Whitlock," he said, emptying his pockets on the table. "Light the student's lamp and read it to me."

"Perhaps Mr. Whitlock don't intend the contents for my eyes."

"Then he had better not send it to me," answered Dinsmore.

Mary lit the lamp, and sat down by the table and, glancing at the letter, burst out laughing. She threw it in Dinsmore's lap, the color flushed up in her face. "I think I was right in assuming that, perhaps, it was not meant for my eyes."

Dinsmore read:

"My Dear Harry:—And so I am to come to you and see the girl whose charm I first discovered and whose fortunes I intended, if all went well, to link with my own, installed as your wife. You understand, I hope, that a compound fracture of the heart and the purse prevented my coming to see you snatch the prize away from me. Well, if she must go to some one else, I would rather that you should have her than any one I know. You're a decent fellow, Harry, and awfully lucky. Was the 'widder' there? To show you that I bear no grudge, I will be with you next week, if you write me that the streams are clear of snow-water.

"Go out and cast a line yourself, and see if they bite. There's a good fellow. I cannot afford very much of a vacation, and I don't want to waste it where there are no trout.

"My respects to the Missus and my love to the Judge, or *vice versa*.

"Yours as ever,

Tom."

"There's no great harm done by letting you see that, I fancy;" and Dinsmore laughed at Mary's blushes.

So Tom came in due time, had some good fishing, and imparted to Mary, various bits of information, according to his lights.

"I assure you, Mrs. Dinsmore, that I was the saving of this truant husband of yours. I opened his eyes to the net that was being spread in his path. You virtually owe him to me; and I ought to be an honored guest in your house."

"Thank you very much, Mr. Whitlock. I can never do enough to pay off such a debt as that."

"Oh! now, you don't believe it; but I tell you, the wool was pretty well over his eyes, when I first came up here. Isn't that true, Harry? Didn't I give you some good advice?"

"Most excellent, from your point of view; and most effective because I didn't need it."

"Weren't you afraid of that winning widow, Mrs. Dinsmore?"

"No, Mr. Whitlock, not in the sense that you mean. I was afraid that some of the village gossips would connect Harry's name with her, so as to hurt his influence; but I never, for a moment, thought that she could make him love her."

"Well, then, you had a great deal more faith in him than I had. I thought him in real danger, and doubted whether he could hold his own."

"I was sure that I could hold my own," answered Mary.

Dinsmore laughed heartily.

"I never thought of your taking that view of the matter," said Whitlock, thoroughly non-plussed, and without any ready answer.

"Suppose we regard this debate as satisfactorily closed," interposed Dinsmore. "It gives one a curious sensation to hear two people discuss one's affections, as though they had them in clinic for dissection. Whatever may have been the doubts or dangers of the past, we have settled them, and reached a conclusion highly satisfactory to the parties chiefly concerned."

And so Dinsmore had the last word.

THE END.